MW00940473

Peter Puckett

& The Amulet of Eternity

R.C. VanLandingham

For my real-life Peter Pucketts
—Dixon, Stafford, and Maxwell!
I pray your journeys end in the
same place as Peter's.

CONTENTS

ACKNOWLEDGMENTS

I want to thank my wife Elena, my sons Dixon, Stafford, and Maxwell, and my parents Richard and Teresa for always being supportive, helpful, and loving.

I want to give a special thanks to Amy Lew Alexander for all of her hard work helping me with this book, from editing to creating the cover illustration. And to Mary VanLandingham for her work on title creation and cover formatting.

I also want to thank Fr. Pete Wait, Bryan Schultz, Richard and Jennifer Lynes, Chris and Christina Kauffman, Amy Hines, Erica Lee, Justine Hicks, Sophia Stanley, and Brian Bailey for the encouragement, assistance, and advice in preparing this book.

I also want to thank Hannah, Jack, Madison, Mary, Morgan, Luke, Jack, Magnus, Zac, and Monty for reading the book early to let me know what they thought of it.

Most importantly, I thank God for all of the many blessings He has given me—especially my salvation—and for the idea for this book. I pray that in some small way, it might bring glory to His holy name.

PROLOGUE
A SAD CHRISTMAS

It was a crisp December morning, just days before Christmas, but Joanna was not in a merry mood at all. She stepped into her grandmother's bedroom and closed the door, shutting out the somber voices and weeping relatives.

Joanna plopped down on her grandmother's bed, buried her face in the palms of her hands and wept. She couldn't understand why her grandmother had died. That's not to say she could not understand the deadly ailment that took her life—after all Joanna was ten years old, clearly old enough to understand that cancer killed. What Joanna could not understand was why God had allowed her grandmother to die.

Joanna's grandmother was the most devoted Christian Joanna had ever known. She went to church every Sunday and sometimes on Wednesday. She and the other ladies in her knitting group knitted hats and scarves for the homeless, and she took meals to shut-ins every other Tuesday. She kept a Bible on her bedside table and said her prayers every night before going to sleep. Joanna never heard her grandmother say a cross word to anyone, and was generally considered one of the gentlest and most generous women in the entire church.

Deep down, however, it was not really her grandmother that Joanna wept for. Sure she missed her grandmother terribly, but the truth was Joanna wept more for her mother who had died a few years earlier when a drunk driver crossed over the center line and slammed into her mother's car head-on.

When Joanna's daddy had told her that mom had gone to live with Jesus, Joanna asked him why Jesus would take her mom away from them. After all, Jesus had the angels and God, His own mother Mary and all of His disciples, and all the good people who had ever died to keep Him company. Why did Jesus need Joanna's mom, too? Her dad couldn't answer the question.

As she sat on her grandmother's bed, Joanna used her fingers to wipe tears from her cheeks, before spying a tissue box on the bedside table, right beside her grandmother's old worn Bible. Joanna reached over and plucked a tissue from the box, brought it to her nose and blew. As Joanna blew her nose, the door to the bedroom swung open and her granddaddy poked his head inside.

"Hey kiddo," Granddaddy said.

"Hey," came Joanna's sullen response. She did not even bother to look up, but kept her eyes on the floor.

"I was wondering where you got off to," Granddaddy smiled as he sat down on the edge of the bed beside Joanna and wrapped an arm around her, pulling her close to him. "I hate these things, too."

Joanna nodded. What was there to like? Everyone just stood around eating snacks, crying, and trying desperately to remember the good times.

"I miss her," Joanna said.

"I imagine you miss your sweet mother, too, don't you?" Granddaddy asked with a gentle smile. Joanna nodded. "Thought so," Granddaddy whispered. "I do, too, but you know, you'll see them again one day," Granddaddy smiled. "In Heaven."

Joanna shook her head. "I'm not sure there is a Heaven," she said.

"What?" asked Granddaddy as his long gray eyebrows rose high on his wrinkled forehead. "No Heaven? Then where do God and the angels live?"

Joanna turned to face her grandfather with a skeptical frown. "Maybe there is no God or angels," she replied.

"What makes you say that?" Granddaddy asked, taken aback.

"Well, everybody says God loves us, right?"

"That's right," Granddaddy replied. "In fact He loves us so much He sent His only son, Jesus Christ, to Earth, to live as one of us and to die for all of our sins."

"If that's true and He loves us so much why does He let us die?" she asked. "Why did he take Mom and Grandma?"

Granddaddy rubbed Joanna's back gently as he attempted a comforting smile. "You know, your grandmother used to ask the same thing."

Joanna's eyes widened with surprise. "Really?" she asked. She couldn't imagine her grandmother ever doubting God.

"Oh, yes," Granddaddy said with a chuckle. "She was French you know."

Joanna nodded. Of course she knew. She'd only been told like a kazillion times.

"When the Nazis invaded France during World War II,

your great-grandparents were able to sneak your grandmother and her little brother out of the country to England."

"I know," Joanna said.

"They were Jews you see," Granddaddy explained, "and the Nazis didn't particularly like Jews."

"Why not?" Joanna asked, genuinely curious. She couldn't imagine anyone not liking her grandmother.

Granddaddy shrugged. "Who knows why people don't like other people. But the Nazis really disliked the Jews. In fact, they tried to kill all of them."

Joanna gasped. She hadn't heard this part of the story before. "Even the children?"

"Oh yes," Granddaddy frowned. "Especially the children."

"They were really bad guys," Joanna said softly.

"Indeed they were," Granddaddy replied. "Unfortunately, your grandmother's parents and her eldest brother were not able to get out of the country. They hid for a while, in the cellar of a nice Christian family, but were eventually discovered."

"What happened to them?" Joanna asked.

"They were taken to a camp, with other people the Nazis didn't like." Granddaddy frowned. "The Nazis didn't like very many people."

"A camp?" Joanna asked. "Like the church camp I go to in the summer?"

Granddaddy shook his head. "No, my dear, not like that. It was a prison camp, where they were kept until they were executed."

"Executed?" Joanna asked. "You mean they were killed?"

"Yes," Granddaddy nodded. "They were killed. Murdered. But thankfully your grandmother and her little brother were safe in England, living with a Christian family there."

"And that's where she met you," Joanna said, proud that she knew that part.

"Yes, when I was stationed in England with the Air Force," Granddaddy smiled.

"And you two got married and she moved back to America with you," Joanna told him.

"That's right."

"But she didn't believe in God?" Joanna asked.

"She did then, yes," Granddaddy said. "But there was a time when she did not. Like you, she couldn't understand why God would allow so much suffering. Why would He allow the Nazis to kill her parents, her older brother, and millions of others?"

"So what happened to change her mind?" Joanna asked.

"One day when she was a teenager, the priest at the church she attended with her foster parents, asked if she was ready to accept Jesus as her Lord and be baptized as a Christian," Granddaddy explained. "She told him no, and explained that she didn't believe in a God that allowed such evil and suffering like her Jewish family endured. She liked and respected Jesus, but if He was really their savior, why hadn't He saved her family and so many others?"

"So what did the priest say?" Joanna asked.

"Well, he sat your grandmother down, pointed to the crucifix behind the altar and asked if she thought Jesus suffered when he was nailed to the cross. 'Oh yes,' she replied. The priest explained that at the moment Christ was nailed to the cross, God was silent. It was the first time in Jesus' life that he did not feel the presence of his Heavenly Father."

"Is that true?" Joanna asked.

"It is," Granddaddy replied. "Then the priest reached into his pocket, produced a small scrap of paper and handed it to her. Your grandmother unfolded it and found a three line poem."

"What did it say?" Joanna asked, her eyes wide with anticipation.

"I'll let you read it for yourself," Granddaddy smiled. "The priest let her keep it."

Granddaddy rose from the bed and crossed the room to the dresser. He took something from the top of the dresser and then returned to the bed and once again sat down beside Joanna. Granddaddy opened his hand revealing a locket composed of silver angel's wings forming the shape of a heart. Joanna recognized it immediately. Her grandmother had worn that locket every day of her life. She always told Joanna that it helped keep God close to her heart.

"Take it," Granddaddy said.

Joanna raised her eyes to meet his before returning them to the silver treasure and scooping it up.

"Open it," Granddaddy told her. Joanna found the small clasp on the side and opened the angel wings up. Inside she found a small, folded, yellowed, piece of paper. She removed the paper as she handed the locket back to Granddaddy.

Joanna unfolded the paper and looked down at the faded words scribbled onto it. She struggled to read it, but eventually made it out. "I believe in the sun, even when it is not shining," she read. "I believe in love even when I don't feel it. I believe in God, even when he is silent." She looked up at her Grandfather.

"The priest explained to your grandmother, that the greatest good that ever occurred, came while God silently allowed the suffering of His son. It was Jesus taking the punishment that we all deserve for the sins we commit, that allows us to go to Heaven to live with Him and His Heavenly

Father," Granddaddy explained.

"Then the priest told your grandmother that the poem she had read had been found in a cellar in France, scribbled on the wall by a Jew hiding from the Nazis. No one knows who wrote the poem, but your grandmother came to believe it was her own father. She believed God had brought her to that particular church, to meet that particular priest who had that particular poem, so that her soul would be saved."

"And it was?" Joanna asked as she wiped tears from her cheeks.

"Yes," Granddaddy said with a grin. "She became a Christian then and there, and told the priest that she wanted to be baptized."

Joanna looked back down at the folded paper as a tear dropped onto it. She folded it back up, placed it gently back into the locket, and snapped the angel wings shut.

Granddaddy smiled and placed the silver chain around Joanna's neck. "I'd like you to keep it," Granddaddy said, "so you can always have God close to your heart."

Joanna nodded as tears streamed down her cheeks and she threw her arms around her grandfather's neck. At that moment she believed. She trusted God and His purpose and knew without a doubt that she would see her mother and grandmother again. One day they would all meet in Heaven.

CHAPTER ONE
THE RED DRAGON

The screeching roar cut through the darkness and chilled Peter Puckett to the bone. Where had it come from? More importantly, what was the source? Peter frantically glanced about in the night, desperately searching for whatever had made that terrifying sound. Then he felt something in his right hand and glanced down to see that he gripped a shining sword, with a golden hilt molded into the shape of a fierce lion's head. The sword's blade was so shiny, in fact, that it appeared to almost glow in the darkness.

Peter didn't remember having a sword. He certainly did not remember taking a sword to bed with him. As he stared curiously at the sword, he noticed his shining silver gauntlets. Gauntlets? His eyes followed the armor covering his arm all the way up to the brilliant silver breastplate covering his chest and emblazoned with a golden lion's head.

Peter suddenly realized that he was covered head to toe in the most stunningly brilliant armor he could have ever imagined. He shone in the darkness, like a lamp on a stand. And that wasn't all, in his left hand, he held a shield—a beautifully crafted instrument divided into fourths by a ruby red cross. Peter lifted the shield to admire it. It too was brilliant and beautiful, and so shiny that Peter could see his reflection. At least it should have been his reflection.

Peter stared curiously at the image staring back at him. It almost appeared to be Peter, it looked similar, but yet it wasn't Peter. His brown hair was covered by a shining silver helmet, but Peter could still tell that the image was older. The person staring back at Peter was a teenager, and Peter most definitely was not a teenager. You see, Peter Puckett was only ten years old. That's when Peter realized that he was dreaming.

He smiled to himself, suddenly enjoying the dream. After all, what little boy didn't want to be a knight in shining armor? Peter hoped he would find a fair maiden to rescue or perhaps a dragon to slay. His enjoyment was short-lived however, as the screeching roar once again cut through the darkness of the night. Peter quickly changed his mind about wanting to slay a dragon. He had no desire to see a dragon or anything else so terrifying.

Fear swept through Peter and he began to run—to flee whatever it was that had produced such a blood-curdling roar. He ran and ran as fast as he could, which was considerably harder than usual considering the heavy weight of the armor.

Peter had no idea where he was running to, but he knew he did not want to be out in the darkness with the roaring creature—whatever it was. He suddenly noticed a light cutting through the night, and saw what appeared to be a city on a hill in the distance. He ran toward it. It seemed a long way off and hard to reach, but he had to try. Who knew what evil lurked out here in the darkness waiting to gobble him up?

CHAPTER ONE

Peter stopped briefly to catch his breath before continuing on toward the shining city. His beating heart competed with his heavy breathing as the noisiest thing in the darkness, but then Peter heard something much louder than either his heart or his breath. The thump thump thump of wings beating the air reached Peter's ears and he spun around to see a giant beast soaring toward him through the darkness of the night.

In his panic, Peter dropped both his shield and his sword as he fled the monster. He ran as fast as he could manage while dropping his helmet, and loosening the leather straps of the breastplate and pulling it off over his head, before dropping it to the ground. Peter jerked off his armored boots and gauntlets, and loosened his belt, allowing anything that might slow him down to fall away from him.

Soon Peter wore nothing but the long superhero pajamas he had gone to bed in. He was lighter now and faster. Much faster. He glanced over his shoulder and saw the beast gaining on him. He gasped as he realized it was indeed a dragon—a fiery red dragon with seven heads and ten horns. Its great wings beat against the night air as it swooped down toward Peter—all seven of its massive mouths opened to reveal long sharp fangs.

Peter knew he could not outrun the red dragon and turned to face it, suddenly wishing—more than anything—that he had not dropped his sword, his shield and his armor. He had thought he would fare better without them holding him back, but now he realized that it was impossible to fight the dragon without his armor and weapons. Unfortunately, it was too late! The giant dragon was upon him. One of its massive mouths—twice the size of Peter's bed—opened wide and Peter screamed in terror as the beast's enormous jaws clamped down on him.

THE RED DRAGON

***

Peter Puckett was still screaming when he found himself sitting up in bed facing a startled Ms. Naomi Parsons. Ms. Naomi leapt back with a wail of her own, so shocked by the screaming Peter, that she nearly tripped over her own feet and fell to the floor. Fortunately, she was able to right herself before she completely collapsed, but by the time Peter realized who she was, she looked completely out-of-sorts.

"Peter!" Ms. Naomi exclaimed as she rushed toward him, wrapping her arms around his shoulders in a comforting embrace. "Are you all right?"

Peter glanced about his room to make sure there were no dragons or other fantastic beasts which might be lurking there to gobble him up. Satisfied that the monsters were all confined to his dreams Peter turned to Ms. Naomi with a calm, but red face. She was so pretty with her dark hair framing her delicate face and oval glasses that Peter thought there was likely not an angel in heaven to match her.

"I had a terrible nightmare," he explained.

"I imagine so," Ms. Naomi replied as she sat down on his bed beside him.

Their conversation was interrupted by a voice from downstairs, inquiring about the sudden screams emanating from Peter's bedroom.

"Is everything all right up there?" called Father Joe Parsons in his proper English accent.

"Yes, darling," Ms. Naomi called back over her shoulder. "Peter was just having a bad dream."

"Very well, but do let me know if I am needed," her husband urged.

"We will, darling," Ms. Naomi replied with an amused

smile. "Meanwhile, you go ahead and eat your cereal before it gets soggy."

She turned back to Peter and laid a delicate palm against his cheek. "Are you all right, my sweet?" she asked. Peter nodded and smiled at her. He loved to hear Ms. Naomi speak. Her voice was soft and beautiful and her British pronunciation of words made everything she said seem so important.

"I'm fine, thank you," Peter replied.

"Well, whatever kind of dream could have made you sit up in bed screaming like that?" Ms. Naomi asked.

Peter shook his head. "The scary kind," he smiled.

Ms. Naomi rose and patted him on the head. "Obviously," she chuckled and then straightened her blue dress, before crossing the room to the window to open the curtains, allowing the sunlight to pour in. "You'd better hurry up and get dressed or you'll be late for school," she reminded him as she stepped over to his door. "And I'd better go let your mother know everything is all right. If she heard all of that screaming she's liable to think we've a demon loose in the house."

Ms. Naomi floated out of the room with a wink, closing the door behind her. Once she was gone Peter tossed the blankets off of him and let his feet drop to the soft carpeted floor. He stood from the bed and began stripping off his pajamas to get dressed for school.

After dressing, Peter placed his large round glasses onto his nose. Peter glanced in the mirror noticing the glasses almost hid the freckles which dotted the bridge of his nose and spots of his cheeks just under his eyes. He ran fingers through his disheveled brown hair which had almost no effect, and then hurried down the steps and into the kitchen where he found a toaster tart and a tall glass of milk waiting for him on the kitchen table. He pulled out his chair and plopped down into it.

"Good morning," he heard and glanced up to see Father Joe smiling at him from the other end of the table wearing his customary black shirt and white collar. The priest had short brown hair—graying a bit on the sides—which he parted to the left. Ms. Naomi sat next to her husband, her hands folded together. The Parsons had already finished their breakfast of sugarless cereal, and Peter's breakfast was the only food remaining on the table. Peter disliked sugarless cereal about as much as a boy could dislike any food, and Ms. Naomi was nice enough to allow him to eat an icing-covered toaster tart with strawberry jam in the middle instead.

"Good morning," Peter replied with a toothy grin as he scooped up his toaster tart and took a bite.

"You haven't said the blessing yet," Ms. Naomi scolded.

"Oh, yeah," Peter said as he laid down his toaster tart and folded his hands in front of his face. "Sorry."

Father Joe chuckled as he watched the boy pray. "Heavenly Father, thank you for all of the blessings you have given us. Especially this food. Amen."

"Amen," Father Joe and Ms. Naomi echoed in unison as they watched Peter take another bite of his toaster tart.

"So how is school going young man?" Father Joe inquired of Peter. "Are you adjusting well?"

Peter nodded between bites. He wasn't really, but he didn't want to worry Father Joe. The priest and his wife had been so kind to Peter and his mother. They really cared for him and if they knew how hard it had been, that would have made them sad. So he kept those things to himself.

Father Joe was the priest at Holy Redeemer, a small church that Peter's grandfather had been raised in and Peter's mother

CHAPTER ONE

had grown up in. Peter's mother had not lived in the town for many years, however. She had married a United States Marine, and as a military family, Peter and his mother lived wherever his father was stationed.

That is until his father's unit was sent to the other side of the world to fight a war. Peter and his mother couldn't go with him and remained in their small apartment just outside of the Marine Corps base in Southern California. A few months after Peter's father had gone off to war, he and his mother received the news that Peter's father had been killed in action. That was two years ago.

Peter and his mother left California soon after to move back east to live with Peter's grandfather. A year ago, they had moved Granddaddy into a home as his dementia had become so bad that Peter's mother could no longer care for him. Six months after that, Peter's mother was diagnosed with cancer. The doctors did not give her very long to live.

She had no one left except Peter, and he wasn't big enough to take care of himself, much less a sick mother. That's when Father Joe—who despite the vast age difference, had been a close friend of Peter's grandfather—invited Peter and his mother to stay with him and his wife Naomi in the rectory where they lived next door to the church.

Peter's mother was reluctant to do so. She wasn't close to the Parsons and only knew them through her father. Besides, it made her somewhat uncomfortable to benefit from such selfless Christian charity, when she herself had stopped believing in God some time ago. She was worried that she would be lambasted with the Gospel every second of her last few months on earth. That was a fate she dreaded almost worse than death itself. She wanted to die in peace, not hearing how she would be banished to the lake of fire for all eternity if she didn't believe in God and Jesus Christ.

Unfortunately for Peter's mother, however, she did not really have any choice in the matter as she had absolutely nowhere else to turn. But after moving in with the Parsons, Peter's mother was pleasantly surprised to discover that Father Joe and Ms. Naomi never tried to force Jesus on her. Sure they prayed over her, taught Peter Bible stories, took him to church and Sunday School, and did their very best to introduce *him* to Jesus, but they never did try to force anything on Peter's mother. The Parsons had been very good to her and her son, and though she appreciated it more than she could express, she was still no nearer to God than she had been when she first came to live with them.

Because Peter's mother was so sick, Father Joe and Ms. Naomi had the job of caring for Peter. Father Joe was in a delicate situation. He wanted to be a father figure to Peter, but realized that he was not Peter's father and certainly did not want to come off as too pushy. He was grateful that Peter, for the most part, was a good kid, but he did worry about the boy, especially since Peter had to change schools when he crossed town to live at the rectory.

Peter always told the Parsons that school was going fine. The truth was Peter didn't have any friends at his new school. Sure, he had some friends from Sunday School and church, but none of them attended the same school as Peter. He tried to make friends at school, but it wasn't always easy being the new kid. Of course Peter had been at that school for a couple of months, so he didn't think he was that new anymore.

Peter crammed the last bite of toaster tart into his mouth—stuffing it so full that it elicited a frown from Ms. Naomi—before washing it down with the remainder of his milk.

"Peter Puckett, one day you are going to choke if you don't

start taking smaller bites," Ms. Naomi scolded him.

"Sorry," Peter apologized as he wiped his mouth with the sleeve of his shirt further frustrating Ms. Naomi.

"I gave you a napkin for a reason," she remarked.

"Oh yeah," Peter said with a good natured smile before picking the napkin up from the table and wiping his hands and face.

Ms. Naomi shook her head as she stood to clear his plate and glass. She leaned over close. "Your mother seems to be doing better than usual this morning, you should go see her before you head off to school," she said softly.

"Yes, ma'am," Peter replied as he stood. He walked toward the living room, but was stopped by Father Joe's voice.

"I'd like to talk to you before you leave, if I could," the priest said.

"Okay, Father Joe," Peter replied and then stepped out of the small kitchen and crossed the living room to the bedroom on the other side.

Peter found his mother lying on a bed, pillows propping her up so that she could watch the television. She didn't notice Peter as he tiptoed into the room, doing his best to be extra quiet, just in case she was asleep. Peter's mother slept a lot, and Peter never wanted to wake her. After all, when he was sick his mother had always told him that he needed to rest. If rest would work for Peter, it should work for his mother, too. Maybe if she rested enough she would get better.

"Peter!" his mother said, clearly startled by him. "You scared me. I didn't hear you come in." She held out her hand for him.

"Sorry, Momma," Peter said as he approached her bed and took hold of her hand. Her fingers were cold and bony. They looked old. Much older than his mother's fingers should have looked given her age.

"It is all right, baby," she replied. "I'm glad to see you this morning. What was all of that screaming about upstairs?"

Peter shrugged. "I just had a bad dream," he told her.

"It must have been pretty terrible," his mother replied.

"I don't really remember," he said.

His mother smiled. "That's what happens with dreams," she told him. "They fade away."

"You look good this morning," Peter said.

This caused his mother to chuckle, but she did look better than normal. Her face was not as white as it usually was, and she seemed to have more life in her eyes. When the cancer was discovered, the doctors had informed Peter's mother that she was too far gone for any treatments to help, and therefore suggested she not weaken her body further by using chemotherapy and radiation to kill the cancer cells. Thus, Peter's mother never lost her hair, as was common for cancer patients undergoing chemotherapy, and it fell in messy rings around her face and pillow. Still, her breathing was laborious and she seemed to strain even to speak and hold Peter's hand.

"Did you do all of your homework last night?" Peter's mother asked him through deep breaths.

"Yes," Peter nodded. "Father Joe helped me with my math."

"Good," his mother replied with a smile, but the smile quickly turned into a grimace. Peter noticed tears stream down her cheeks as she winced with a pain Peter realized must be very intense. She released Peter's hand as she squeezed her eyes shut and gripped the sheets tightly while emitting an agonizing groan from her lips.

"Momma," Peter said in a voice full of concern. "Momma are you all right?" But his mother didn't answer. Instead she moaned in agony as pain surged through her body. "Momma, how can I help you?" Peter pleaded as tears began building up in his own eyes and streaming down his own cheeks.

Peter heard footsteps behind him and then felt a hand on his arm as Ms. Naomi gently moved him from the side of the bed. "You go on to school, darling," Ms. Naomi said with a comforting smile. "I'll take care of your mother."

"But, I can…" Peter began as he looked at his mother lying on the bed writhing in pain.

"Not now, Peter," Ms. Naomi said firmly, and her eyes told Peter she meant it. Ms. Naomi turned away from Peter toward Peter's mother.

"Come on, my boy," came Father Joe's voice from behind causing Peter to turn around. "How about I walk you to school this mornin'?"

Peter nodded as he wiped the tears from his eyes. Father Joe wrapped an arm around Peter's shoulder leading him away. Before he left, Peter stole one more glance into the room. His mother was weeping into her hands, as Ms. Naomi lifted her cell phone to her ear.

"I'm calling the nurse now," Ms. Naomi informed Peter's mother, and that was the last Peter heard before Father Joe whisked him through the living room, into the kitchen, where he grabbed his book bag, and out the door to school.

CHAPTER TWO
THE GIRL IN THE OVERSIZED GLASSES

The air was cool, but the sun was shining brightly as Father Joe walked Peter to school. The church and rectory were less than half a mile from school, and so Peter walked there every day that the weather wasn't bad. Often times he walked alone, but sometimes—like today—Father Joe or Ms. Naomi walked with him.

"The nurse will do the best she can to make your mother comfortable, Peter," Father Joe told him as they walked along the sidewalk.

"I know," Peter replied. "I just wish there was something I could do to help her."

The priest placed an arm around Peter's shoulder. "There are things you can do, Peter," he said.

"Like what?" Peter asked as he glanced up at Father Joe with a curious face.

CHAPTER TWO

Father Joe peered back at Peter with a friendly smile. "Well, what do you think?" he asked the boy.

Peter shrugged. "She likes it when I visit her," he replied.

"Indeed she does," Father Joe agreed. "And keeping her spirits up helps more than you can know."

Peter nodded. "I suppose I could draw her a pretty picture."

"That's an excellent idea, my boy. What else?"

Peter contemplated the question for a while. "I suppose if I make good grades and don't get in trouble, that would help."

"Yes, it would," Father Joe agreed. "Your mother certainly doesn't need to be worrying about your school marks."

"But I wish there was something I could do to help save her," Peter said.

Father Joe stopped walking and bent over to look Peter in the eye. "There is, Peter. And its the best thing you can do for your mother, or for anyone else for that matter."

Peter cocked his head to the side, perplexed at what Father Joe could be talking about. "What's that?" he asked.

Father Joe laid a hand on each of Peter's shoulders and looked deeply into the boy's eyes. "You can ask God to help her."

Peter frowned. "Does that really work?" he asked skeptically.

Father Joe straightened back up. "Of course it works," he said. "If you trust in God He will always answer your prayers." Then Father Joe thought for a second. "Though He does not always answer them the way you intended. Nor does He always answer them right away."

"Well, how long does it take?" Peter asked.

Father Joe laughed as he placed an arm around Peter's shoulder once more, guiding him toward the school.

THE GIRL IN THE OVERSIZED GLASSES

"Sometimes it can take quite a long time, my boy," Father Joe told him.

"Really?"

"Oh, yes," Father Joe answered. "Ms. Naomi has been praying that God would bless us with a child the entire 19 years of our marriage."

"But you still don't have one," Peter said.

"That's right. But it doesn't stop Ms. Naomi from asking, every single night, that God give us a child to love and raise and protect."

"She hasn't given up yet?" Peter asked.

Father Joe chuckled. "Hardly," he said. "Ms. Naomi does not give up easily, in case you hadn't noticed."

Actually, Peter had noticed. Ms. Naomi was nothing if not persistent.

"Besides," said Father Joe, "Abraham and his wife Sarah didn't have a child until they were old and gray."

"Really?" asked Peter, remembering the names from his Sunday School lessons. Abraham was the father of the Jewish people, so he obviously had children. "How old?"

"Well," thought Father Joe, "Abraham was a hundred and his wife Sarah was around ninety."

"Wow!" exclaimed Peter. "That's really old."

"Indeed," Father Joe remarked. "And of course you remember John the Baptist from Sunday School?"

"Yeah, he was Jesus' cousin," Peter said. "He ate bugs with honey on them."

Father Joe laughed. "That's right, he ate locusts and honey and dressed in camel hair. But did you know his parents were really old when he was born?"

"How old were they?" Peter inquired. "Like a hundred?"

"The Bible doesn't tell us exactly how old they were, but

John's father Zechariah described himself as an 'old man.' So old in fact, that he refused to believe the angel who told him that he and his wife would have a child. As punishment for not believing, Zechariah lost his voice and could not speak until the day his son John was born."

"How long was that?" Peter asked.

"At least nine months I would imagine."

"Wow, that's a long time," Peter replied. "I guess you should always believe an angel."

Father Joe chuckled. "Good words to live by, Peter," he said. "The point is that nothing is impossible for God," Father Joe said. "And Jesus tells us to be persistent in our prayers. So if you really want God to save your mother, keep praying for it and praying for it."

Father Joe stopped walking because they had reached the school. He turned and looked down at Peter. "Do you understand, Peter?" he asked.

Peter nodded.

"Good boy," Father Joe smiled and patted him on the back. "Have a good day and I'll see you after school."

"Okay," Peter said, somewhat sadly, and then turned and walked away, down the small hill leading to the school playground. As he reached the playground he turned around to look at Father Joe, but the priest had already left, returning to the rectory or the church.

As Peter continued toward the school, he noticed Dylan Bodi speaking with some of his friends over by the slides. Peter hurried past, too scared to use the slide and hoping that Dylan and his gang wouldn't notice him. Dylan was a lot bigger than Peter and nearly a year older, going through fourth grade for the second time. He was also the class bully, picking on all the kids all the time. He especially liked to tease Peter, because Peter was the new kid. The new kid always got it worse, and besides physically beating Peter up and playing pranks on him, Dylan teased him with mean names like "four eyes" because Peter wore glasses. In fact, Peter thought that he might have friends at school except that the other kids were worried that they would be mercilessly teased if they played with him.

Thankfully, this morning Peter was able to slip past Dylan and his friends undetected. He found a spot on the far side of a large oak tree where a boy might hide somewhat from other students, especially the bullies. Peter often hid there playing by himself in the dirt before school and during recess, reenacting scenes from his favorite cartoon shows, or building houses for ants.

This morning, however, Peter didn't really feel like playing in the dirt. He was still upset about his mother's pain. His hopes had been raised when she had seemed brighter and more alive that morning, but when the pain started, it dashed all of those hopes. Tears began to well up in Peter's eyes and he pushed back his glasses to wipe them away.

Peter loved his mother very much and did not want her to die, but more than that, he was afraid to be left all alone. His father had already died, his grandfather's mind was so sick he couldn't even feed himself or recognize Peter, and if his mother died Peter wouldn't have anyone. Peter would be completely alone.

Peter couldn't hold back the tears anymore. They poured from his eyes and down his cheeks creating small rivers over his freckles and across his soft white skin. Peter didn't know what he was going to do. Then he remembered what Father Joe had said. Peter remembered that his father and mother used to pray with him every night before bed before his father had died. And while his father was off at war, he and his mother prayed every night that God would bring him home safely. But Daddy never came home, and Momma stopped praying. She stopped reading Peter Bible stories and attending church. She stopped believing God existed at all.

Peter shook his head. If Father Joe was right, then why did God let Daddy die? After all, Peter and his mother had prayed and prayed that God would save him and bring him home. They were certainly persistent. Peter began to doubt that Father Joe knew what he was talking about and was just about to give up the idea of praying, but a nagging feeling tugged at him, convincing him that he had nothing to lose. Momma's life was worth trying anything.

So, Peter rolled over onto his knees in the dirt behind the oak tree and began to pray. "God," he said. "Please save my mother. Please don't let her die. Don't let me be alone." He wiped the tears from his eyes. "And if it's not too much trouble, please give Father Joe and Ms. Naomi a child to raise. They sure do love children." He was about to finish with an "Amen" when he remembered something. "Oh yeah, and if you could send me a friend at school, that would really be nice. Thank you. Amen."

Peter used his fingers to cross himself like Father Joe had taught him at church. He wiped the remaining tears from his face and stood up. He was just about to turn around when he heard words that made his heart sink.

"Hey there Four Eyes!" Dylan's voice taunted viciously.

Peter sighed. He'd been spotted.

"Look at that dork in the huge glasses!" Dylan and his friends cackled.

Peter slowly turned around to face them, ready for their torment. But to Peter's great relief, he realized the bullies were not looking at him. In fact, they were looking in the opposite direction. Peter cocked his head in puzzlement.

"I bet she can see Mars with those things!" laughed one of Dylan's friends—a redheaded, freckle-faced boy that liked to shoot spit-balls at Peter when their teacher, Mrs. Downing, wasn't looking.

Peter was taken aback. Did he say "she?" Peter peered past the crew of bullies to see a small, shy girl with long blond hair pulled up with a red bow, wearing a blue and red dress and the most oversized glasses Peter had ever seen perched upon her nose. The girl did not look up, but kept her eyes on the ground as she quickly moved past the bullies mocking her.

Peter didn't recognize the girl. He was certain he had never seen her before. That meant that she was new. Peter smiled to himself. This might be his lucky day. With a new kid in school, especially one with glasses so big they didn't even fit her head, maybe he would finally be off the radar of Dylan's crew.

The bell rang, and Peter lifted his book bag over his shoulder to run to the building with all of the other kids. As he found his classroom, he was elated to see the new girl was in his class. Now Dylan and his friends could shoot spitballs at her instead of him. Maybe God was smiling on him after all.

Peter placed his plastic tray of food on top of the pea green cafeteria table before sitting down in a small chair. He sat at the end. That's where the other kids had relegated him—all alone at one end of the table, with the seats right beside him always remaining empty.

Peter looked down at his tray to see a small pepperoni pizza, a scoop of potatoes, and a few green beans. He sighed.

CHAPTER TWO

It wasn't the best meal, but it wasn't the worst either. Peter opened his carton of chocolate milk and scooped up the pizza ready to take a bite. He never said the blessing at school, because he was afraid the other kids would make fun of him.

Just as Peter was swallowing the piece of pizza, someone sat down right beside him. Peter turned his head to see Danny Fields smiling at him.

"Hi, Peter," Danny said.

Peter stared at Danny for a long moment. He was unsure of what to say. None of the other kids had ever said hello to him before. Before he could speak, Zack Trevor sat down in the seat across from him.

"Hey Peter, hey Danny," Zack smiled.

Peter was so surprised he nearly choked on his pizza. Then Peter suddenly got very suspicious. They were trying to play a prank on him. Dylan must have put them up to it.

"Why are you guys talking to me?" Peter asked accusingly.

Zack laughed. "Because we can now."

"What?" asked Peter.

"Look, Peter, we like you," Danny said. "You're a nice kid and we've always felt bad that nobody would play with you, but until you arrived, Dylan used to terrorize us."

"Yeah," Zack nodded. "You got us off the hook, and we knew if we came anywhere near you that Dylan would set his sights on us again."

"So now you want to be my friends?" Peter asked somewhat skeptically.

"Of course," Danny replied with a broad smile. "In fact, Zack and I are going over to my house after school to play video games. Do you want to come?"

Peter couldn't believe this. Of course he wanted to go play video games with Zack and Danny. "Yeah, that would be great!" Peter said as the elation washed over him. Father Joe was right—God did answer prayers, and he answered this one a whole lot faster than Ms. Naomi's prayers to have a child of her own.

"So what made you start talking to me now?" Peter asked. He wanted to know how God worked and was curious if they had heard a voice from Heaven, or if God had just placed the idea in their heads.

"Because you aren't the object of Dylan's teasing anymore. She is," Danny said as he pointed down the table.

Peter's eyes followed Danny's finger to the other end of the table where he saw the new girl in the oversized glasses sitting all alone, the chairs around her empty. He also saw Dylan and his crew laughing as they kept glancing at her, making jokes about how silly she looked. She never looked at them, but kept her eyes focused on her tray of food. Peter saw her push her glasses up and wipe her eyes. He knew she was trying desperately not to cry. It's the same thing Peter did when he was mercilessly mocked by Dylan and his friends.

"I kinda feel sorry for her, but what are we supposed to do?" asked Zack.

"Yeah," Peter said softly.

"It was the same thing with you," Danny explained. "We wanted to be your friends, but we sure liked not having Dylan pick on us anymore."

"But now you're safe," Zack smiled.

"Yep and we can be friends," Danny agreed.

Peter nodded. He would finally have friends. But he couldn't help feeling angry at them for never speaking to him before. They had let him sit all alone with no one to talk to while bullies tormented him day after day. Would people that truly wanted to be his friends do that?

CHAPTER TWO

Peter sighed. He knew that if Father Joe found out that he had made friends at the expense of another kid's torment he'd be disappointed in Peter. He'd tell him that Jesus wouldn't like that because Jesus loved everyone. Especially those who didn't have any friends.

Suddenly Peter stood up, picked up his tray, turned and walked toward the other end of the table. Dylan and his crew watched him, but Peter didn't care. He simply shot them a cold glare. Peter walked all of the way to the other end of the table and stood across from the new girl. She slowly looked up at him, over her gigantic glasses.

"Can I sit down?" Peter asked politely. The girl did not speak, but nodded her head up and down as she kept her eyes fixed on Peter's. Peter placed his tray on the table and then sat down in the chair across from her.

"Hey look Four Eyes loves Four Eyes!" shouted Dylan. "Their children will have eight eyes!" Dylan and his friends roared with laughter until they were silenced by another voice.

"Dylan Bodi, that is enough out of you!" came Mrs. Downing's firm voice. "One more word and you will be going to the principal's office. Do you hear me?"

"Yes, ma'am," Dylan said sheepishly, and he and his friends turned back to their trays of food in silence.

Peter smiled to himself at Dylan's scolding. He then turned to see the new girl was staring at him. In fact, she hadn't taken her eyes off of him since he sat down.

Peter gave her a friendly smile. "My name's Peter," he said. "What's yours?"

The girl smiled shyly. "Ariel," she said as she pushed her glasses high up on her nose.

"Did you just move to town?" Peter asked.

Ariel nodded. "Just this morning."

THE GIRL IN THE OVERSIZED GLASSES

"Today?" Peter asked. "Wow, and you started school, already? What do your parents do?"

Ariel shrugged. "What do your parents do?" she asked.

Peter looked down at his tray. "My Dad was a Marine, but he was killed in the war. And my mom is really sick, so she just stays in the bed."

"I'm sorry, Peter," Ariel said as she reached across the table and patted his hand gently with hers. "That must be hard. But I promise you, one day things will get better."

Peter glanced up, and his eyes met hers. He saw past her newness and glasses for the first time and realized how pretty she was. He smiled. Things were getting better already.

CHAPTER THREE
THE GOLDEN KEY

After school, Peter plodded slowly back home. For the first time since he and his mother had moved in with Father Joe and Ms. Naomi, Peter wasn't in a hurry to get back. What he really wanted to do was talk to Ariel some more. At recess that afternoon he had shown her where he liked to hide behind the big oak tree so that Dylan wouldn't notice him and spend the entire recess tormenting him. He and Ariel had sat cross-legged in the dirt talking. If Peter were being honest, he would have to admit that he had done almost all of the talking.

Peter had told Ariel all about his father and mother and how they had moved around a lot because his father had been in the military. He told her how brave his father was to go and fight the bad guys, and how much he missed him. He told her about his grandfather and his mental problems and how he would likely die soon, too. And then Peter began talking about his mother.

Peter loved his mother more than all the others. He loved

her more than anything. When he began telling Ariel about his mother's cancer tears came to his eyes. He tried to hold them back, but they broke free and flowed down his cheeks. To his surprise, Ariel hadn't made fun of him or called him a cry-baby. Instead she had reached up and wiped the tears from his face with her fingers, much like his mother used to do before she got sick.

Peter sat in the dirt staring into Ariel's eyes for a long time. There was something about her that was beautiful and amazing, but Peter couldn't quite put his finger on it. She made him want to tell her everything, and he did. He told her that that very morning before the bell rang he had prayed to God asking God to save his mother. He told her that he had also asked God to send him a friend. He smiled at her as he had explained that she had walked on campus right after he asked for a friend.

Peter looked down at the ground fearful that she would think he was crazy and was suddenly embarrassed that he had confessed so much. But she didn't think he was crazy—not at all. In fact, to Peter's delight, Ariel had replied: "Isn't God just the most amazing person EVER?!? I mean he simply said "Bang," and not only did the entire universe burst into existence, but it all fell into perfect place, so that every meteor would collide with a planet at the exact moment God wanted it to. So that every bug would eat the exact leaf at the exact time that God wanted it to. So that everything always works out exactly as he intends."

"You really believe that?" Peter asked.

Ariel had nodded vigorously. "Oh yes, it is true, Peter," she smiled. She then turned to the large oak tree they were sitting under. "When God planted this tree, two-hundred and eighty seven years ago, he knew that the two of us would be sitting here, today, talking about the exact things we are talking about."

Peter's eyes popped wide. Father Joe and Ms. Naomi had spoken to him about how amazing God was many times, but they had never put it into that perspective. Peter suddenly felt such awe for his creator, and felt quite confident not only that God *could* save his mother, but also that God *would* save his mother. After all, God had already answered one prayer today—why not another? And for the first time in a long time, Peter felt joy in his heart.

Ariel had been very interested to hear about the church and the rectory where Peter and his mother lived with Father Joe and Ms. Naomi. He promised to show it to her sometime and suggested that she and her parents should attend the service there that Sunday.

But it wasn't Sunday yet and Peter walked home, alone. He wanted to get home quickly, hoping that his mother was already healed, but he also wanted to talk to Ariel, just one more time. She had disappeared in the flood of students after the bell rang and Peter assumed she had gone to the bus or to meet her parents. Still, he walked slowly keeping an eye out for her, just in case.

"Peter!" came a sweet voice behind him and he spun around to see Ariel walking quickly to catch him. Peter's heart raced as a big, toothy grin spread across his face. "I've been looking all over for you," Ariel smiled when she reached him.

"Oh yeah?" he asked.

"Don't you want to show me the church?" she asked.

"Sure," he said excitedly, but then frowned. "But don't you need to get home to your parents?"

"No," she replied. "My parents aren't there."

"Oh," Peter exclaimed. Assuming Ariel's parents both

worked and she wouldn't want to go home alone, he decided to invite her home with him. "Well, why don't you come meet Father Joe and Ms. Naomi. I'm sure Ms. Naomi will give us a snack. Then I can show you the church."

Ariel nodded with excitement. "That sounds wonderful," she said.

"And we can check on my Mom to see if God has healed her yet."

Ms. Naomi had been delighted to meet Ariel and happily fixed her and Peter glasses of milk and a plate of chocolate chip cookies. Ariel smiled broadly as she took her first bite, her eyes lighting up like a Christmas tree.

"Did you know that chocolate chip cookies are the only cookies that British people call cookies?" Peter asked Ariel, showing off some of the British trivia he'd learned since moving in with Father Joe and Ms. Naomi.

"What do they call other cookies?" Ariel asked.

Peter snickered and stole a glance at Ms. Naomi to see her chuckling. "Biscuits," he said causing Ariel to giggle.

The girl turned to Ms. Naomi. "These are amazing!" she said.

"Well, thank you, Ariel," Ms. Naomi replied proudly. "They just came out of a tube."

Peter washed his last cookie down with the tall glass of cold milk and then—much to Ms. Naomi's displeasure—wiped his mouth with the sleeve of his shirt.

"Peter Puckett, how many times do I have to tell you to use your napkin?" Ms. Naomi scolded.

"Sorry," Peter replied.

Ms. Naomi frowned as she cleared the cookie plates and

glasses from the table, but Ariel smiled brightly, and her joy was contagious.

Ms. Naomi returned the smile. "Why are you smiling so big?" she asked the girl.

Ariel used her forefinger to push her oversized glasses further up her nose with a sweet laugh. "I was just thinking about what a wonderful mother you are going to be," she replied.

Ms. Naomi stopped cold and stared at Ariel for a moment as her smile reluctantly faded from her face. She quickly spun around, away from the children, as she set the plates in the sink. Then Peter heard a sniff and saw her wipe her cheek and he knew she was crying.

After an awkward minute, Ms. Naomi composed herself and turned back to face Peter and Ariel. Her eyes were red and her cheeks were still damp, but the bright smile had returned to her lips. "So what do you two have planned for the rest of the afternoon?" she asked.

"Ariel would like to see the church," Peter explained.

"Well, that sounds nice," Ms. Naomi replied.

"I want to check on Momma first, though," Peter told her.

Ms. Naomi seemed reluctant, but conceded. "All right, but just for a moment, Peter," she said. "Your mother needs her rest, and she is in her room with the nurse and Father Joe right now."

Peter slid down from his seat and Ariel followed him. He walked out of the kitchen and into the living room, crossing it to his mother's bedroom. Ariel stayed back a few paces, so as not to interfere.

When Peter peeked into the room he saw his mother lying flat on her back staring at the ceiling and breathing heavily, while Father Joe and the nurse stood at the foot of the bed speaking in hushed tones. Father Joe watched Peter's mother, with pain etched onto his face.

"If she lasted more than twenty-four hours, I would be shocked," the nurse explained to the priest.

Peter gasped. "No," he said weakly, calling attention to himself.

Father Joe's eyes met his and Peter saw surprise there.

"Peter," the priest said, but Peter didn't wait to speak to him. He turned and bolted away, past Ariel, through the living room, into the kitchen and out through the kitchen door. Ariel followed. Peter dashed down the wooden steps leaping over the last one to land on the grass below. He turned and sprinted for the church. Ariel pursued him.

Peter burst through the front doors of the small white building with its pointy steeple jutting into the air above. Light spilled into the church as Peter was welcomed by empty pews and a larger-than-life crucifix attached to the wall behind the altar. Besides the light beaming in through the now-opened front door, the only other light that managed to illuminate the mostly darkened church came through the stained glass windows in the front of the church and along the side walls.

Peter stared at the crucifix, a large statue of Jesus hanging on the cross. He wiped the tears from his eyes as he strode down the center aisle between the pews toward the altar, at the front of the church. Peter stopped when he reached the altar. His eyes were fixed on Jesus.

"Why won't you save her?" Peter asked as his vision blurred with tears once again. "Why won't you save her?" he shouted, but the figure of Jesus refused to answer.

"Peter," he heard his name called and spun around to see Ariel standing in the doorway. Peter wiped the tears from his face with the back of his hand. He watched her as she walked down the aisle toward him. She reached him, stood up on her tip toes and placed her arms around his neck, pulling his head down onto her shoulder.

"It's all right to cry," she whispered into his ear. "It demonstrates your love and compassion." As if they had been waiting for Ariel's permission, a flood of tears poured forth from Peter's eyes as he wrapped his arms around Ariel's waist and wept on her shoulder. While he cried she patted his hair like his mother used to before she got sick.

"It's not fair," Peter said with a giant sniff.

Ariel lifted his head off of her shoulder so that she could look deeply into his eyes. "Who is to judge what is fair except God? He will show favor unto those He wishes to show favor."

Peter wiped his eyes. "Why won't He show favor on my mother?" he asked.

Ariel smiled gently as she pushed a strand of Peter's hair back from his face. "Oh, He has, Peter," Ariel said, her voice filled with joy. "The Lord God is going to answer your prayer to save her."

Excitement, mixed with disbelief rushed through him. "He is?" Peter asked, a bit confused.

Ariel nodded excitely as she reached over the collar of her dress and down the front to pull out a golden key which hung from a golden chain around her neck. She pulled the chain up over her head twisting it around her hair before handing the key to Peter.

Peter stared at the key he held in his hand. It was large and heavy and unlike any key Peter had ever held before. It looked more like a key to the door of a tower where a fairytale princess might be locked away in some enchanted story.

"What's this?" he asked as he glanced up from the key, his

eyes meeting Ariel's.

Ariel frowned, genuinely perplexed that Peter did not know what he held in his hand. "It's a key," she said.

Peter rolled his eyes. "I know it's a key, Ariel," he smirked. "What does it unlock?"

Ariel turned her head toward the altar, but looked past it. "It unlocks that door," she told him.

Peter's gaze followed Ariel's, but the only door he saw beyond the altar was the door to the sacristy—the place in the church where the communion wine and bread were kept and prepared. Peter frowned. He had been inside of the sacristy more than once with Father Joe or Ms. Naomi and knew that the key that opened it looked like a regular key, not a souvenir from a renaissance fair.

"I don't think this key is going to open the sacristy, Ariel," Peter told her.

Ariel turned to look at him with an amused expression on her face. "Not the sacristy, silly boy," she laughed. "It opens the other door. The one beside the sacristy."

"What door?" he asked seeing absolutely no doors except for the door to the sacristy.

"What do you mean, 'what door'?" Ariel asked and Peter could hear the exasperation building in her voice. "THAT door!" she exclaimed pointing to the empty space of wall beside the door to the sacristy.

Peter turned to her with his eyebrows raised. "Is this a joke or…?" but before he could finish they both heard Father Joe's voice calling his name.

"Hide the key," Ariel commanded, and Peter thought he detected a bit of hurried panic in her voice. "Put it around your neck and keep it hidden under your shirt."

"Why?" Peter asked.

"Stop asking questions, and just do it," Ariel shot back. Peter chuckled at her, but complied, slipping the chain over his head and around his neck. He tucked the key beneath his shirt and just as he did so, Father Joe walked up the steps and into the church.

"Here you are," the priest said with a smile as he stepped through the still open front doors to the church. He turned to his left and flipped a switch on the wall. The lights overhead flickered, but soon the entire building was bathed in light. "That's better," Father Joe remarked.

"Are you all right?" Father Joe asked Peter.

"Yes, I'm fine," Peter replied.

"Are you sure?" the priest asked.

"Yes, I'm sure."

Father Joe smiled broadly and then turned his attention to the small girl standing beside Peter. "And who do we have here?" the priest asked in his proper English accent.

Peter smiled. "This is my friend from school, Ariel," he informed Father Joe.

Father Joe seemed utterly delighted. "What a beautiful name you have, my dear," Father Joe smiled. "Do you know that legend claims there is an angel by that name?"

Ariel smiled. "I do, as a matter-of-fact," she replied.

"Excellent!" Father Joe exclaimed.

"So what brings you two to the church?" Father Joe asked with a bit of suspicion.

"Um," Peter began, "Ariel, uh, wanted to see the church."

"Is that right?" Father Joe asked somewhat doubtfully.

"Oh yes," Ariel replied. "I just love churches, and your stained glass is amazing. I love how they are composed of the stations of the cross."

This changed Father Joe's tone immediately. "It is quite

lovely, isn't it?" he remarked as he glanced around the sanctuary. "All to the glory of God, of course."

"Of course," Ariel replied.

"What are the stations of the cross?" Peter asked.

Father Joe frowned. "I see that I am failing miserably in your education, my boy," he remarked. "We shall have to remedy that, and there is no better time than the present. Come along."

Father Joe led the two children over to the side of the church to stand in front of the first stained glass window. Peter recognized the depiction of Jesus in the window, but not the other people. They were gathered around Jesus and looked awfully angry.

"The stations of the cross represent each step of the crucifixion, from the moment Jesus was condemned to die by the Roman governor Pontius Pilate to the time Jesus' lifeless body was laid in the tomb," Father Joe explained.

"Why did they want to kill Jesus?" Peter asked.

"For a variety of reasons," Father Joe replied. "Jealousy for one, but I think mainly they didn't like what He had to say."

"What do you mean?" Peter asked.

"Jesus showed the world a different way to live—to love God and serve your fellow man. Instead of accumulating wealth at the expense of the poor, Jesus taught to give your wealth to the poor. Instead of seeking power and to have others serve you, Jesus taught to humbly serve others. If Jesus was the Son of God and the Jewish king—that they called the Messiah and the Greeks called Christ—then He would overturn the entire order of those in power, both Jewish and Roman."

"God came to Earth in the person of Jesus Christ, to live as a man, to suffer as a man, to be tempted as a man. He came to love the weak and save the wicked from their own evil and sin, and humanity nailed Him to a cross to die," Ariel added. "You can see in the first window, Governor Pilate handing Jesus over to be crucified."

"That's right," Father Joe said as he led the two children to the next window. "The second station depicts Jesus carrying His cross." Peter stared at the large colorful window, and the beaten man struggling to haul an enormous wooden cross up a hill. Peter felt sympathy for Him.

They moved on to the third window, and Peter saw a depiction of Jesus lying on the ground, the cross on top of Him and a Roman soldier beating Him with a whip. "What happened here?" Peter asked.

"This is the first time Jesus fell," Ariel informed him.

"The cross was quite heavy, you see," Father Joe explained. "And Jesus had been whipped and beaten savagely by the Roman soldiers. He had lost a lot of blood. It's actually a wonder He was able to carry the cross at all."

At the fourth window, Peter saw a woman reaching out to Jesus as He carried the cross. "Who is that?" Peter asked as he pointed to the woman.

"That is His mother, Mary," Father Joe replied.

"Mary watched as her son was flogged, and sent off to be crucified," Ariel told him. "She stayed to watch Him as He was nailed to the cross and hung up like a common criminal." Peter turned to see Ariel wiping a tear from her eye.

At the fifth window, Father Joe explained that a man named Simon the Cyrene, had helped Jesus carry the cross the rest of the way, because Jesus had become too weak to carry it on His own. At the sixth station, Peter saw a woman, whom Father Joe told him was named Veronica, wiping Jesus' face. The seventh window depicted the second time Jesus fell.

That was all the windows on that side of the church so Father Joe led them across the sanctuary to the windows on the other side. The eighth station depicted Jesus meeting the women of Jerusalem. The ninth station showed Jesus falling a third time, with the Roman soldiers whipping him mercilessly.

"What is going on there?" Peter asked when they reached the tenth station.

"Jesus is being stripped naked," Father Joe explained. "Prisoners were crucified without any clothing to completely humiliate them."

Peter did not have to ask any questions about the eleventh station. It was clear what was happening. The Roman soldiers were driving nails through Jesus' hands and feet. At the twelfth station, Peter saw Jesus hung on the cross. "And that's where He died," Father Joe said solemnly.

"He died for His friends," Ariel said, and Peter turned to see she was crying. "But all of His friends abandoned Him. They were afraid, you see, because they did not have faith. Not even a tiny amount, as small as a mustard seed. Despite their boasting they did not have the faith and courage to follow their Lord into death. But later they would," Ariel smiled happily. "After Jesus ascended to Heaven He sent the Holy Spirit to His disciples, and the Spirit gave them all of the courage and faith they would need to willingly die for Christ."

In the thirteenth station, Peter saw men and women weeping as Jesus was taken down from the cross. In the fourteenth station, Jesus was being laid inside the tomb where he was buried.

"That's it?" Peter asked.

"Those are all of the stations of the cross, yes," Father Joe replied. "But that's not all there is." He then led them back to the center of the sanctuary and pointed to the beautiful circular window above the crucifix behind the altar. "That is the Resurrection. On the third day Jesus rose from the dead."

All three of them stood staring in awe at the depiction of Jesus arising from the tomb until Father Joe glanced down at his watch. "It'll be supper soon," he said and then turned to Ariel. "Will you be joining us young lady?"

Ariel turned toward the open church doors. The sun was setting. She turned back to Peter and Father Joe. "I had better not," she said. "Thank you for your hospitality, but I will be going now."

Ariel began walking toward the door with Peter and Father Joe close behind. Father Joe flipped off the lights as the three of them stepped outside into the setting sunshine. He pulled the doors closed and locked them.

Ariel and Peter had continued toward the rectory, and Father Joe jogged to catch up. "Let me drive you home," Father Joe said to Ariel.

"It's not far, I can walk," Ariel replied.

Father Joe smiled. "Well then let me walk you home," he said.

"That's probably not a good idea," Ariel remarked.

"Ah yes," Father Joe smiled. "Smart girl. Don't go off with some strange man you just met. But I don't want you going alone. I'll have my wife walk you." He then turned to Peter. "Say good-bye, then go get a start of your homework, Peter. I'll just go inside and fetch Mrs. Parsons to walk your friend home."

"I don't…" Ariel began, but Father Joe would have none of it. He was determined that Ariel not go home alone. He ignored her and bounded up the steps of the rectory to enter through the kitchen door searching for Ms. Naomi.

"Ms. Naomi is nice, you don't have to worry about her,"

THE GOLDEN KEY

Peter promised.

"I know," Ariel smiled.

"I guess I'll see you tomorrow," Peter said.

Ariel leaned close and whispered in his ear. "Maybe sooner," she said and then patted the key hanging against his chest.

Ariel turned to walk away. "Aren't you going to wait for Ms. Naomi?" he asked.

"No," Ariel replied.

"You forgot your book bag!" Peter exclaimed, suddenly realizing it. "Wait here, and I'll get it."

Peter rushed up the steps and through the kitchen door. He walked around the kitchen table and found Ariel's book bag on the floor, leaning against the chair where she had sat eating cookies. He scooped it up just as Father Joe was reentering the kitchen with Ms. Naomi.

Ms. Naomi led the way outside through the kitchen door to walk Ariel home followed by Father Joe and Peter carrying the girl's book bag. When they stepped outside, however, Ariel was nowhere to be seen.

"Ariel!" Ms. Naomi called, but received no answer.

"I suppose she did not want you to walk her home either," Father Joe said to his wife.

Ms. Naomi turned to him. "A woman can be just as scary to a girl as a man," she explained.

Father Joe chuckled. "Yes, dear, you are terrifying," he smirked. "She's probably worried you'll bake her more fresh chocolate chip cookies or something equally horrific."

Ms. Naomi laughed at her husband's joke as she led him back inside. Peter stood on the steps alone for a moment staring at the street. He glanced down at the bag he still held and decided he'd take it to Ariel the next day at school.

CHAPTER FOUR
THE DOOR TO ANOTHER WORLD

After supper, a bath, and homework Peter sat by his mother's bedside, holding her hand as she stared at the ceiling. She would occasionally acknowledge him, telling him she loved him through pained gasps. Peter assured her that he loved her too, as tears ran down his cheeks. Most of the time though, she said nothing, and only stared at the ceiling.

After a while, Ms. Naomi came into the room and told Peter it was time to go brush his teeth and get ready for bed. Peter reluctantly left his mother and plodded up the stairs to his room. A few minutes later, with his teeth brushed and wearing a fresh set of pajamas, Peter slid under the blankets on his bed. Ms. Naomi and Father Joe came into his room to say good night, and Ms. Naomi leaned over kissing his cheek. She turned and left as Father Joe ruffled Peter's hair.

THE DOOR TO ANOTHER WORLD

"Could you check the closet?" Peter asked. He had asked Father Joe to check the closet every night since he and his mother had come to live in the rectory. He needed to be sure that no monsters were hidden in there. Like many little boys, Peter was afraid of the dark, and it helped him fall asleep if Father Joe made sure that nothing was hidden in his closet waiting to leap out and pounce on him once the Parsons had gone to bed.

Father Joe smiled and nodded. He opened the door to the closet and poked his head inside, moving the clothes out of the way and searching for any sign of monsters. Suddenly, he froze as his eyes caught sight of something. "Oh no!" he exclaimed causing Peter to bolt upright in bed.

"What is it?" Peter asked, scared that a goblin was ready to pounce.

Father Joe turned to face him. "This closet's a mess," he smiled as he stepped to the side so that Peter could see for himself. Sure enough, clothes and toys were just piled up on the floor in a heap. "If Ms. Naomi sees this, you'll be in for it," Father Joe whispered—much too loudly—as if he were trying to keep a terrifying secret from his wife. "I suggest you clean it up soon before she does. The last time she cleaned my closet, she donated all of my favorite shirts and jeans to the homeless."

Peter lay back down with a chuckle. "All I ever see you wear is a black shirt with your white priest's collar and khaki pants," Peter told him.

"That's because that's all she left me with," Father Joe explained. "That and my tweed jacket."

Father Joe closed the door to the closet and turned back around to face Peter. "Have no fear, my boy. Your closet is 100% monster free."

"Thank you, Father Joe," Peter smiled.

Father Joe gave him a wink. "Try to get some good sleep, Peter," he said. "Tomorrow might be a long day." Peter nodded, and Father Joe turned to leave the room, stopping by the door to flip off the light. "Good night," he said over his shoulder, but before he could go, Peter stopped him.

"Father Joe," Peter said.

"Yes?" the priest asked.

"I prayed for Momma to get better, just like you said to, but she hasn't. She has gotten worse."

Father Joe crossed the room and sat down on the side of Peter's bed. He patted Peter's hand reassuringly. "Prayers do not always work out the way we want them to."

"I also prayed that God would send me a friend," he said.

"Oh yeah?" Father Joe asked. "I thought you had lots of friends. I see you playing with kids every Sunday after the service."

"Oh, I have friends at church, but not at school," Peter explained.

"But you told me things were going well," Father Joe reminded him.

"I know," Peter said softly, "and I didn't mean to lie. I just didn't want you and Ms. Naomi to worry."

"Well, that is sweet of you, Peter, but we would rather know what is really going on. We can't help you if we don't know you are hurting," Father Joe explained.

"I do have a friend at school now," Peter said. "Right after I asked God to send me a friend, Ariel walked across the playground."

Father Joe smiled. "See, God does answer prayers."

"Then why wasn't my mother healed?" Peter asked. "I wanted that more than a friend."

THE DOOR TO ANOTHER WORLD

Father Joe nodded. "I know you did, Peter, but sometimes God doesn't give us what we want and instead gives us what we need."

"I need my mother," Peter said as he started to cry.

"Well then, you keep praying," Father Joe suggested. "She hasn't left us yet. Remember, Jesus told us we need to be persistent in our prayers."

Peter nodded as he wiped the tears from his eyes.

Father Joe patted him on the leg and then stood and crossed the room to the door. "See you in the morning, Peter," he said.

"Good night, Father Joe," Peter replied as Father Joe gently closed the door.

The room was dark except for some small pools of light cast by the night light plugged into the wall, and the moonlight streaming in through the window. Peter glanced around the room to make sure that no monsters had suddenly materialized in the darkness with the door now closed. He didn't see any, and settled down, staring up at the ceiling.

"Jesus tells us to be persistent in our prayers," Peter said to himself, echoing Father Joe. Peter knew that meant to keep doing it. So he decided he would pray all night. He wouldn't even sleep. He would just keep praying and praying, begging God to save his mother until Ms. Naomi came in to wake him up for school.

"God, please save my mother," he said. "Please, please, please. I'll do anything you want if you just please save her." He prayed like that for about half an hour, until he finally drifted off to sleep.

Peter's eyes popped open as he was awakened by a noise.

CHAPTER FOUR

He turned to look at the red numbers glowing from the clock on his bedside table. It was nearly midnight, so the Parsons would have long since gone to bed. Peter lay completely still listening to the night, but all he heard was his own breathing and beating heart.

After a long while, Peter determined that he must have dreamed the sound and closed his eyes to sleep again. Just as he did so, he heard something again. This time there was no mistaking it for a dream. Peter heard a rustling, and was certain it was coming from his closet. He lay in bed completely frozen with fear.

Suddenly, the closet door popped open, and Peter was just about to scream, but stopped himself when he saw that it was not a monster that had stepped out of the closet. Peter sat up, turned on the lamp by his bed, and snatched his glasses off of the bedside table, pushing them onto his face. He turned back toward his closet and smiled as he saw Ariel smiling back at him.

"What are you doing in my closet?" Peter asked with an amused chuckle.

"Coming to see you," Ariel said. "Now you need to get up and get dressed."

"What?" Peter asked. "It's late."

"We've got to go, Peter," Ariel explained as she tossed him a pair of pants and a shirt she had found while inside the closet.

"Go?" Peter asked. "Go where?"

Ariel stopped and stared at him intently. "To save your mother," she said matter-of-factly.

"What are you talking about?" Peter asked with a yawn. "And how did you hide in my closet? Father Joe checked it."

"Look, Peter," Ariel said firmly, "I can explain everything

later, but right now, we need to go. It's dark outside."

"I know it's dark," Peter said. "But what does…?" he began, but Ariel cut him off.

"They are more powerful in the dark," she said while she glanced over her shoulder as if to make sure nothing was sneaking up on her.

"What are more powerful in the dark?" Peter asked.

"The demons, Peter—now hurry up and get dressed."

"Demons?" Peter asked in disbelief.

"I had hoped to do this when the sun was still out but we were interrupted by Father Joseph," she said.

"Do what?" Peter asked.

Ariel was done explaining. "Peter Puckett, stop asking questions and put your clothes on, right now!" she snapped at him, sounding a lot like Peter's mother used to, before she got sick, when she had lost her patience with Peter.

Peter nodded, stood from the bed and began to pull off his pajamas, but then remembered Ariel was staring at him. "Could you at least turn around?" he asked.

Ariel sighed. "Very well," she said and turned her back to Peter.

A minute later, he announced that he was finished, and she turned back around.

"What about socks and shoes, Peter?" she asked. "Are you going to run around all over creation in your bare feet?"

"Oh, sorry," he replied before rushing over to his dresser and pulling out a pair of white socks with blue stripes.

"Where is that key I gave you?" Ariel asked him, and he scooped it up from the top of his dresser and showed it to her. "Good," she smiled. "We're going to need it to open the door."

"What door?" Peter asked as he put the chain over his

head, around his neck and tucked it beneath his blue shirt.

"The door in the church that I showed you this afternoon," she said.

Peter frowned as he pulled his shoes on. He hadn't seen a door in the church that afternoon and was beginning to wonder if Ariel were crazy. After all, she was talking about demons, mystery doors, and saving his dying mother.

Once he had his shoes on, he was about to ask her what was really going on, but she didn't give him a chance. Instead she tossed him a brown jacket from his closet, rushed to the door of his bedroom, and yanked it open. She moved quickly but quietly down the stairs and Peter had no choice but to follow her.

Once they were in the kitchen, Ariel whispered to him. "We'll need Father Joseph's key to the church," she said.

"I don't know about this," Peter began, but Ariel placed a finger against his lips.

"Peter, if you want your mother to be saved it will take faith. A lot of faith."

"All right," Peter whispered. He crossed the kitchen to the key rack, removed Father Joe's key chain from it, and then slipped the church key off the ring.

Ariel smiled and then led him out of the kitchen door into the cool air outside. Once on the grass, she took hold of his arm. "We need to hurry to the church before they come for you," she said.

"Who?" Peter asked.

"The demons," she replied. "Haven't you been paying attention?"

The two children raced across the large lawn toward the church, when Ariel suddenly halted, stopping Peter with her. She stared at the shadows beside a pine tree, and Peter suddenly saw them move. A black figure stepped forth, as if the darkness itself had come to life. The figure appeared to be a man, but there was something strange about its head. The head was shaped like that of a dog. No, not a dog. A wolf! A chill shot down Peter's spine. Was this a demon? He wanted to run, but Ariel held him steady.

"I'll handle this," Ariel said in her soft voice as she released Peter's trembling arm and stepped toward the creature. The creature continued to move toward her as well.

"In the name of the Lord God Almighty, I command you to stand aside!" Ariel commanded firmly.

Peter was impressed with her bravery, but also frustrated with her apparent foolishness.

"Ariel!" he shouted. "Let's run back to the house! Father Joe will know what to do."

But Ariel ignored him and instead kept striding confidently toward the creature in front of her.

"This is your last chance, night stalker!" she shouted at it. "Stand aside or I shall strike you down!"

The creature released a blood curdling howl from its lips before dropping to all fours and charging toward Ariel. Panic surged through Peter.

"Ariel!" he shouted as he watched the creature she'd called a night stalker race toward her ready to kill the little girl.

Ariel did not flee, however, but instead rushed toward the creature as if she were a Marine charging enemy positions.

"No!" Peter shouted, terrified that his new friend was about to be killed, when suddenly something strange happened. Ariel spun around, and as she did, light flashed all around her. When the light faded, Peter's mouth dropped open. The little girl who had been there before was replaced with a grown woman, her skin and clothes so brilliant that they glowed in the darkness. In her right hand she carried a shining sword—in her left a small silver shield, and from her back appeared two beautiful white wings.

When Ariel met the creature, there was not even a fight. One swift swing of her sword and the beast fell motionless in two pieces upon the lawn, before fading back into the darkness. Ariel spun back around to face Peter.

"Peter, come on!" she shouted as she waved her hand for Peter to join her. Her voice was no longer that of a little girl. It was a woman's voice, but not just any woman's voice. It was the most beautifully melodic voice Peter had ever heard.

But Peter did not move. He stood completely still, his mouth hanging open as he realized what he was staring at. His friend Ariel had not been named after an angel—she *was* an angel. A real life angel!

"Peter!" Ariel shouted again, snapping the boy out of his trance. "There are more of them—hurry!"

Peter suddenly heard growls behind him and peered over his shoulder to see at least six more of the wolf creatures galloping toward him on all fours. Peter screamed a high pitched panicked noise before running toward Ariel as quickly as he could. He hid behind her wings, where he thought he'd be safest.

"Get to the church," she said. "They will not enter there."

Peter nodded, turned, and sprinted for the church as quickly as he could while Ariel remained in place to protect him from the night stalkers that were after him. Peter reached the church and shot his hand deep into his pocket to pull out Father Joe's key. As he did so, he heard howls of pain, and he smiled to himself, assuming Ariel was chopping the monsters to bits.

Peter fumbled with the key, trembling so badly with fear

that he struggled to insert it into the lock. He heard Ariel scream in agony and turned to see a wolf creature ripping a chunk of her wing off from behind, while she fought another in front of her.

The key slipped from Peter's fingers and fell with a clang. "Oh, no!" he cried as he dropped to his hands and knees, desperately searching for it.

"Hurry, Peter!" he heard Ariel's voice call and looked up to see she had defeated the creatures that had attacked her. Now she was running toward him. At first, he was relieved, but then he noticed the lawn erupt with scores of the beasts, all chasing after Ariel. Could she defeat that many?

Peter's fingers finally found the key, and he picked it up and slid it into the keyhole. He turned it and opened the door, stepping inside just before Ariel reached him. She joined him inside and then slammed the door shut. "We'll be safe in here," she said softly. "Night stalkers cannot enter consecrated ground." As she spoke, Peter noticed cuts, bites, and claw marks, dotting her shining white skin with dark painful looking sores.

Ariel slid her sword into a golden sheath hanging on her belt, and slipped her shield into a sling positioned between her white wings. The angel then fell down to her knees, bowed her head, and squeezed her eyes closed. Peter began to rush toward her, fearful that she would collapse onto the hard wooden floor of the sanctuary, but then he realized she had not dropped to her knees from exhaustion but rather to pray. As she did so, Peter, noticed the wounds fade from her skin. She smiled, mouthed the word "Amen," and then stood, staring at Peter.

Peter stared back, trembling with excitement and fright. Ariel was at least six feet tall, with soft golden hair held off of her face by a shining golden band instead of the bright red bow she had worn as a little girl. She wore a white dress tied at her waist by a golden belt. The dress fell to her knees and golden metal boots covered her feet, shins, and calves. On her wrists were a pair of golden bands, and the oversized glasses she had worn as part of her disguise were gone. In fact, the only feature that could connect the little girl Peter had met to the beautiful woman before him was her soft golden hair. "You're an angel," he said with wide eyes, his voice cracking nervously.

"Yes," Ariel said in her sweet melodic voice. Peter had never heard a voice as beautiful in his life.

"A real angel," he said.

"Yes, Peter, I am a real angel," she said as she dropped to one knee so as to not present an imposing figure peering down at him. She gently placed a hand on his shoulder. "I know you have a lot of questions and I will answer the ones that I can, but right now we need to leave, before the others show up."

"But I thought you said they couldn't enter the church," Peter said.

"The night stalkers outside cannot, but other kinds can, and trust me, you do not want to meet them tonight."

Peter nodded. "So where are we going?" he asked.

Ariel stood and stepped past Peter, walking down the aisle between the rows of pews, toward the altar. As she passed, Peter noticed her wing, where the wolf thing had ripped part of it off. The wing had not healed like the rest of her.

"Your wing is still damaged," Peter said, and Ariel turned toward him.

"Yes," she answered.

"Why didn't it heal like the rest of you?" Peter asked, clearly confused.

THE DOOR TO ANOTHER WORLD

"The Lord God, will heal what it pleases Him to heal, when it pleases Him to heal it," she said.

"That's not fair," Peter frowned.

Ariel smiled as she bent over to look Peter in the eyes. "Trust me, Peter, you want love and mercy from God, not fairness." She then straightened back up and pointed past the altar.

"We'll use the key I gave you this afternoon to go through that door," she said.

Peter stared past her, following her finger, but he still did not see any door other than the one leading to the sacristy.

"What door?" he asked, growing frustrated. "I don't see a door, Ariel!"

Ariel lowered her arm and cocked her head to the side as she stared down at Peter. She was clearly perplexed. "After all you have just witnessed, you still do not believe?" she asked.

"Believe what?" he asked in response.

"Believe that there is a door there," she said.

"How can I believe there is a door there when I can't see it?" he asked.

Ariel placed a hand on his shoulder. "You will not be able to see the door, *until* you believe," she explained.

Peter sighed. That made absolutely no sense to him. Ariel was patient with him, however. She stepped behind him, turning him to face the wall behind the altar where she insisted the door was. She placed a hand on each of his shoulders and leaned forward, whispering into his ear.

"Close your eyes," she instructed and Peter complied, squeezing his eyes tight. "Do you believe that I am an angel?" she asked.

"Yes," Peter replied.

"Why?" she asked.

"Because I have seen you in your angel form."

"Do you believe your mother loves you?" Ariel asked.

"Yes," Peter replied.

"Why?" Ariel asked. "You cannot see love."

"But she's my mom," he said. "Of course she loves me. She tells me so. And I can see how much she loves me, because of how she treats me and kisses me and stuff."

"So, even though you cannot see your mother's love, you still believe it, because you trust her and can see the effects of her love?"

"Yes," Peter said.

"Do you trust me?" she asked.

Peter nodded.

"And haven't you seen that what I have told you has been true?" she asked.

"Yes," he replied.

"And haven't you seen that I am an angel?" she asked.

"Yes," he replied.

"So trust me now, Peter, when I tell you there is a door. Believe the door exists. After all, why would I lie about it?"

That made sense to Peter. Why would she lie about it? If Ariel the warrior angel said there was a door, there must be a door.

"Do you believe it now?" she asked.

"Yes," he replied.

"Good," she said. "Open your eyes."

Peter opened his eyes and gasped when he saw a large, beautiful door made of what appeared to be gold and encrusted in shimmering jewels.

"Insert the key," she said.

Peter nodded and removed the key from around his neck. He stepped away from Ariel, past the altar to the jewel encrusted door. He inserted the key into the large keyhole and turned it. The door opened, and light filled the room, momentarily blinding Peter. Once his eyes adjusted he was amazed at what he saw.

"Let's go, Peter," Ariel said. "Step through."

Peter swallowed hard, took a deep breath, and stepped through the door.

CHAPTER FIVE
EVERMORE

Peter stepped through the shining door into a grassy meadow at the top of a small hill. Before him stood a stone altar of primitive design and construction, but that was not what was impressive. It was the looming mountain behind the altar that so impressed Peter. The mountain was enormously tall with snow covering its peaks, surrounded by a blue cloudless sky.

Peter felt the tip of Ariel's wing brush against him as she stepped past and into the meadow. He turned around to see the inside of the small church through the doorway.

"This is amazing!" Peter exclaimed as he kept looking back and forth from the church to the mountain and back again.

"Remove the key and close the door," Ariel instructed.

Peter nodded, removed the key from the keyhole, and replaced the chain around his neck before gently closing the door, keeping his head close to it so as to watch the inside of the church until the very last second. When it was completely closed, Peter took a step back to admire the amazing gem encrusted door.

Unlike the door in the church, this side of the door was not against a wall. In fact, nothing but a door and a door frame were standing in the meadow beside the altar. Peter walked around to the other side of the door and saw nothing except the back of the door, but without a knob. He then spun around to face Ariel with amazement.

"How did we do that?" he asked. "Is this key magic?"

Ariel shook her head. "Oh no," she replied. "Magic is evil. Never dabble in such dark arts as magic, witchcraft, or sorcery. And run away from anyone who does."

Peter frowned. "But I like magic," he protested. "Father Joe can make a coin disappear in his hand and then reappear behind my ear."

Ariel laughed. "That isn't magic, Peter, but simply a trick. There is no harm in that," she explained. "Real magic—the type witches, wizards, and sorcerers practice—is dark and very, very dangerous."

Peter stared at her, perplexed for a moment. "Then how did we step through a door in the church back home and end up here in a meadow, on a hill at the foot of a giant mountain?" he asked as he pointed from the door to the mountain.

Ariel thought for a second before answering. "I cannot explain the how to you," she said at last. "But, these doors are not magical. They are simply doorways that the Lord has placed throughout His creation, linking different worlds."

Peter's eyes popped wide. "Wait," he said excitedly. "We're not on Earth anymore? We're on a different planet?"

Ariel sighed. "No, Peter, this is not what you would call an alien planet. It's more like a different plane of reality. Or a different realm."

"Oh like another dimension," he said proudly.

"All right," she replied. "You may call it that. Whatever helps you to understand."

Ariel held out her hand to Peter. "Come," she smiled and he stepped forward and took it.

"Where are we going?" Peter asked.

"To see Nicholas," she replied.

"Who is he?" Peter asked.

"He is a friend," Ariel answered. "We need to get you better outfitted for your quest and he can help with that."

"Where is he?" Peter inquired.

Ariel smiled. "Up there," she replied as she pointed up toward the snowy peak looming high above them.

"How are we going to get way up there?" Peter asked.

Ariel pulled him close to her body and wrapped both arms around him. "We're going to fly, Peter," she smiled as she spread her wings wide. "Now hold on tight." Peter obeyed, wrapping his arms around the angel's waist and squeezing his eyes tight as she flapped her wings, lifting off the ground.

"Ow!" Ariel screamed in pain as she dropped back down onto the grass.

"What's wrong?" Peter asked.

"My wing," Ariel replied as she looked at the tear where the night stalker had bitten her. "The demons must have wounded me worse than I thought." She let out a sigh as she dropped to one knee and said a silent prayer.

"Did you ask God to heal your wing?" Peter asked.

"No," Ariel replied. "The Lord God shall heal my wing when the time is right. I simply prayed that He watch over us and give us the strength to complete our journey." Ariel stared at Peter for a long moment as if she were expecting him to do something. When he did nothing but stare back she finally spoke.

"It would not be a bad idea for you to offer a similar prayer," Ariel suggested.

"Oh," Peter said. "Right." He squeezed his eyes closed and prayed. "Lord, please watch over us and make us strong enough for the, um, I mean, our, um, journey," he said. "Amen." Then his eyes popped open, and he looked at Ariel.

"How was that?" he asked.

She nodded. "Not bad, Peter, but we'll keep working on it." She then turned and began walking down the hill toward the mountain. "Come along," she called to Peter. He darted after her, catching up and walking beside her.

"So why were those demon werewolf things trying to kill me?" he asked.

"Because, God has selected you for a very important mission," Ariel explained. "Demons always do their best to thwart the servants of the Lord and prevent us from doing His perfect will."

"Wait, God has a mission for me?" Peter asked in disbelief.

"Yes," Ariel replied.

"What's the mission?" Peter asked excitedly, his mind already racing.

"The Lord God, in His infinite wisdom and mercy has chosen you, Peter, to retrieve a very special item which some call the Amulet of Eternity. It lies past the deep dark depths of the Leviathan in the Realm of the Goblins."

"Wait a second, that sounds pretty creepy," Peter said warily, suddenly not liking this mission. "Why would God need me to go and get this amulet? Can't he just like snap His fingers and make it appear?"

Ariel threw back her head and laughed. "Yes, of course He

can Peter," Ariel said. "God does not need you to retrieve the amulet for Him. Nor does God even need the amulet. God does not need you or me or anyone or anything else for anything. To the contrary, it is we who need Him."

"Then why does He want me to go into this dark Levia-whatever-thing realm with goblins and get it?" Peter asked.

"Because sometimes our Lord graciously allows us the privilege of being instruments of His will. We receive the honor of serving Him, even though He truly has no need for servants. It is all part of His generous nature."

"But why me?" Peter asked.

"Because you prayed for it," Ariel replied.

"When did I pray to go find an amulet?" Peter asked.

"You didn't pray to go and find an amulet, Peter," she explained. "You prayed to God that He would mercifully save your dying mother."

Peter nodded. "But what does that have to do with getting this amulet? Is he making me prove myself worthy or something?"

"No, of course not," Ariel replied with an amused chuckle. "You certainly are not worthy of God's grace and mercy and could never prove otherwise. None, but Jesus Christ Himself, God's own Son, is worthy."

"Then why am I doing it?" Peter asked.

"Because, the Amulet of Eternity, as some call it, will save your mother," Ariel replied matter-of-factly.

Peter stopped walking and after a couple more steps Ariel stopped as well, turning to look at the boy. He was pale with a nervous expression on his face.

"Is that true?" he asked.

"Of course it's true, Peter," she replied. "I do not lie."

"You promise me that if I get this Amulet of Eternity thing, it will heal my mom's cancer?"

"No, Peter, I do not promise that," Ariel said. "What I promise is that if you trust in the Lord, retrieve this amulet and return with it to your mother, before she dies, then God's Holy Spirit will use the amulet to save her."

Peter nodded excitedly as he bit his bottom lip. Then he had a thought and it was a heart-breaking thought.

"How far is this amulet?" Peter asked.

"It will be quite a long journey, Peter," Ariel said.

"But the nurse said my mother would probably die in twenty-four hours and that was like eight hours ago," he said. "We'll never make it back in time." Tears began to build up in his eyes as his hopes collapsed. He had been foolish to think his mother might actually be saved. How could some amulet do what the doctors couldn't do?

Ariel stepped over to him, knelt down and placed her arms gently around his shoulders, pulling him tight to her in a comforting embrace. "Oh, Peter, do not fear," she said "What you perceive as time does not exist here."

Peter stopped crying and pulled back to look at her. "What do you mean?" he asked.

"Time is something that the Lord God created in the universe you inhabit, but it does not exist here. So when you step out of the door, back into your world, it may be the exact same time you stepped through the door into this one."

Peter wiped the tears from his eyes and sniffed. "How is that possible?" he asked.

Ariel cocked her head to the side in puzzlement. "How is it not?" she asked. Peter only shrugged. Ariel stood and straightened her dress. "But do not let that be an excuse to dawdle," she said firmly. "Now come on, let's get to that mountain."

CHAPTER FIVE

Ariel began to walk once again and Peter hurried to catch up. "What's the name of this place anyway?" he asked.

"Most call it Evermore," she replied.

Peter smiled. He liked that name.

They had traveled quite a distance, yet the mountain still seemed a long way from them, when Peter noticed the light in the sky beginning to fade, as if night time were approaching. Ariel must have noticed the fading light too, as she tilted her face toward the sky. "It will be darkfall soon," she explained. "We do not want to be out in the open after dark if we can help it. The forces that come out after the light has faded here are…" she let her voice trail off.

"Are what?" Peter prodded.

Ariel stopped walking for a moment and looked down at her young companion. "Many are much more terrifying than the night stalkers you saw back at the church."

Peter stood staring at her wide-eyed and white with fear. How could that be possible? "Like what?" he asked. He didn't really want the answer, but asked the question all the same.

"Demonic powers of all sorts," she replied. "Goblins, se'irim…"

"What are s-se-se'irim?" Peter asked, struggling with the word.

"Se'irim are large beasts with humanoid faces and bodies, but dark red skin, sharp fangs, hooves for feet, pointed tails, and enormous horns like those of a ram protruding from their disfigured heads. If they catch a little boy like you, they'll most likely have you for their supper."

Peter swallowed hard. He glanced around to make sure there were no se'irim sneaking up on them at that very moment. "W-what are we going to do?" he stuttered with fear.

"There is a dwarven village just over the next rise, Ariel replied as she pointed toward a small hill. "We'll find a room there for the night."

"Dwarven?" Peter asked. "You mean like little people?"

Ariel nodded. "Yes, only, you shouldn't call a dwarf that to his face, if you know what's good for you," she replied. Ariel then turned and began walking toward the dwarven village.

The light had nearly faded when they crested the hill, and Peter saw the small dwarven village ahead of them. Around the village was a wall made from logs with pointed ends at the top to prevent people (or other things) from easily climbing over the top. It reminded Peter of the pictures of forts on the American frontier in his school history books. The wall likely stood no more than ten feet high, but to Peter—and he assumed the dwarfs—it was massive. As Peter and Ariel approached the village they noticed the gate beginning to swing closed.

"Hold the gates!" Ariel called and Peter saw two small men, no taller than himself, jump out and point menacing spears toward him and Ariel. The dwarfs wore long beards, and sour expressions upon their faces. They were outfitted in chain mail armor, with helmets atop their heads. When they noticed the angel striding toward them, their sour expressions quickly gave way to welcoming smiles.

"Beggin' your pardon, Your Grace," said one as he struggled against his armor to bow at the waist.

"We did not realize who you were when you called," explained the other. "Please do come into our humble little village."

"Yes, quickly, Your Grace," said the other. "The dark is beginning to fall."

Both dwarfs stepped aside with polite bows as Ariel led

CHAPTER FIVE

Peter through the gates and into the small dwarven village. Once both she and Peter were safely inside, the two dwarf guards completed the task of closing and locking the gate. The light in the sky peeped out just as the latch was secured, and Peter noticed Ariel's skin glowing in the darkness.

"There," said one of the guards, satisfied that the gate was secure. Both dwarfs then spun to face Peter and Ariel.

"Tis an honor to have you here, Your Grace," one of the guards told Ariel and then turned to Peter. "And your young companion."

"My friend and I are deeply grateful for the shelter, dear sirs," Ariel told the dwarfs.

"Think nothing of it, Your Grace," one of the dwarfs answered as he waved it off.

"You'll be wanting the inn?" inquired the other.

"Yes, thank you," Ariel replied.

A big toothy grin spread across both of the dwarf's faces. "Straight down the middle, on the right," one informed them as he pointed. "You can't miss it, Your Grace."

"Thank you for your kindness," Ariel replied, causing both dwarfs to beam happily. "Come Peter, let's be going."

Peter nodded and followed Ariel as she turned and walked along the dirt road between two rows of wooden buildings until they at last came to the inn. It was not a very large inn— of course nothing in the village was very large. A sign hung over the door, identifying the establishment as *The Dancing Gopher*. Peter could hear raucous voices coming from inside the inn and it made him a bit nervous. Ariel glanced down at him, gave him a comforting wink, and then stepped through the door.

CHAPTER SIX
THE DANCING GOPHER

Ariel had to duck her head to step through the doorway of *The Dancing Gopher* and once inside, her head was only an inch or two below the ceiling. Peter followed the angel inside and found a small, dark tavern—the air thick with pipe smoke and the smell of something that reminded him of apple cider. With her impressive height and radiant skin, Ariel stood out in the tavern filled with dwarfs wearing long beards that dropped well below their waists and over-sized noses that slipped inside of the large mugs from which they drank. Several of the dwarfs puffed on long pipes, sending rings of smoke into the air as they huddled together at the bar or around tables speaking in low voices. Peter sensed a feeling of discomfort and even dread permeating the room.

When the dwarfs noticed Ariel and Peter, a hush fell over the tavern so suddenly that Peter was certain that had a record been playing it would have skipped. Every eye in the room fixed on the large, winged angel that stood just inside the doorway. Even Peter's eyes were drawn up to Ariel, but they quickly returned to the room as the dwarfs set down their cups and slowly rose from their seats.

Peter feared that these short yet dangerous looking men were going to draw weapons and kill him and Ariel right there on the spot. To Peter's surprise and delight, quite the opposite happened. Instead of attacking him and Ariel, the dwarfs suddenly broke out in joyful cheers. Everyone in the tavern pressed close to Ariel, bowing at the waist and thanking "Her Grace" for visiting their humble little village.

Ariel's mere presence had changed the mood of the tavern from one of gloom to one of joy as smiles replaced scowls and laughter replaced fear. Music reached Peter's ears as a pair of dwarfs with lute and guitar played a merry tune. Even Peter was welcomed as an honored guest with everyone assuming he must be someone of importance because he accompanied an angel.

The sea of dwarfs parted as a small, round dwarf with a long beard and dirty apron pushed his way through, followed by another dwarf in a dress. The second dwarf looked very much like the first except for the dress and lack of beard, which made Peter assume she was a female. When the pair stood before Ariel, they both bowed low at the waist, their foreheads nearly touching the floor.

"Welcome to *The Dancing Gopher*, Your Grace," the bearded dwarf said as he straightened. "And your young companion," he added with a toothy grin aimed at Peter.

"Thank you, Master...?" Ariel asked politely.

"Grifeth," the dwarf replied with another bow as he introduced himself. "Owner and operator. And this is my lovely bride Griselda," he added as he pointed a knobby thumb at the second dwarf.

THE DANCING GOPHER

"It is such a pleasure to make your acquaintance, Your Grace," Griselda smiled and Peter noticed at least three front teeth were missing.

"You and your young companion will be spending the night I hope?" Grifeth inquired.

"Yes," Ariel replied.

"Well, you will have Room 3--it's the best in the inn!" Grifeth said proudly.

"Master Sooth is staying in Room 3," Griselda reminded her husband.

Peter noticed frustration wash over Grifeth's face as he turned toward his wife. "Then move Master Sooth to Room 2. Do you expect a Messenger of the Lord to sleep in a small room?" he demanded.

"Are you going to tell him?" Griselda inquired causing Grifeth to sigh.

Grifeth turned to the crowd of dwarfs. "Sooth!" he shouted above the laughter and music.

"Yeah?" came a gruff reply from the back of the room.

"We're moving you to Room 2, so that Her Grace can have Room 3!"

"Anything Her Grace wants," Sooth called back, his voice no longer gruff but sweet.

Grifeth gave his wife an "I told you so" look before sending her off to ready the room for their guests. He then led Peter and Ariel to a round table from which he shooed three other dwarfs, all happy to give up their seats for a "Messenger of the Lord."

Once Peter and Ariel were seated, Grifeth smiled broadly at them. "Would you like something to eat?" he asked. "The stew is nice and hot."

"None for me," Ariel smiled. "But my companion needs to

eat."

"Very, good," Grifeth replied. "And a cup of cider for the lad?"

Ariel frowned. "Best to stick with water, I imagine."

"Yes, Your Grace," Grifeth replied with a bow and then quickly moved away to fetch Peter's dinner.

With Grifeth out of the way the other dwarfs began to press in again. One younger dwarf—Peter could tell because his beard was shorter—fell down on his knees before Ariel, a white cloth in his hands.

"Looks like you've been on a long journey, Your Grace," the young dwarf smiled. "Your boots are all dirty. May I shine them for you?"

"You may," Ariel replied with a friendly smile.

"Thank you, Your Grace," the young dwarf smiled happily as he took the white cloth and began to polish Ariel's armored boots.

Ariel noticed Peter's perplexed expression as he watched the dwarf cleaning her boots. She leaned over to him and spoke softly. "The Lord blesses those who humbly serve others," she said.

"Really?" Peter asked as he stared down at the young dwarf joyfully cleaning dirt and grass from Ariel's boots, as if he'd been bestowed a great honor. Peter didn't understand. Cleaning someone's boots seemed to Peter, to be a very lowly, even humiliating thing to do.

As if reading his thoughts, Ariel said, "Humbly serving others is one of the noblest things one can do."

That didn't sound right to Peter. "How is shining someone's boots noble?" he asked.

"Those who want to be kings and queens in the next life, must be servants in this life," she replied. "Even the Christ

THE DANCING GOPHER

Himself knelt down and washed the feet of His disciples."

"Are you serious?" Peter asked in surprise. "Jesus washed his disciples' feet?"

"That's right," she answered. "As Christ explained, He came not to be served, but to serve others."

Their conversation was interrupted when Master Grifeth returned with a wooden bowl of steaming stew and a shiny metal cup filled with water. He set both down in front of Peter, then produced a metal spoon from the pocket of his apron and handed it to the boy.

Peter happily accepted the spoon. He was starving, having not eaten since the supper Ms. Naomi had prepared, which seemed like ages ago. He leaned over the stew and gave it a sniff. It smelled delicious, but Peter was unsure if that was caused by the flavor itself or his own empty stomach. No matter, he thrust the spoon deep into the stew and scooped out a heaping helping, bringing it close to his mouth before Ariel abruptly stopped him.

"Are you not going to even bother to thank the Lord God for this food?" she asked with disappointment ringing in her voice.

Peter's eyes cut from the spoonful of stew to Ariel then to Master Grifeth and the other dwarfs who looked on with anticipation. Peter sighed as he laid his spoon back into the bowl, folded his hands and prayed.

"Dear God, thank you for this food, and thank you for my new friends Ariel and the dwarfs," he said. "Amen."

"Amen!" echoed the entire tavern.

Peter turned to Ariel to find her smiling at him. He then picked up the spoon again and shoved the stew into his mouth. It was not as good as his mother's, but Peter still liked it.

"This is quite good," he told Master Grifeth, causing the

dwarf to smile. "What's in it?"

Grifeth opened his mouth to answer, but Ariel shook her head to shush him. Grifeth got the hint and smiled. "Family secret, young Master," he told Peter.

He then turned to Ariel. "And do not worry about payment," he told her proudly. "Everything is on the house."

"You are most generous, Master Grifeth," Ariel said with a polite bow of her head. "And I doubt everyone at the inn receives metal cups and spoons."

Grifeth blushed, slightly embarrassed. "You are correct, Your Grace," he said. "We keep those for special guests and special occasions."

"We are certainly honored," Ariel replied.

"Yes, thank you," Peter added through a mouth full of stew, before gulping down a large swallow of water.

"It is we who are honored," Grifeth told her. "It isn't every day a Messenger of the Lord comes to our humble little inn."

Ariel smiled and nodded. "I suppose not," she said, realizing that even though she thought of angels as nothing impressive at all, others found them to be magnificent. Many believed angels to be the closest one could come to the divine without meeting the Lord Himself.

"And we are grateful to Almighty God that he answered our prayers," Grifeth continued, eliciting a confused look from Ariel.

"How has God answered your prayers?" she asked.

"The Lord sent you to protect us," he replied matter-of-factly.

Now Ariel was really confused and so was Peter.

"Protect you from what?" Peter asked the dwarf.

"The shedom," another dwarf offered and the music came to an abrupt end as dread once again fell over the tavern.

THE DANCING GOPHER

"What's a shedom?" Peter asked before thrusting another spoonful of stew into his mouth.

"If you don't know, believe me when I say you don't want to know," Griselda told him as she stepped up next to her husband, clearly having finished preparing Room 3 for their guests.

"What shedom?" Ariel asked.

Master Grifeth leaned in close. "During the past several darkfalls, it's come into the village, slipping past the guards as if they weren't even there, and creeping all around the village, checking rooms like it's looking for something."

"Or someone," Griselda added.

"Yeah," Grifeth agreed. "And it's someone specific, too, because it leaves everyone else alone, as long as they don't get in its way."

"So the Lord God answered our prayers and sent you to protect us from him," Griselda smiled.

Peter shook his head. "Actually we are on our way to…" he began but Ariel interrupted him.

"Why did we walk here instead of fly?" she asked Peter.

"Because your wing was injured fighting those wolf things," he replied.

"If my wing had not been wounded, we would have flown to the top of the mountain without ever stopping at this village, correct?"

Peter nodded. "Probably," he agreed.

"Don't you think that might be the reason the Lord God did not heal my wing when He healed the rest of my body?" she asked. "So that we would come this way and help these good people?"

Peter hadn't thought of that.

"God often engineers our paths for us," Ariel explained.

CHAPTER SIX

"We don't understand why certain things have occurred, but He does. Our only duty is to follow the path He has set before us in humility and obedience."

Peter nodded demonstrating that he understood.

"So you are going to help us?" Master Grifeth asked.

Ariel smiled. "I'm certainly going to try," she replied. "And if it be God's will, I shall succeed."

A great cheer erupted throughout the tavern and the music and laughter began once again.

"On behalf of everyone at *The Dancing Gopher*, please let me extend my deepest gratitude to Your Grace," Grifeth said, once again bowing deeply at the waist.

Ariel smiled. "Give thanks to God," she instructed him.

"Of course," Grifeth said. "We are always most grateful for the protection provided by Almighty God."

He then turned to Peter who had just finished his stew and sat slumped back in his chair patting his full belly.

"How was the stew, young Master?" Grifeth asked.

"Very good, thank you," Peter replied.

"I'm glad you liked it," Grifeth smiled.

"Because you're likely to get nothin' else at *The Dancing Gopher*," laughed a dwarf at a nearby table.

"Don't need nothin' else!" Grifeth shot back. "The stew is just fine!"

"Master Grifeth," Peter said.

"Yes?" the dwarf asked.

"Why is your inn called *The Dancing Gopher*?" Peter asked.

A broad smile spread across the dwarf's face. "Did you hear that?" Grifeth shouted to the room. "The lad wants to know why I named this place *The Dancing Gopher*!"

Uproarious laughter filled the tavern.

"Should we show him?" Grifeth asked.

THE DANCING GOPHER

"Aye!" came the amused cries from the patrons as they raised mugs of cider.

Master Grifeth smiled at his honored guests. "Sit back and relax," he told Ariel and Peter. "You're about to see the greatest show on this side of the mountain!"

Grifeth and his wife quickly disappeared as a fife and oboe joined the lute and guitar. The melody picked up, and the crowd fell into silence as two dwarfs placed a square table right in front of the table where Peter and Ariel sat. Atop the table, they set a wooden crate that had a piece of black cloth covering the side facing Peter and Ariel.

The music suddenly stopped, and everyone stared at the crate. Then the music started again, playing quickly, and Peter saw the black cloth begin to wiggle as if someone or something were moving it from behind. Suddenly, the cloth parted in the middle like curtains on a stage and out jumped a small brown animal. The creature stood up on its hind legs waving to the crowd, like a *prima donna* at the opera, but stood just over half a foot tall.

The crowd cheered wildly, and Peter turned to Ariel with a large amused smile. "It's a gopher!" Peter laughed to a nod from Ariel. Peter quickly turned his attention back to the gopher as the music slowed. To Peter's surprise, the gopher bowed at the waist toward him and Ariel, just as the dwarfs had. Then the small rodent began to sway in rhythm to the music.

The dancing began slowly, but as the beat of the music picked up, so did the gopher's dancing. Soon he was leaping and spinning all over the table, and then to Peter's surprise and delight, the small creature leapt from his table onto Peter's table. The gopher landed on his knees and slid toward Peter before rolling over onto his back and then performing a backward somersault.

The gopher held out his hand to Peter and Peter shook it as if the animal were a person. The gopher then turned to Ariel extending his hand to her as well, but when Ariel reached out to shake it, the gopher leapt onto her arm, scurrying up to her shoulder, then onto her head. It remained atop her head for but a moment before leaping several feet through the air to snag the chandelier. The chandelier spun round and round with the weight of the gopher until the gopher eventually let go, flying through the air once more.

The gopher performed an impressive flip, landing on the tavern bar to enthusiastic cheers, and raised his front legs up like arms. He kept dancing to the quick pace of the melody, shaking his hips back and forth and turning somersaults and flips. The gopher leapt onto the beard of a dwarf sitting on a stool by the bar, surprising the dwarf so much he almost spilled his cider.

The gopher slid down the dwarf's beard to land on the floor, once again rolling into a somersault before scrambling up the leg of the table from whence he had begun. Once on top of the table his dancing slowed once again with the rhythm of the music. Then came the finale. The gopher sprinted across the table as if he were going to leap onto Peter's table again, but instead, spun around and sprinted back. Just before he reached the crate, he twisted around and performed a back flip over the curtain and back into the empty crate. The gopher jerked the curtains closed as the music ended and the crowd erupted into joyous cheers.

After a brief moment, the black curtains parted once again and the gopher stepped out. He bowed to the cheering crowd, again and again. He smiled at Peter and Ariel as they clapped their hands, and leapt across the table onto theirs.

THE DANCING GOPHER

"That was amazing!" Peter shouted.

"Well, thank you, sir," the gopher replied.

Peter stopped clapping and stared wide-eyed at the gopher for a moment before turning to Ariel. "It talks!" he exclaimed.

Ariel chuckled. "Of course he talks," Ariel said. "Why wouldn't he?"

"But I mean, I can understand him. He speaks English," Peter replied.

Ariel shook her head. "No, he speaks gopher, and the dwarfs speak dwarfish."

"Then how do I understand them?" Peter asked.

"It's called speaking in tongues," Ariel explained.

"What's that?" Peter inquired.

"Do you know where you got the name Peter?" Ariel asked.

"Mom and Dad named me after Jesus' disciple Peter," he replied.

"And did you know the disciple Peter spoke in tongues?" Ariel asked.

"No," Peter replied.

"He once spoke to a crowd of men from different countries, and as he spoke, they could understand his speech in their own tongue, or what you'd call a language," Ariel explained. "That is what happens here. Each creature speaks in his or her own tongue, but everyone else understands it in the language they speak."

"That's incredible!" Peter said before turning back to face the gopher. "My name is Peter," he said as he extended a hand, introducing himself.

"It's a pleasure to meet you, Peter," the gopher replied. "My name is Euripides."

"Nice to meet you as well, Euripides," Peter smiled.

"That was a very entertaining performance, my furry little

friend," Ariel said.

"Thank you, Your Grace," Euripides replied with a gracious bow toward the angel. "It was certainly an honor to dance for you."

"The honor was ours my friend, but if you will excuse us, I believe my young companion needs to get some rest. We have had a long day, and I need to find that shedom."

CHAPTER SEVEN
THE SHEDOM

Peter collapsed onto the dwarf-sized bed in Room 3, exhausted from the long journey. While the bed would have been a tad too short for Ariel, it was perfect for Peter. He didn't think he had ever walked that far before in his entire life, but feared his walking days were not yet behind him. He knew they somehow had to get to the top of the mountain to see this Nicholas, and after that who knew where Ariel would take him.

Still, as tired as he was, Peter was not ready to fall asleep. He was much too excited and had a million questions for Ariel. The one that was bothering him at the moment was how nighttime could exist if time itself did not.

"What does one have to do with the other? You call it nighttime and daytime," Ariel said emphasizing the word *time*. "But in Evermore the two are commonly called darkfall and lightrise. Unlike in your world, however, the darkness in Evermore does not fall because of the march of time, nor does the light rise. The length of a darkfall is dependent on the power darkness has in this world, not on the revolution of the Earth as it does in your world."

Peter stared at the angel as she stood in front of the window, watching for the shedom. The thought of a demon that terrified the dwarfs as much as the mention of the shedom did, sent shivers up Peter's spine. He chose to focus on getting to the bottom of the time mystery so as to avoid thinking about demons.

"What do you mean that the length of a darkfall is dependent on the power of darkness in this world?" he asked, still perplexed.

Ariel turned to look at him. "Christ Jesus is the light here, not the sun," Ariel explained. "In fact there was a time when no darkness reached Evermore. Christ's light shone constantly. Then the darkness began to creep in, slowly, little by little. One day, Christ will completely cast out the darkness, but until that day arrives, darkness grows more and more powerful, and the nights grow longer and longer."

That made Peter's head hurt, so he thought of a different question. "I saw a movie once and when time stopped everyone froze. Nothing moved. The clocks didn't tick, the birds didn't fly. Nothing moved at all. Why doesn't that happen here if there is no time?" Peter asked.

"Because time is not frozen here, Peter," Ariel explained. "Time does not exist at all."

Peter frowned, having difficulty coming to grips with the concept of a lack of time.

"Close your eyes," Ariel said. "You need some sleep. We'll have quite a long journey after lightrise."

"But I don't want to," Peter said as he fought back a yawn.

"Peter," Ariel said, fixing him with a stern glare.

"Okay," Peter relented and closed his eyes. He fell asleep

almost instantly, snoring gently on his bed. Ariel watched Peter for a while, suspecting she knew the reason the shedom had been terrorizing the dwarven village. If she was correct, she would be able to set a trap for it. She pulled the blankets over Peter, gently kissed his forehead like a mother saying goodnight, and then left the room, closing the door behind her.

Peter did not awaken to the door being closed, but simply continued to snore as he slept soundly in his bed. Once Ariel left, nothing was inside the room except for Peter and the darkness. Yet there was suddenly movement in the room. It was as if the darkness itself was somehow alive.

The darkness slowly twisted itself into the figure of a man. Well not quite a man. It appeared as a black armored figure, covered with a long dark cloak, the hood of which concealed its face. From beneath its cloak, the demon produced a long, jagged, dark-bladed sword. It stepped toward Peter's bed and raised the sword up over its head, ready to thrust downward and kill the boy.

Night after night, the shedom had searched for this boy, knowing Peter was on a quest that would take him through Evermore. Finally, the boy had arrived and the demon could complete the mission its master had given it—kill Peter Puckett.

The shedom was just about to thrust its sword into the blankets when it noticed a soft glow of light coming from behind it. That could mean only one thing!

The demon spun around, sword raised high to find Ariel behind it ready to strike. "Mal'akh!" the demon shrieked as it deflected Ariel's blow with its own dark blade, causing a loud thunderous clang that jerked Peter awake.

Peter sat up in bed as he saw Ariel locked in fierce battle

with what appeared to be the darkness itself. The demon slammed its heavy sword against Ariel's, knocking hers to the side and then swung back in the other direction, narrowly missing her throat, as she ducked backward out of the way. The shedom took the opportunity to slam its black-armored shoulder into Ariel's chest, knocking her backward, out through the open door, from whence she had appeared.

The shedom, slammed the door closed and then turned its attention back toward Peter who still sat in bed. Peter screamed as the shedom leapt toward him, its jagged sword raised high above its head ready to cut Peter in half. Peter screamed again when he looked beneath the hood covering the demon's face. There grinning wickedly at Peter was a black-armored faceplate molded into the shape of a human skull. A terrified Peter managed to scramble out of the way, just as the blade came down, chopping the bed in half.

Peter dashed for the door, but it burst open before he reached it as Ariel stepped through, sword in hand, and a determined look upon her face. "Get out of here!" she commanded Peter, and he eagerly complied, scurrying past her and down the steps to the tavern below. When he reached the tavern, Peter saw several customers still patronizing the place, smoking pipes and drinking cider. He almost slammed into Master Grifeth who was on his way up the stairs to investigate the sounds of the battle.

"What's going on lad?" asked Master Grifeth.

"Ariel is fighting the shedom!" Peter replied to wide eyes. Each of the dwarfs put down their mugs, pipes or musical instruments and drew weapons as Peter ran and hid beneath the table he and Ariel had sat at earlier. The dwarfs rushed to the stairs, none wishing to miss an opportunity to assist the angel in killing the shedom. After all, the tale of this night would be told for generations.

Suddenly, the shedom materialized from the darkness inside the tavern. It turned from side to side searching for Peter, finally noticing him hiding under the table. The shedom moved in for the kill, flinging the table away with one hand to reveal a terrified Peter, his arms wrapped around his knees. The shedom raised its dark sword to kill Peter, but suddenly stopped and shrieked a blood-curdling scream. Peter noticed Master Grifeth beside the demon, thrusting a kitchen knife into its hip. The shedom slammed the back of its armor-gloved hand against the dwarf, sending him flying across the tavern to land in a clump on the floor.

The shedom didn't have time to turn its attention back to Peter before the other dwarfs began to attack. Before the demon could retaliate, Ariel rushed downstairs leaping across the room and slamming an armored boot into the shedom's chest, knocking it backward. She was on it with a flurry of blows, forcing the demon back toward the door. While the shedom was distracted, Griselda managed to slip behind it and open the door to the tavern. Ariel forced it outside and kept up her attack.

The shedom did not stay on the defensive long. It vanished into the blackness and reappeared behind the angel, nearly slicing her in half with the jagged blade of its sword. Then the dwarfs began to pelt it with anything they could get their hands on: bowls, knives, boots, even a cat. The shedom held up an armored arm to protect itself and Ariel took advantage, swinging downward and slicing through the demon's chest. The armor protected it, however, and the shedom turned once again to go on the offensive. It was so strong that it eventually knocked Ariel's sword out of her hand. She fell to the ground attempting to dodge the next blow.

CHAPTER SEVEN

"Die!" the demon shrieked as it raised its dark blade high above its head, but before the blade dropped, the shedom's vision was suddenly obscured as Euripides the gopher leapt on top of its face, covering its eyes. The shedom screamed in frustration, as it grabbed Euripides with its free hand and tossed the tiny gopher away.

Euripides had bought Ariel enough time, however. As the shedom turned its attention back toward the angel, it found her recovering her sword and swinging the blade toward its head. The shedom jerked its head back to dodge the blow, but was not able to get completely out of the way. Ariel's sword knocked the demon's helmet right off its head revealing its true face beneath.

Peter, who was watching the battle through a window from inside the tavern, gasped when he saw the shedom's face. It appeared to be a veil of darkness pulled tight over a human skull. The shedom was furious now, and charged toward Ariel with a terrifying cry, but before it reached her, a beam of light cut through the darkness.

"The lightrise!" Peter heard Master Grifeth shout excitedly. The shedom turned to look at the sky which was quickly turning from dark back to light. It shrieked the most hideous scream Peter had ever heard before vanishing back into the darkness from where it had come.

The sky began to fill with light and dwarfs rushed from their homes cheering the angel and their own brave warriors. Ariel gave a sigh of relief as she saw a living, breathing and apparently unharmed Peter, rushing toward her. The boy threw his arms around her waist.

"You saved me," he said.

"Of course," Ariel replied as she returned his embrace. "That's what I'm here for."

THE SHEDOM

"Lightrise came quicker than it has of late," Master Grifeth said as he joined Ariel and Peter. "I don't remember a darkfall that short in a long time. Looks as though the Lord was with you."

Ariel nodded. "He always is," she replied with a smile.

"Euripides!" Peter cried as he released Ariel and sprinted over to the small gopher who lay motionless on the ground several yards away. Peter dropped down to his knees on the green grass beside Euripides and bent over to look closely at the small creature.

"Euripides, are you all right?" he asked. "Please be all right."

Euripides released a moan as he turned over onto his back. "Wow, I've never been thrown that far before," he said. The gopher then turned again and pushed himself to his feet. "I think, I'm all right. Nothing appears to be broken." He wiggled each of his legs and then his dancing hips just to be sure.

Ariel joined them and knelt down beside Peter. "You're my hero, Euripides," she said. "You saved my life."

Euripides blushed. "It was nothing, Your Grace," he smiled. "Happy to help."

Ariel stood and surveyed the dwarfs who had all come out to enjoy the lightrise and to see the Messenger of the Lord. "As I suspected, the shedom came to the village looking for Peter," she told them. "Once we leave, you should not have trouble from it again."

"Where are you going?" Master Grifeth asked.

"We are going to the top of the mountain to see Nicholas," she replied. "But I can't fly as my wing is injured."

"You'll have to take the tunnels," one of the dwarfs shouted out.

"That's what I'm afraid of," she replied.

"What's wrong with the tunnels?" Peter asked.

"They are dark," Euripides told him.

"Dark?" Peter asked. "So more shedom?"

"Don't worry, lad," Grifeth told him. "I've been in the tunnels hundreds of times and have never seen a shedom in there."

"Good," Peter said, the relief evident in his voice.

"You're much more likely to run into a band of se'irim," Grifeth added.

Peter remembered Ariel's description of se'irim as large red devil looking creatures with horns and fangs that ate little boys like him. Peter suddenly had no desire to go to the tunnels.

"How bad is it?" Ariel asked.

"It's getting worse," Grifeth told her. "As the darkfall gets longer and longer, the demons and other dark forces get bolder and bolder—but the early lightrise is a good sign."

"Yes," Ariel agreed. "We shall trust in the Lord, and he will get us through any hardship. Thank you all for your hospitality, but we should be going while the light is up."

The dwarfs gathered around her and Peter, thanking Ariel for ridding them of the shedom, and wishing both of them a safe journey. Suddenly, Euripides was on Ariel's shoulder, having scurried up her leg and arm.

"I shall go with you, Your Grace," the gopher announced. "You may need my skill once again."

"That is very…er…noble of you, Euripides, but…" Ariel began but Peter interrupted, begging that she let Euripides come with them.

"Oh, please," Peter said, his hands folded together as he pleaded with her.

"It's not my decision, Peter," Ariel said. "Grifeth is his

master, and Euripides has a duty to him."

Euripides leapt from Ariel's shoulder, bounced off of Peter's head and landed in Grifeth's beard. "Please, can I go with them?" Euripides begged the dwarf.

"But who will entertain my customers?" Grifeth asked.

"I know a squirrel that sings," Euripides offered.

Grifeth frowned. "I don't want an inn called *The Singing Squirrel*," he complained. "That would be ridiculous."

"Oh, please, Master Grifeth," Peter said. "Besides I doubt anyone will miss the dancing gopher, as good as that stew is."

Grifeth considered it for a moment, and finally relented. "Very well, gopher," he said.

"Thank you!" Euripides cried.

"It's all right," Grifeth replied. "I hear tale of a juggling badger near the Three Forks, that I've been wanting to talk to."

Master Grifeth gave Peter and Euripides some bread, apples, and a flask of water for their journey. Then Peter, Ariel, and Euripides said their good-byes and started out. They made for the tunnels which dug deeply into the side of the mountain and could even take them to the mountain's peak. But Peter desperately worried about what they would find in the darkness there.

It was a long walk from the dwarven village to the nearest entrance to the tunnel, but they arrived before another darkfall came upon them. Euripides had ridden on Peter's shoulder most of the way, and thus could not understand why Peter was so tired when they reached the entrance to the tunnels.

"Here we are," Ariel announced.

Peter looked up from the grass he'd been staring at as he walked, to see the side of the mountain. It was a sheer cliff, but there appeared to be a doorway behind a steel gate. Beside the gate was a dwarf with a long dark beard sitting in a little wooden chair leaned against the mountainside. The dwarf appeared to be asleep.

"Go and wake him and ask him to open the gate," Ariel instructed Peter.

Peter nodded and walked over to the dwarf who snored loudly in his little chair.

"Excuse me, sir," Peter said, but that didn't wake him. "Sir," Peter said a bit louder, but the dwarf just continued to snore.

Tired of waiting, Euripides leapt from Peter's shoulder and onto the dwarf's rather large nose. The dwarf awoke to see the small gopher staring him in the eye. The dwarf screamed and tried to stand, causing the chair to collapse onto the ground, along with the dwarf and Euripides.

Euripides hopped off the dwarf's nose, and quickly scurried back up Peter's leg and onto his shoulder. The dwarf huffed as he glared at the boy with a gopher perched on his shoulder as if it were a parrot. He pushed himself to his feet and then dusted off his clothes. "What do you want?" the dwarf asked angrily.

"We'd like you to open the gate, sir," Peter said.

"Oh, you do, do you?" the dwarf asked. "What business does a little boy and a troublesome gopher have in the tunnels?" he asked "Besides becoming a meal for hungry se'irim."

Peter swallowed hard. "We're trying to get to the peak of the mountain," Peter told him.

"And what's at the peak of the mountain?" the dwarf asked.

"We're going to see Nicholas," Peter said.

The dwarf laughed. "See Nicholas, huh? Hoping he'll give you a rocking horse are you?"

"What?" asked Peter, clearly confused, but the dwarf

ignored his question.

"What have you got as payment?" the dwarf asked. "Ruby? Diamond? Emerald?"

Peter reached deep into his pockets, turning them inside out. "I'm sorry, sir, I did not know I needed any of that."

"Oh no?" the dwarf asked. "Expected passage for free did you? You children today, always expect to get things for free. Those tunnels didn't dig themselves you know," he explained. "Took a lot of dwarfs a long time to construct them. But you think we should just let you use them for free, huh?"

"Oh, no, sir, I just..." Peter began.

"Just what?" the dwarf interrupted as he glared at Peter and Euripides. "Take your gopher and be going, boy," the dwarf said as he repositioned his chair so that he could sit down again.

"How about three emeralds?" came Ariel's voice from behind Peter. "One for each of us."

The dwarf leaned over to look past Peter and Euripides at the angel standing behind them. He leapt to his feet and rushed past Peter.

"No, uh, no need, Your Grace," he said as he bowed low at the waist. "There is no charge for a Messenger of the Lord." He held out his arm to invite her to walk toward the gate. "But I must warn you, the se'irim have taken control of many of the passages. We've roped off the more dangerous ones, and our patrols do the best they can to keep the tunnels clear, but the devils are still in there."

"Thank you for the warning, Master dwarf," Ariel said.

The dwarf nodded as he rushed to the gate and pulled an enormous key out of his pouch. He slipped the key into the lock, turned it, and opened the gate. "Take the middle tunnel all the way up to the peak," he instructed.

CHAPTER SEVEN

"Thank you again," Ariel said.

"My pleasure, Your Grace. May the Lord be with you," he said as they stepped through.

"And with your spirit," Ariel replied.

They heard the gate close and lock behind them, and Peter felt a shiver dance up his spine as they stepped into the darkness.

CHAPTER EIGHT
INTO THE TUNNELS

As fear swept over him, Peter immediately regretted stepping into the dark tunnel. He couldn't see anything except Ariel, and even though her amazingly radiant skin glowed in the darkness, it was not enough to illuminate the dark tunnel. Peter stepped close to Ariel and took hold of her hand, prompting the angel to give his fingers a comforting squeeze. Holding Ariel's hand made him feel better, but it still did not quiet all of his fears. Peter's imagination began to run wild as he stared into the blackness recalling the warnings about se'irim in the tunnels.

"How are we even going to find the right tunnel if we can't see?" Peter asked in a trembling voice.

"That is odd," Ariel said.

"What is?" Peter inquired.

"There should be torches along the walls, lighting our way," she explained.

"I can see," Euripides remarked proudly. "Gophers live

much of their lives underground. I'm used to this."

Ariel turned to stare at the small creature perched atop Peter's shoulder. "Perhaps we should tie a leash around your neck and you can guide us," she laughed.

Euripides gruffed at that suggestion. "I'm not a dog!" he exclaimed, clearly offended.

"Well, then," Ariel replied. "I suppose we'll do it my way." With that, she released Peter's hand, drew her sword from its sheath and slammed it down onto the stone floor, pointy end first. A wave of light burst forth from her sword and rolled along the floor and up the walls, covering all of the tunnel. In its wake, the wave of light left the walls and floor of the tunnel glowing like a full moon.

"That was cool!" Peter exclaimed.

"Yes, it was," Ariel smiled at him. She returned her sword to its sheath with a clang and then held her hand out for Peter. "Come, let's get moving."

Peter nodded eagerly as he reached out and took hold of the angel's outstretched hand. Ariel led him along the tunnel, and Peter marveled that no matter how far they walked, the walls and floor were still illuminated. He turned around to see that as they passed a section of the tunnel, the illumination slowly faded away.

After walking for what seemed like an eternity to Peter, they finally came to a large cavern. The walls of the cavern were illuminated by the light from Ariel's sword just like the walls of the tunnel. The cavern reminded Peter of the inside of a domed cathedral he'd once visited in California, complete with carvings of angels battling demons, alongside dwarfs and what Peter assumed to be giants.

"Why don't we rest here, so that you and Euripides can eat," Ariel suggested. "We're about to get to the difficult part."

INTO THE TUNNELS

Peter was happy to rest. His feet and legs already hurt, and he certainly wasn't looking forward to the "difficult part." He pulled the bread the dwarfs had given him from his pouch and broke off a piece for Euripides.

Peter was about to take a bite when he remembered that he had not thanked God for it. "Dear Lord, thank you so much for this bread and water, and for keeping us safe," Peter said.

"Amen," Euripides added and then dug into his piece of bread. Peter also opened up the flask of water and drank heavily before pouring some into the cap for Euripides to drink.

As he ate, Peter's gaze rose to the ceiling of the cavern, and he gasped when he saw the enormous mural painted there in bright colors. The mural depicted a man holding seven stars in his hand, with a double edged sword coming out of his mouth. The man was beautiful with brilliant white hair that was as pure as the new fallen snow. His face shone like the sun, and his eyes appeared to be burning with fire. He wore a flowing white robe with a golden sash across his chest. His feet were as perfect as polished bronze and beneath them was a dragon—a red dragon with seven heads.

Peter gasped when he recognized the red dragon from his dream. However, unlike his dream, the monster in the painting had clearly been defeated and was being crushed under the feet of the man.

"Who's that?" Peter asked Ariel as he pointed up at the mural on the ceiling.

Ariel lifted her eyes to see the mural. "That is Jesus Christ," she informed him. "And not a bad rendering either."

"What about the dragon?" Peter asked.

"Oh I do not like the dragon at all," Euripides remarked. "It gives me the creeps."

Ariel frowned as her eyes narrowed. "Yes, the Red Dragon," she sneered. "He is the enemy, the wicked one. He is a great serpent and the ruler of the demons."

"The ruler of the demons?" Peter gasped.

"Yes," Ariel replied. "He is Christ's great adversary, but as the painting shows, our Lord will be victorious in the end. He will lead a great army from Heaven and will crush the Red Dragon and his demons under His feet."

"How do you know?" Peter asked. "How do you know that Jesus will defeat the Red Dragon?"

Ariel gazed down at her young companion and placed an arm around his shoulder. "Because the Lord God Almighty has said so," she said confidently. "The Lord God Almighty created everything and controls everything. If He wills that it happen, then that is how it will happen."

Peter nodded. "And if God wants to use the Amulet of Eternity to save my mother, He will," he said.

"That's correct," Ariel smiled. "And with that in mind, let us continue our journey."

Peter turned his attention to the tunnels exiting the cavern. There were seven. Three on the right, three on the left, and one straight ahead, in the center of the others.

"The dwarf told us to take the center tunnel," Euripides reminded them.

"So he did," Ariel agreed, and Peter suddenly realized that of the seven tunnels, only the one in the middle was illuminated. The other six were as dark as a moonless night.

"Well then, let's go find this Nicholas so we can get back and save my mother," Peter said.

Ariel nodded. "Good plan, Peter," she agreed as she helped the boy to his feet. She led the way across the cavern and into the center tunnel. The tunnel began to ascend and soon the smooth floor disappeared, evolving into steps. "These steps should lead us all of the way to the top of the mountain."

"Wow," Peter mumbled as he wondered to himself how many steps that might be. After all, when he had stood at the base of the mountain peering up, it appeared as though the mountain rose up forever. "How long will this take?" Peter asked.

Ariel chuckled. "I have no idea," she replied. "I usually fly."

Peter sighed. His young mind's exaggerated sense of time imagined it would take a year or more to walk that many steps, and his legs hurt already. As they rose higher and higher the steps became steeper and steeper. Peter noticed entrances to other tunnels on the left and the right.

"Where do these other tunnels go?" he asked.

"Everywhere!" Euripides told him.

"Everywhere?" Peter asked, certain that could not be true.

"Not exactly everywhere," Ariel said. "But Euripides is correct that the mountain tunnels really are quite extensive."

"But you never know what's hiding in the dark," Euripides reminded them. "As the darkness grows stronger, the dark forces grow bolder and bolder."

"Why doesn't Jesus just defeat the darkness now?" Peter asked. "What's he waiting for?"

"He's waiting on the appointed time," Ariel replied. "Only God the Father knows when His Son Jesus Christ will defeat the darkness. Even Christ Himself doesn't know."

"But why would He wait so long?"

Ariel turned and peered down at her young companion. "Perhaps He is giving those who are currently living in darkness and wickedness a chance to repent of their evil sins and turn to Jesus."

Peter nodded. That made sense to him. "Because God wants everyone to live in Heaven with Him," he said.

"That's correct, Peter," Ariel replied. "But as merciful and generous as He is, the Lord cannot allow evil and wickedness to dwell in His presence. So those who choose the darkness over the light will be cast out into that darkness for eternity."

Peter shivered, and Euripides put words to his thoughts. "That doesn't sound very pleasant," the gopher frowned.

"I agree," Ariel replied. "That is why you must make sure that you love and trust in Jesus Christ, obeying His commands and turning from your evil ways."

Peter beamed proudly. "Well, I'm safe," he remarked. "I don't have evil ways."

Ariel stopped in her tracks, causing Peter to stop as well. She turned and fixed him with a stern glare. "You don't have evil ways?" she asked.

"No," Peter replied confidently with a shake of his head. "I'm a good boy."

Ariel chuckled. "As far as boys go, you are pretty good, Peter Puckett," she said and then bent over so that her nose was only a few inches from Peter's as she stared him in the eyes. "But know this, and don't forget it, only God Himself is truly good."

"But I am good!" Peter said. "I mean, I sometimes forget to say the blessing and 'yes sir' and 'no ma'am,' but I am certainly not evil."

Ariel straightened back up as she narrowed her eyes. "How did your father die, Peter?" she asked.

Peter's head bowed in sadness. "He was killed in the war," he replied.

"How was he killed?" Ariel asked.

Into the Tunnels

Peter shrugged, refusing to meet her eyes. "I guess a bomb blew up and killed him."

Ariel nodded. "Was it an accident?"

Peter shook his head back and forth. "No, the bad guys did it," he said, and Ariel could hear his voice crack as he pushed up his glasses and wiped the tears from his eyes.

"And how do you feel about these bad guys that killed your father?" Ariel asked gently. "Do you love them? Do you forgive them for what they did?"

Peter jerked his head up to glare at Ariel, tears streaming down his cheeks. "No!" he shouted. "I hate them! I want them to die! I can't wait to grow up and become a Marine and I'm going to go over there and I'm going to kill them all."

"And what about that bully at your school, the one who always picks on you?" Ariel asked. "Dylan. Do you hate him too? Do you wish he were dead?"

"Yes!" Peter shouted. "I wish he'd get hit by a bus so that he couldn't hurt me anymore." When the words left his mouth, Peter dropped to the stone floor of the tunnel sitting down, wrapping his arms around his knees, and sobbing. Euripides leapt from his shoulder and scurried a few feet away. As Peter wept, Ariel slowly lowered herself to her knees beside him. She wrapped an arm around his shoulders and pulled him close to her breast. He sat there crying for a long time, until he eventually calmed himself and wiped the tears from his eyes.

Ariel slipped a finger beneath his chin and pulled his face up to look her in the eyes. "You see, Peter," she said softly. "There is evil in you."

Peter nodded. He realized she was right. As good as he thought he was, something wicked lurked beneath.

"Everyone has some darkness in them," Ariel told him.

"Even you?" Peter asked.

CHAPTER EIGHT

Ariel nodded. "Yes. Unfortunately, even angels can turn to the darkness. And when we fall, giving into that darkness instead of following the light, we twist into demons."

Peter's eyes went wide in shock. "An angel can become a demon?" he asked.

"Yes, Peter," she replied. "Everyone has the capacity for evil, and if we do not fight the darkness and keep our eyes on the light of Christ, we become monsters."

"So what can I do?" Peter asked.

"Keep your eyes focused on the light of Jesus Christ. Think about good things, like love and kindness, instead of evil things like hate and revenge. Beg God's forgiveness for your wickedness and ask Him to help you fight against it. Then you will be well on your way to Heaven."

Peter nodded. "I will," he said.

"Good," Ariel replied as she stood up and helped Peter to his feet. Ariel kissed Peter gently on the top of the head. "Come on," she said. "Let's get moving so we reach Nicholas' house before darkfall."

Peter nodded as Ariel turned to lead the way up the steps. As they walked along, something pungent reached Peter's nose. He sniffed the air and almost gagged. It smelled to him like a sweaty horse covered in rotten eggs.

"What is that smell?" he asked.

Ariel suddenly froze in her tracks. "Se'irim!" she sneered as she drew her sword. Fear gripped Peter as Ariel turned to look back at him. "Hurry we've got to…" she began, but did not get a chance to finish the sentence.

Something enormous crashed out of a nearby tunnel and slammed into Ariel, knocking her against the wall of the tunnel. Peter heard her sword clang against the stone floor and knew it had been knocked from her hand. Peter screamed in terror when he saw the se'irim. The creature towered above the boy as it attempted to bring the blade of its giant battle axe up and into Ariel's throat while Ariel held it at bay.

"Her sword!" Euripides shouted to Peter snapping him out of his terror.

Peter saw the sword lying on the stone floor and rushed to it, scooping it up into his hands. Then with a courageous battle cry on his lips he charged the giant beast. The angelic sword penetrated the se'irim's dark red skin and the monster howled in pain. It turned and slammed the back of its giant hand into Peter, knocking him backward to land on the floor of the tunnel.

Peter lifted his head to see that he had indeed helped Ariel. While the se'irim was distracted, Ariel had managed to reach down and yank her sword from the creature's thigh. She then shoved it upward into the beast's body. The monster staggered briefly before collapsing onto the ground.

Ariel turned to Peter with a warm smile. "You saved me," she said proudly.

Peter pushed himself to his feet and was about to run over to her for a hug when two more se'irim appeared from the tunnel behind the angel.

"Ariel, look out!" Peter screamed.

Ariel spun, barely blocking the blow from a giant mace with her sword. Peter scanned the ground for Euripides, worried the gopher would get trampled during the melee, when he suddenly felt giant hands grab him from behind, lifting him up off his feet.

"Help!" Peter cried as he was carried away into a dark tunnel.

CHAPTER NINE
A CAGE WITHOUT BARS

A terrifying panic coursed through Peter as he was carried through the darkness of the tunnels by giant red hands with long black fingernails that resembled the talons of a bird-of-prey. He screamed until his throat hurt and then screamed some more, partly hoping for someone to rescue him and partly out of sheer terror. The se'irim that carried him seemed to enjoy Peter's screams, as if the terror and torment that produced them thrilled it.

The se'irim was enormous—at least seven feet tall—with dark red skin, giant horns similar to those of a ram, yellow eyes that seemed to glow in the darkness, horrifying fangs, and hairy legs with hooves instead of feet. Swishing behind it was a long red tail, that was pointed at the end like the tip of a spear. Worst of all was the smell! Peter had never imagined that anyone—man or beast—could possibly smell as bad as the se'irim did.

Peter continued to scream until the se'irim stepped out of

the darkness of the tunnel into a giant cavernous room illuminated by torches, a chandelier made from deer antlers, and a flaming fire in the hearth. The flames cast lights and shadows in a terrifying dance around the room. A large, wooden table was situated near the fire with four bowls set on top of it. Apparently, the se'irim would be having dinner soon, and Peter suddenly feared that he would be the main course.

After entering the room, the se'irim leaned its long, menacing spear against the wooden table and grinned wickedly at Peter. However, instead of killing Peter, the large monster opened what appeared to be a giant birdcage hanging by a chain from the ceiling in the center of the room. The giant beast tossed Peter inside of the cage and then closed the door before locking it with a key on a large ring that hung from the se'irim's belt.

Peter cowered inside of the cage as the se'irim chuckled. It stared at Peter for a brief moment and then turned and left the room. Once it was gone, Peter stood up in the cage, walked over to the door and tried to open it. It was no use—Peter would never be able to open the door without the key. He peered over the edge to the stone floor below and estimated he was about ten feet off the ground. That was an intimidating height for a boy of only ten years old.

"Help!" Peter shouted as loud as he could. "Ariel! Help!" After shouting for a while he finally gave up and collapsed onto the floor of the cage, wrapped his arms around his legs, and began to cry. He was so scared that he didn't know what else to do. He was certain that the se'irim were going to cook and eat him. Peter's weeping was interrupted by hearty laughter behind him. He lifted his head, wiped the tears from his cheeks and turned to see the source of the laughter.

When he did so he saw a dwarf sitting on what appeared to

be an enormous scale. The scale consisted of two large metal disks on either side of an equally large wooden arm. The dwarf sat on one side of the scale and on the opposite side of the scale was a pile of shiny stones of various colors. Peter stood and turned to stare at the dwarf. He looked similar to the dwarfs Peter had already met at the small dwarven village. He had an oversized nose, dark red hair, and a long red beard.

"What's so funny?" Peter demanded as the dwarf's laughter faded.

"Not funny, exactly," the dwarf said. "It's just that I am stuck here on this giant scale and I prayed to the Lord God to deliver me and my treasure and then suddenly here you are."

Peter cocked his head to the side, unsure of what the dwarf meant.

"You see, lad, these se'irim were going to eat me for their dinner tonight, but then they found you."

"What does that have to do with anything?" Peter demanded.

"Well, everyone knows that a se'irim would prefer to feast on a tender young boy such as yourself than a gristly old dwarf like me," the dwarf said happily. "So, you bought me some more time to figure out a way to escape."

Peter frowned as he stared at the dwarf. The dwarf was not in a cage. He could simply jump off of the scale any time he chose to. "I don't see any cage holding you," Peter remarked.

The dwarf nodded. "Right you are lad. This cage is not as visible as yours. But most cages in life do not have actual bars and locks, do they?" the dwarf asked.

Peter had no idea what the dwarf was talking about. How could it be a cage if it didn't have bars and locks?

"You see, I am balancing up here over a high ravine," the dwarf explained. Peter looked more closely and realized he was right. The dwarf hung over a ravine about six feet in width. "It is probably two hundred feet to the bottom," the dwarf estimated.

"Yes, but you could easily jump to safety," Peter told him. "You are only a couple of feet from the edge. Just jump off. You could save yourself and then save me."

"Aha," the dwarf smiled. "But if I do that, the scales will tip and my treasure of precious stones will fall to the bottom of the ravine and be lost to me forever. Besides why would I care what happens to you?"

Peter frowned at that last remark, but understood his point. He didn't know Peter. Perhaps Peter could befriend him. "What's your name?" he asked.

"Strom," the dwarf replied.

"It's nice to meet you, Master Strom. My name is Peter," he said. "Peter Puckett."

"Did I ask?" the dwarf snapped. "Do I care what your name is, boy? You will be in a se'irim's belly soon. And I've got to figure out how to escape *with* my treasure before it's my turn."

Peter turned his back on the dwarf and sat down on the floor of the cage with a huff. He didn't like this dwarf. Strom wasn't nearly as nice as the dwarfs at *The Dancing Gopher*. In fact he was a real jerk. And who would care so much about their treasure of precious stones that they would let themselves die for them?

Even though Strom was in the same room with him, Peter felt completely alone. Without the key, there was no way out of the iron cage in which he hung. Unless Ariel managed to find him, the only person who could get the key and save him was the dwarf, but Strom was uninterested in saving even himself without his treasure, much less saving Peter.

CHAPTER NINE

Peter placed his face in his hands and began to cry again. Oh how he wished he had a friend now. Oh how he wished he wasn't alone. But then he remembered something. He wasn't alone. Father Joe had told Peter that Jesus was always with him, even when Peter couldn't see Him. Peter decided that the only way to get out of the predicament he was in, was to ask Jesus for help.

Peter slid onto his knees, bowed his head, and folded his hands together. As the tears rolled down his cheeks, he began to pray. "Jesus, I'm in big trouble. The se'irim are going to have me for dinner if I don't get out of this cage. You've been so nice to me in answering my other prayers, and I know I forgot to say thank you. I'm not very good at remembering to say thank you—Momma always has to remind me. But I really do appreciate it. If you could please help me now and save me from the se'irim, I would be very, very, very grateful." Peter thought for a moment. "I suppose you could just unlock the cage for me, or teleport me to another place. Maybe you could just make the se'irim disappear. However you do it, Jesus, please save me from these monsters. I really don't want to get eaten. Amen."

Peter then sat back down and waited for Jesus to open the door to the cage, or to make the key suddenly appear or be teleported back into the tunnel with Ariel. But nothing happened. Peter sighed but didn't give up. "I need to be patient," he said to himself. "Jesus will save me. He has to."

Peter waited and waited, wondering what was taking Jesus so long. Then, just when he had decided Jesus wasn't going to save him at all, Peter heard a soft voice call his name.

"Peter," the voice said, but Peter knew it did not belong to Jesus. He rushed to the side of the cage and peered over the edge to see a small brown gopher standing up on his hind legs staring at him.

"Euripides!" Peter shouted excitedly. "How did you find me?"

"I told you gophers can see in the dark," Euripides reminded him. "Plus, it is pretty easy to follow the scent of a se'irim."

Peter imagined that was true. The creature's stench probably lingered in the tunnels for a long while. "Where's Ariel?" Peter asked.

"I don't know," Euripides told him. "She was still fighting a couple of se'irim, so I decided I had to rescue you myself."

"Euripides, the se'irim are going to eat me!" Peter told him.

"Not if I can help it," the small gopher said bravely. "I just need to find the key to that cage, and I'll get you out of there." Euripides scanned the room, hoping to see the key somewhere.

"One of the se'irim has the key," Peter told him.

Euripides stopped searching the room and looked up at Peter in his cage. "Oh," he said, the disappointment and fear evident in his voice.

"It was on a large keyring on its belt," Peter explained. "You'll have to sneak up and take it from him."

Peter and Euripides heard boisterous laughter and turned to see Strom slapping his knee.

"What's so funny?" Peter demanded.

"Imagining that little gopher taking a key from a se'irim and rescuing you," the dwarf replied. "More likely, the se'irim will be having gopher stew tonight along with you, boy."

Peter turned back away from Strom and peered down at Euripides once more. "Don't listen to him, Euripides," Peter said. "I know you can do it."

Euripides nodded. Peter's confidence in him bolstered the confidence he had in himself. "I'll get that key, Peter,"

CHAPTER NINE

Euripides said. "Don't worry, I'll be back soon."

As Euripides scurried away, Strom began to laugh again.

"Oh, be quiet!" Peter snapped at him.

Euripides hurried along a tunnel leading into another room within the se'irim's cavernous lair. He came to an opening on his left and slowly sneaked up to it and peered inside. The room held a rack of weapons—battle axes, spears, maces and the like—but no se'irim. Euripides continued on as quickly as his little legs would carry him.

Euripides finally encountered a much larger room where he found three se'irim, playing a game. At least, he assumed it was a game. It was rather odd for a game, but Euripides couldn't think of what else it could possibly be.

Two se'irim stood in the middle of the room with their backs to each other, about ten feet apart. A third stood away from them, by a wall, clearly observing the game, but not participating. The two playing the game took turns tossing large stones over their respective heads, each trying to hit the other. Because they had their backs to one another neither se'irim could aim at the other, and had to guess where to throw the stone.

The floor was littered with stones that had missed their target, and Euripides suddenly realized that se'irim were not incredibly bright creatures. Eventually, a large stone crashed down onto the head of one of the se'irim, landing right between its horns. The beast screamed in pain, and the other spun around, laughing at its friend and bragging that it was the winner.

The se'irim struck by the stone wobbled away to sit on the floor, its back to the wall, while the se'irim observing the rock tossing match took the loser's place in the game. The two participants turned their backs to one another and once again began tossing stones over their respective heads.

Euripides turned his attention to the monster sitting against the wall and holding his sore head. The gopher smiled when he noticed a large key ring attached to the se'irim's belt. "The Lord is clearly with me today," Euripides said to himself, and then slowly crept forward, crawling on his belly toward the giant red-skinned beast.

When Euripides finally reached the se'irim, he examined the keyring and surmised that it hung from a metal hook attached to the monster's belt. Euripides had to stand up on his hind legs to lift the key ring over the hook to free it from the se'irim's belt. The key ring was enormous—at least it was enormous to Euripides. It was almost as big as he was, but to a creature as large as a se'irim it would have been quite manageable.

Euripides used all of his strength to lift the heavy ring off the hook but struggled to get it high enough to clear the hook. Even standing on his tip-toes, Euripides just wasn't tall enough to remove it from the hook. As Euripides held onto the key ring, the se'irim suddenly stood up. Euripides rose up into the air with the rest of the keys. Apparently, the other match of rock throwing was over and they were switching opponents again.

Euripides released the ring, landed on the ground, and scurried behind some of the rocks before he was noticed by one of the se'irim and turned into a stew. While the loser of the previous match nursed a sore head, the other two se'irim turned their backs to one another and resumed tossing the large stones. Stone after stone was tossed, and Euripides had to stay alert to avoid being crushed beneath one of them.

CHAPTER NINE

After each se'irim had thrown about ten stones, one finally crashed atop the head of the se'irim carrying the key ring. This time, however, the se'irim did more than just stumble and rub its head. In fact, the creature completely collapsed onto the floor of the cavern with a heavy thud. Its companions laughed, deep guttural laughs, as their friend laid unconscious on the hard stone floor. Not wanting the game to end, both of the other se'irim stepped over to the unconscious monster, lifted him up and carried him to the side and out of the way. When they did so, the key ring fell from the hook on the creature's belt and onto the stone floor.

"Praise God," Euripides smiled to himself and dashed out from behind a large stone, grabbing hold of the ring and hurrying back to his hiding spot before the se'irim turned and spotted him. Just after Euripides made it back to cover, the se'irim returned to the game and once again began tossing the large stones.

Euripides took advantage of their distraction and dashed quickly from rock to rock before finally reaching the door to the room and running as fast as he could while holding onto the large key ring. Euripides ran back along the tunnel until he reached the room in which Peter was imprisoned.

"Peter! Peter!" Euripides shouted excitedly. "I have the key!"

Peter peeked out of the cage and beamed broadly when he saw his friend holding the large key ring. "Wonderful, Euripides!" Peter exclaimed.

Both of them heard a laugh behind them, as the dwarf amused himself at their expense. "So the little gopher somehow managed to get the key from the se'irim did he?" the dwarf asked. "Well, now let's see him fly ten feet off of the ground to unlock the cage."

A Cage Without Bars

Euripides glanced around the room and quickly formulated a plan. "That's the easy part!" he exclaimed. The gopher slung the key ring over his shoulder and across his chest and then hurried to the table, climbing the table leg all the way to the top. Once on top of the table, Euripides charged the long spear that the se'irim had left leaning against it. The gopher leapt onto the spear, his momentum causing it to fall forward. Euripides rode the falling spear, leaping off of it to grab hold of the chandelier. Euripides' momentum caused the chandelier to spin round and round just as it had when he was dancing at the inn. As the chandelier spun around once again, Euripides released it and flew through the air and right into Peter's cage.

"That was incredible!" Peter shouted to the small gopher. He removed the key ring from Euripides' body and hurried across the cage to the door. Reaching his arm in between the bars of the cage, Peter was able to insert the key into the lock and turn it. The cage door opened, and Peter shouted excitedly as the small gopher scurried up his leg to rest on his shoulder.

"Now all you've got to do is jump," Euripides said.

Peter peered over the edge at the floor below.

"It's pretty high," he said.

"You can do it, Peter," Euripides assured him.

Peter nodded and leapt out of the cage. He landed on his feet but fell over. Unhurt, he quickly scrambled to his feet and made his way to the door and freedom. But then something stopped him. He slowly turned around to see the dwarf sitting on the scale, his arms crossed in front of his chest, a scowl on his face.

Peter crossed the room to stand in front of Strom. He offered his hand to him. "Come on, Strom," he said. "Just jump off."

CHAPTER NINE

"I've already told you, I'll lose my treasure if I do!" the dwarf shot back.

Peter shook his head in confusion. "So this treasure is worth more to you than your life?" he asked.

"A little boy wouldn't understand!" Strom said. "I've worked all my life in these tunnels, digging and mining to amass that treasure and if I leap off the scales, I'll lose it all."

Peter nodded. "Yes, Strom. You will lose some pretty, colorful, shiny rocks if you leap off the scale, but you will gain your life. If you love your treasure more than your life, you will surely die," Peter said and the dwarf considered the boy's wisdom for a moment. "What good will those shiny rocks do you after you're dead anyway? You can't take them with you."

Strom looked up at Peter and gruffed.

"When you are cooking over the se'irim's hot fire, you are going to realize just how worthless your treasure really was!" Peter shouted in frustration.

Strom stared at Peter for a long moment considering this. He then glanced over at his treasure. The shiny rocks were so beautiful. He had spent most of his life collecting them, but the thought of being cooked for the red devil's meal was enough to jar him into action. The fire burned hot and Strom looked at it, imagining it burning his skin. He turned back to Peter. "You're right," he said. He glanced once more at his pile of precious stones representing his entire life's savings. "Treasure is no good to me if I am dead."

Strom rose to his feet, took hold of Peter's outstretched hand, and leapt off the scales. When he did, the side with the precious stones tipped, dumping the red, blue, yellow, and green gems into the ravine and causing a considerable amount of noise. Strom almost regretted his decision as he watched his treasure disappear into the darkness.

A CAGE WITHOUT BARS

Suddenly, the three of them heard a terrifying roar from down the corridor. The se'irim had heard the crash. "Uh oh!" Peter said.

"We'd better hurry!" Strom exclaimed, once again propelled to action from fear of being cooked and eaten. The dwarf led the way out with Peter close on his heels, and Euripides riding on Peter's shoulder. They ran as quickly as they could into the dark tunnel.

"I can't see!" Peter shouted.

"Hold on to me, boy!" Strom instructed, and Peter reached out and placed a hand on the dwarf's shoulder. Even though they were running as fast as they could manage, Peter could hear the se'irim gaining on them, their hooves banging against the stone floor sounding like a horse galloping on cobblestones.

"They've almost caught us!" Peter shouted as he heard the heavy breath of the creatures right behind him. Just as he thought he was about to be snatched up and taken back and eaten, the tunnel walls and floor suddenly illuminated. Then Peter saw Ariel charging toward them. Strom and Peter ducked to the side, and the angel leapt past them, sword raised.

Peter turned to see Ariel and the two se'irim doing battle. The angel fought fiercely and quickly. She stabbed one and then spun and sliced behind the leg of the other causing it to drop to a hairy knee with a howl of pain. Ariel then brought her gleaming sword down killing the se'irim instantly.

She stood still a moment, remaining in a fighting position standing over the fallen se'irim and waiting to see if any more were coming. Once Ariel was satisfied that there were none she sheathed her sword and turned back to Peter and his companions. Ariel stepped forward and threw her arms around the boy, scooping him up into a big embrace.

"I was afraid I'd lost you," she said. "But the Lord in His mercy led me to you."

"God also sent Euripides to help me escape," Peter told her. Ariel released Peter and looked at the small gopher perched on his shoulder.

"Well done, Euripides," Ariel said as she patted him on the head. "It seems the Lord meant for you to join our quest." Euripides beamed proudly.

Ariel then turned to Strom. "And who is this?" she asked.

Peter stepped over to the dwarf and patted him on the back. "This is my new friend Strom," Peter said. This took Strom totally off guard. Nobody ever wanted to be his friend, and Strom had been very mean to Peter.

"It is a pleasure to meet you Master Strom," Ariel said.

Strom dropped to his knees before her. "The pleasure is mine, Your Grace," he said. "And thank you for dispensing with those se'irim. Nasty creatures."

Ariel smiled. "My pleasure," she said. "Now rise, Master Strom. We still have a ways to go to reach Nicholas." Ariel then glanced around. "Unfortunately, I'm not entirely sure where we are."

Strom rose from his knees and smiled proudly. "Do not fear, Your Grace," he said. "I know every tunnel there is and will have you to the peak of the mountain before darkfall."

"Well then, lead the way," Ariel said, and Strom turned and led them away from the se'irim's cavern.

CHAPTER TEN
NICHOLAS

Peter's new dwarf friend, Strom, led the way up the steep steps along the illuminated tunnel toward the peak of the mountain. The climb was difficult as the stairs grew gradually steeper, but Strom continued climbing them as if he were simply walking along flat ground. Peter, on the other hand, struggled mightily and kept having to ask the dwarf to slow down.

"We want to get there before darkfall, don't we?" Strom asked.

"Yes," Peter agreed. He certainly had no desire to see another shedom.

"Then we must hurry," the dwarf told him.

Peter turned to see Ariel following them, and she gave him a reassuring wink. He turned back and pressed onward and upward.

Not only did Strom climb steps like they were nothing at all, but he also talked the entire time. He told them his entire

CHAPTER TEN

life story, how he had been born in a small village on the other side of the mountain, but had joined the miners at a young age and spent most of his adult life digging in the tunnels. His singular pursuit had been the accumulation of treasure.

"But thanks to young Master Peter, I have come to realize that perhaps treasure is not the most important thing there is," Strom explained. "I mean, I nearly ended up in a se'irim's stew pot. What was I thinking?" He then stopped and turned back to face his new friend. "I am sorry for being so mean to you in the cavern, Peter."

Peter smiled. "That's okay, Strom," Peter said. "We were in a tough spot."

The dwarf nodded before turning to Euripides. "And it was mean of me to tease you, gopher," he said.

"It's all right," Euripides smiled. "It's not the first time I have been teased."

"You have some truly amazing skills," Strom commented.

"You should see him dance," Peter laughed.

Strom joined him in laughter. "Perhaps one day." He then turned back around and continued walking up the steps. "But we need to continue moving," he said.

"So you don't think treasure is that important anymore?" Ariel asked.

Strom shook his head. "No, Your Grace," he said without turning to face her. "At least not important enough to lose my life for. But to be honest, part of me still aches to go and find it, to retrieve it from the ravine."

"That would be very dangerous," Peter cautioned him.

"Indeed it would, lad," Strom agreed. "But you must understand, I spent most of my life accumulating that treasure. I've lost everything. Don't get me wrong, I'm happy to be alive, but the prospect of starting over, accumulating treasure again is overwhelming. And what if I end up losing that treasure as well?"

"That is a puzzlement," Ariel agreed. "What you need is a treasure that you cannot lose."

Strom stopped and turned to face the angel. "What do you mean?" the dwarf asked. "What kind of treasure is that?"

"Heavenly treasure," Ariel replied.

"Heavenly treasure?" Strom repeated, his eyes wide with excitement. "Please tell me about this Heavenly treasure, Your Grace."

"Yes, Ariel, I want to know about it, too," Peter said.

"Heavenly treasure is the greatest treasure there is," she explained. "It cannot be lost or destroyed. It does not rust or tarnish. It lasts for all eternity!"

"Where can I dig up this Heavenly treasure?" Strom asked.

Ariel smiled brightly. "Our Lord Jesus Christ explained that when we stop loving our earthly treasures, whether they be precious stones," she said and then turned to look at Peter, "or a new bicycle, and are willing to just give them away to help those in need…When we start loving God more than anything and loving others as much as we love ourselves, then we will build up treasure in Heaven."

"That sounds easy," Peter said.

"Humph! It doesn't sound easy at all," Strom said. He turned back around and once again began ascending the steps. "In fact, it sounds very difficult. I can't imagine caring so little about my treasure that I could just give it away."

"It is difficult, Master Strom," Ariel agreed. "But it is also worth it. When you die, you will care nothing for the treasures of this world. But you will long for the treasures of Heaven."

Strom frowned to himself, and kept walking, deep in thought.

CHAPTER TEN

Finally, they reached the end of the tunnel—a giant iron door. Strom reached out and turned the handle, pushing the door open. It was difficult to open, not only because of the heavy weight of the iron, but also because of the snow that was packed around it.

Peter shivered as he followed Strom through the doorway into the knee deep snow. He looked out over Evermore, and felt he could see the entire world from way up there. But he soon forgot about the view as the wind cut through him like a knife. It was cold on top of the mountain—very cold. Peter's jacket was not thick enough for this type of weather and he tried to keep warm by wrapping his arms around himself. He turned to look at Ariel, and noticed that she did not seem fazed by the cold at all.

The angel scanned the sky. "We need to move quickly," she told them. "Darkness is beginning to fall."

"How far is it?" Peter asked.

"Not very," Ariel replied as she pointed to the mountain peak at a massive red brick house with white trim enveloped by the snow. Except for the enormous size, the house looked as though it would not be out of place in most suburban American neighborhoods.

"Let's hurry!" Strom urged, but was quickly out of breath, the high elevation and deep snow taking its toll on him. Peter followed him at a snail's pace, struggling against the wind and cold. Euripides remained perched on Peter's shoulder, pressing his body against Peter's hair to try and stay warm.

"I don't think I can make it," Peter said. The cold was biting, and he struggled to breathe in enough oxygen. Suddenly, he felt two arms reach around him, picking him up. Ariel pulled Peter in close and wrapped her beautiful white wings around him.

NICHOLAS

"Hold on," she said. "We're almost there."

Strom finally reached the house, and pulled himself up the snow-covered steps to the enormous wooden double-doors. He pulled back the giant knocker and slammed it twice against the door. He waited a few moments as the others joined him on the porch and then gave another knock. This time, the doors opened, seemingly on their own. Strom smiled as warm air rushed past his face. As they stepped inside they were greeted by a long, empty hallway.

The doors slammed closed behind them, plunging the hallway into darkness except for a tiny bit of light from flickering candles mounted on the walls. Ariel set Peter's feet on the soft carpeted floor.

"What do we do, Your Grace?" Strom asked, and Peter could hear the nervousness in his voice.

Ariel shrugged. "I suppose we find someone," she said. Ariel led the way along the dark hallway. Peter was as nervous as Strom, and he thought even Ariel seemed a bit on edge. She didn't draw her sword, but she let her hand rest on its hilt, ready to draw quickly if necessary. As they walked carefully along the hallway, Peter heard soft voices whispering somewhere, perhaps coming from inside the walls. The voices gave him the creeps, and he was glad he had Ariel with him.

"Hello!" Ariel called out in the darkness. "Nicholas?" The only thing they heard in reply was her voice echoing in the empty corridor.

As they walked, Peter noticed the hallway was lined with dark red wooden doors, but Ariel did not stop at any of them. Instead, she continued—as if she knew exactly where she was going—to a set of large, red double doors at the end of the hallway. When they reached the doors, Ariel rapped gently. "Hello?" she called again. She was about to knock once more when the doors opened on their own to reveal a pitch black room. Ariel led the others inside.

"Can you see anything?" Peter whispered to Euripides.

"Yes," the gopher replied. "There is someone in here."

From the darkness, Peter heard movement. A lot of movement.

"Sounds like a lot of someones are in here," Strom said.

The doors slammed closed behind them, and they suddenly heard giggles from all around.

"It's a trap!" Euripides shouted.

There was a sudden burst of light, and the room illuminated. Peter leapt back as he realized they were surrounded. Surrounded…by elves? The room was filled with tiny people no more than a foot in height dressed in red and green clothing, with big heads and disproportionately large, pointy ears that poked up from under their cone-shaped hats.

"The elves have taken over!" Strom shouted frantically.

Suddenly, the elves leapt forward, but they didn't attack. Instead they broke into song. The elves sang a catchy tune in unison while performing a difficult synchronized dance that included acrobatics so impressive they even made Euripides jealous. Several elves leapt on top of Peter, spinning around his head before diving off and landing on the floor in a somersault. Then the elves gathered for the finale, singing and dancing in complete unison.

> He knows what is deep in your heart
> Best beware, be on your guard
> Or you'll end up with a bag of sticks,
> Here he is, Jolly Ole Saint Nick!

There was a flash of light and a poof of smoke and suddenly standing before them was a tall man with a long white beard in a flowing red and white robe.

NICHOLAS

Peter heard Ariel laughing and turned toward her. "You knew what was happening this whole time, didn't you?" he asked and the angel nodded.

"All first-time visitors meet Nicholas the same way," Ariel smiled. "With song and dance."

"That was the greatest thing I've ever seen!" Euripides exclaimed as he clapped his little paws together. "Oh Master Grifeth would no doubt love to have a few of these elves at *The Dancing Gopher!*"

The old man with the white beard stepped forward. "Ah, Peter Puckett, it is so wonderful to have you in my home," he said.

"Peter, this is Nicholas," Ariel said.

"Nicholas?" Peter replied. "Saint Nick?" Nicholas nodded. Peter's eyes popped wide as his mouth fell open with the realization of who he was talking to. "You're Santa Claus!"

Nicholas threw back his head with a hearty laugh. "Yes, my boy, there are many who call me Santa Claus."

Peter shook his head. "I didn't think you were real," he said. He then turned to see the hundreds of elvish eyes staring at him. "And you really do have elves!"

Nicholas chuckled. "Well I wouldn't say that I have them," he said as his gaze swept in all of the elves in the room. "It's more like they have me."

"What do you mean?" Peter asked.

"Well if I were a king, one might call them my royal guard," Nicholas laughed.

"You're guarded by elves?" Peter asked in disbelief.

"Indeed," Nicholas replied.

Peter snickered. "You must not be that important if these happy little creatures are your guards."

"Peter, no, elves are..." Strom tried to warn him, but it was too late. Nicholas clapped his hands, and before Peter could blink, a score of elves had closed on him at blinding speed, tripping him with tiny, but extremely strong rope. Peter crashed to the floor, and the elves then bound him up completely. Peter felt himself jerked into the air as the elves pulled him upward, feet first toward the ceiling with a strand of rope. Peter hung upside down from the ceiling in the middle of the room, swinging back and forth.

"I take it back," Peter said.

Nicholas laughed boisterously as he stepped up to the suspended Peter. "Actually, I am not very important and cannot understand why the Lord, in His generous mercy, would bestow such a wonderful honor on me, to be guarded by some of the fiercest warriors in all of Evermore." Nicholas then turned to the elves. "Let him down, please," he said. The elves complied and soon, Peter was back on the floor, with the elves unwrapping the rope.

Peter pushed himself to his feet as Strom and Euripides introduced themselves to Nicholas. The old man then turned to Ariel. "The boy must be outfitted!" he said with a wave toward Peter.

Ariel smiled. "That is why we are here, Nicholas," she said.

"Of course," Nicholas replied, and then turned back toward Peter. "Well my boy, let us go see what we can find."

Peter nodded excitedly. He had no idea what Nicholas was talking about, but if it came from Santa Claus, it had to be good.

"Nicholas is Judge of the Western Province of Evermore," Ariel explained to Peter as they walked through the enormous house.

NICHOLAS

"A judge?" Peter asked. It seemed odd to think of Saint Nick presiding over court.

"Not like you think of a judge," Ariel explained. "He is more like Lord Protector."

"Oh," Peter said. "How many provinces are there?"

"Just four," Ariel explained. "The North, South, East, and West."

"So you are like in charge of this province?" Peter asked Nicholas.

"Not exactly," Nicholas replied without turning around. "I am more of an administrator. The Lord God is in charge."

"So you don't really bring gifts to girls and boys on Christmas?" Peter asked with a hint of disappointment in his voice.

Nicholas stopped cold in his tracks and spun to face Peter. "Of course I do," he said. "But not dolls and video games and other nonsense like that."

"Then what?" Peter asked with a shrug of his shoulders.

Nicholas leaned down, bringing his face close to Peter's. "Whatever gifts the Lord God in His never ending generosity wishes to bestow," Nicholas smiled. "I have the honor and pleasure of taking gifts from God to His people. Not just boys and girls either. Moms and Dads, Grandmas and Grandpas, too."

"Like what?" Peter asked, annoyed that Nicholas appeared to be dodging the question.

Nicholas smiled. "I gave you the gift of generosity when you were a very small boy," he said and then tapped Peter's chest with his pointer finger. "Placed it right there in your heart while you were asleep in your crib."

"Generosity is a gift?" Peter asked perplexed.

Nicholas straightened. "Of course it's a gift," he said. "It is a wonderful gift. Think of how horrid the world would be if no one ever received that gift."

"But why did you give me the gift?" Peter asked. "Why didn't the Holy Spirit just give it to me Himself?"

"He could, of course. He could bestow the gifts without any assistance from me, just as He could save your mother without any assistance from you. And oftentimes He does. But sometimes…" Nicholas paused and smiled at Peter.

Peter continued. "Sometimes He gives us the honor of taking part in His work," Peter said, remembering what Ariel had explained to him earlier.

"That's right," Nicholas said as he clapped his hands together.

"How do you know about my mother?" Peter asked.

Nicholas laughed once more. "You might be surprised at how much I know, my boy." He then spun on his heel and continued walking. "But come along, now. We have things to do."

Nicholas led them into a grand room, with twenty foot ceilings and walls of green and gold wallpaper adorned with grand portraits of seemingly ordinary people in enormous gilded frames. There was a portrait of a mom and her children dressed in dirty and torn Elizabethan era clothing that reminded Peter of the actors from a "Shakespeare in the Park" production his parents had taken him to in California a few years ago. There were other portraits of an old lady on a park bench, a dirty girl holding a baby that looked like she was from a commercial for a Christian children's charity, a small boy and his dog, and a balding man with wire rimmed glasses sitting behind a stack of papers on a desk. All of the portraits were displayed as if they were paintings of kings and queens.

"Who are these people in the pictures?" Peter asked.

Nicholas turned to him with a smile. "Oh, these are some of the most wonderful people I have ever met. Songs will be sung of their greatness!"

"Really?" Peter asked. He had expected that someone like Saint Nicholas would have met truly amazing people, like the Queen of England or George Washington. These people didn't seem special at all. They looked like the people Peter had known all of his life and ran into every day.

"Oh yes, they are extraordinary," Nicholas assured him, as he himself admired the portraits.

"Why don't I recognize any of them?" Peter asked.

Nicholas turned toward him. "Why would you?" the old man chuckled. "The world cares little for them. They are not self-indulgent movie stars or power-hungry politicians. They do not boast in their possessions or achievements and certainly do not demand nor even crave the adoration of others."

"Then what makes them so great?" Peter asked with genuine curiosity.

Nicholas smiled broadly. "Their hearts, their love, their generosity. They have compassion for their fellow man and do not crave glory. They put others before themselves and love God with all of their hearts. That, my boy, is what makes them great."

Peter stared at the portrait of the small boy and his dog. "What about him?" Peter asked.

Nicholas beamed as he stepped closer to the large painting. "Oh yes, Tommy, is one of my favorites," Nicholas explained. "He did some truly extraordinary things."

"Like what?" Peter asked.

"Well, did you know that every day during school lunch, Tommy would give his pudding snack to his little friend whose parents could not afford such luxuries? Every day! Tommy never held back."

"Wow, that was really nice," Peter said.

"Extremely," Nicholas agreed. "And he loved Jesus so much that for his eighth birthday, instead of asking for the usual toys, Tommy asked people to buy backpacks and school supplies for poor Christian children in India." Peter's eyes went wide. He couldn't imagine a birthday without getting a present for himself.

"Tommy was a truly selfless child," Nicholas continued. "And when he was nine and all he wanted for Christmas was a puppy, you can bet that I made sure he received one."

"So what's he doing now?" Peter asked. "Is he all grown up?"

Nicholas looked at Peter, and Peter saw tears gleaming in his eyes. "Tommy never grew up," Nicholas said. "He got leukemia and died at age eleven."

Peter was shocked. He stared at Nicholas and then looked back at the portrait, then back at Nicholas. "But why?" Peter asked in disbelief. "If he was so good, why did God let him die so young?"

Nicholas considered this for a moment. "Well, sometimes the Lord in His wisdom allows the good children to grow up so that they can be good adults and help the rest of the world—to demonstrate the love of Christ. But other times, he takes them home to Heaven, so that they do not have to suffer through all of the trials of the first life like the rest of us. I imagine He loves them so much He wants them with Him."

Peter nodded. That made sense to him. But it was still sad. "So Tommy is in Heaven?" he asked.

Nicholas chuckled happily. "Oh yes, he most certainly is. He trusted in Jesus as much as anyone ever could I suppose. Even when he lay in the hospital bed dying, he was not afraid.

NICHOLAS

He told his mother and father not to worry—Jesus would take care of him until they got there, and that he would watch them from Heaven."

"And so he has," Ariel added.

Nicholas wiped tears from his eyes and then turned toward a sitting area with four wing backed chairs of red velvet set near a roaring fire in an impressive hearth. "Enough about that," he said. "We have other matters to discuss. Come, sit."

Nicholas took one of the chairs nearest the fire as Peter sat across from him and Ariel beside Peter. Strom joined them in the fourth chair and Euripides lay down in front of the hearth, curled up into a furry ball on the rug and went to sleep.

Peter looked at Nicholas. On one side of him was a small table with a pipe, matches, and round little spectacles set upon it. On the other side was a giant red bag. Nicholas placed the spectacles on his nose before picking up the pipe. He turned to Strom.

"Would you care for a smoke?" he asked the dwarf.

"Very much, sir, if it pleases you," Strom replied.

"Indeed it does," Nicholas smiled. "Help yourself." He pointed toward the round table beside Strom's chair. The dwarf turned to see a small wooden box. He opened it and found a slender wooden pipe, tobacco, and matches.

"Well thank you, sir," Strom smiled happily as he removed the pipe from the box and began to stuff tobacco into its bowl.

Nicholas brought a lit match to the bowl of his own pipe and puffed away as the flame lit the leaf. When the pipe was lit, Nicholas waved the match through the air extinguishing it before laying it on the table. He then turned his attention to Peter.

"So here we have Peter Puckett," Nicholas smiled. "On a quest to save your mother, eh?"

CHAPTER TEN

Peter nodded his head up and down. "Yes, sir."

"Are you ready for what lies ahead, young man?" Nicholas asked.

Peter glanced at Ariel before turning back to Nicholas. "Well, to be honest, I don't know what lies ahead," Peter remarked. "So I can't tell you if I'm ready or not." This answer amused Nicholas, and he began to chuckle as he puffed on his pipe.

"A fine tobacco, sir," Strom remarked and Peter turned to see the dwarf enjoying his pipe.

"Yes, the finest, in fact," Nicholas replied. "Turkish." He then turned his attention back to Peter. He stared at the boy for a long moment as he puffed on his pipe. The old man appeared to be considering something, or everything. Eventually, Nicholas removed the pipe stem from his mouth and looked at Ariel.

"You know where he is going and what he must do," Nicholas said. "What do you think he'll need?"

Ariel's eyes darted from Nicholas to Peter and back again. "I think, more than anything at this point, he needs a shield," she said.

Nicholas' eyebrows rose high on his head as he nodded his agreement. "Yes, he could use a shield, most assuredly," he said as he looked at Peter. "But I fear he is not yet ready."

Peter glanced at Ariel and then back at Nicholas. He agreed with Ariel that a shield would be good idea. If he was going to be coming face-to-face with any more of those shedom or se'irim, he wanted not only a shield, but a sword.

"I'm ready," Peter asserted.

"Are you now?" Nicholas asked with an amused laugh. "Very well." He set his pipe down on the table, turned to the other side of the chair, and opened the large red bag. He reached deep inside and pulled out a beautiful shield which gleamed brilliantly in the firelight. The shield was divided into fourths by a ruby red cross, and Peter recognized it from his dream about the red dragon. In his dream, he had carried that exact shield. That is, he carried it until he dropped it, because it was too heavy and was weighing him down. "Well come and get it, my boy," Nicholas said as he laid the shield down on the carpeted floor.

Peter climbed down from his chair and walked over to the shield. He bent down, slipped his fingers beneath it, and lifted. At least, he tried to lift it. The shield moved a little off the ground, but not very far before Peter released it and allowed it to drop back down on the floor.

Nicholas chuckled and patted the boy on the back good naturedly. "See, my boy, you are not quite ready."

Peter looked up at him. "It's just too heavy," Peter said. "I could probably use a smaller shield."

"Oh no, Peter," Nicholas said, "The weight has nothing to do with the shield's size or with your strength. It's a matter of faith, you see. You simply do not have enough faith to lift the shield. Even if you could, I fear that you would not have enough faith to wield it in battle. In the face of the enemy you would drop it because it is too heavy for you."

Peter remembered his dream. When he had seen the red dragon, he had dropped his shield. Not only his shield, but his sword and all of his other armor as well. Peter sighed, realizing that Nicholas was right. He didn't have enough faith. He slumped back into his chair with a pout. He felt defeated.

"I'll never have enough faith to lift the shield," he whined.

"Well, not if you don't seek it," Ariel said.

"What do you mean?" Peter asked.

"Faith doesn't come from within you," Ariel said. "It

comes from the Holy Spirit. Sometimes He gives it to us suddenly and completely. Sometimes He gives us a little bit at a time. But if you want it, if you seek it and pray for it, I promise you, the Holy Spirit will give it to you, when the time is right."

"How will I know when the time is right?" Peter asked.

"You won't," Ariel replied. "Only God will know."

"I believe young Master Peter needs a night," Nicholas said. Ariel nodded her agreement.

"What do you mean?" Peter asked.

"It has been a long journey Peter," Ariel explained. "Perhaps you should rest before you are outfitted."

Peter did feel tired and his legs were sore. He was also hungry and could feel a rumble in his belly.

As if sensing his hunger Nicholas spoke up. "But before you rest, let us feast!" he smiled.

"A feast?" Strom shouted excitedly as he jumped to his feet. "That is something I most certainly would not want to miss."

"Nor would I," Euripides agreed, suddenly awake and scurrying across the carpet. He hurried up Peter's leg to rest on the arm of the boy's chair.

"Then what are we waiting for?" Nicholas laughed boisterously as he rose from his chair. "Let's eat!"

CHAPTER ELEVEN
AN ELVISH KNIGHT

The Great Hall was ornately decorated with cream colored wall paper printed with small golden designs that reminded Peter of snowflakes. More portraits of seemingly ordinary people adorned the walls and an enormous fireplace covered much of the far wall. Red carpet covered the entirety of the floor giving the impression of royalty. A long cherry wood table sat beneath a beautiful crystal chandelier and was topped with the most delicious foods Peter had ever seen. Turkey and dressing with brown gravy, pink smoked hams, grapes piled high in bowls and glistening with droplets of water, long green beans, golden crusted pies, steaming custards, cakes dripping with icing, potatoes covered in melting butter, and crispy golden rolls were all laid out from one end to the other. After a blessing thanking the Lord for the meal and for protecting them on their journey, Peter, Strom, and Euripides were finally allowed to dig in.

The feast was prepared and served by another race of little

CHAPTER ELEVEN

people. Smaller than dwarfs but larger than elves, munchkins were a kind and darling people—happy to help and always eager to serve. The myths were confused, Nicholas explained. Legend claimed that elves worked in Saint Nick's workshop, but as Peter had already discovered, the elves were Nicholas' royal guard. The munchkins were the labor, though they did not busy themselves constructing dolls and wooden trains. Instead they kept the manor in order, administered the books, cooked and served the meals and fed and cared for the reindeer.

"Wait!" Peter stopped as he was just about to take a bite out of an enormous, golden-brown turkey leg. He turned to stare wide-eyed at Nicholas. "You really have reindeer?"

"Of course," Nicholas replied, happily amused by Peter's excitement. "How else do you think I travel around?"

"But do they fly?" Peter asked with a skeptical eye.

Nicholas laughed joyfully. "Of course they fly," he smirked. "What else would be the point of having them way up here on the tippy top of this mountain?"

Peter shrugged and then bit into the turkey leg. "So how did people outside of Evermore learn so much about you anyway?" he asked as he chewed.

"Peter Puckett," Ariel scolded like an embarrassed mother. "Do not talk with your mouth full."

"Sorry," Peter apologized and then swallowed his food.

Strom laughed at him from across the table before raising his stein and gulping down a swig of cider.

"Do you think you are the first person to cross over into this world, Peter?" Nicholas asked.

Peter thought about it for a moment. "I suppose not," he replied.

"No, you are not, my boy," Nicholas said. "In fact I am

from your world as well."

"Really?" Peter smiled before taking a drink of thick, creamy and warm chocolate milk.

"Oh yes," Nicholas said. "I lived in a different place and time than yourself. I was a bishop in the Greek city of Myra in the early fourth century."

Peter's mouth dropped open. "Wow, that was a long time ago!" he exclaimed.

Nicholas chuckled. "Indeed it was. In fact, Myra no longer exists and the location in your time is present day Turkey."

"No wonder you have such a long white beard," Peter joked, causing the entire table to laugh.

"It also helps keep my face warm in the snow," Nicholas chuckled.

"And you do really deliver gifts all over the world?" Peter asked.

"Yes, indeed," Nicholas replied.

"But how is that possible?" Peter asked as he turned to Ariel. "You told me that time didn't exist here and that I would arrive back in my world at the same time I left."

Ariel shook her head. "You are correct that time does not exist in Evermore, but I did not say you *would* arrive back in your world at the same time you left. I said you *may* arrive back at the same time you left. You will return to your world at the exact moment the Lord wills you to return."

"And not a moment later or earlier," Nicholas smiled. He then leaned forward and gave Peter a wink. "You can explain that to scoffers who ask how I can deliver gifts to everyone in the world in a single night."

"The Apostle Peter, after whom you were named, once declared 'one day is with the Lord as a thousand years, and a thousand years as one day,'" Ariel explained. "God created time and exists outside of time. Time does not bind Him as it binds you."

Peter yawned as he set down his turkey bone. He was suddenly finding it very difficult to keep his eyes open.

Ariel turned to Nicholas. "I think we should call it a night," she replied. "We can finish our discussions tomorrow."

"Good idea," Nicholas agreed. "Young Master Peter appears as though he might fall over."

Peter chuckled as he rubbed his eyes. "I feel like it, too," he confessed.

"Very well," Nicholas replied. He summoned one of the munchkins to him. "Kindly show our guests to their rooms," he instructed.

"Yes, Your Excellency," the munchkin said with a curtsy. She then turned to Ariel. "If Your Grace will follow me," she said. Ariel and the others stood and followed the munchkin from the room. The munchkin opened a large door—which Peter estimated must be ten feet high—and led Ariel, Peter, Strom, and Euripides into a long hallway. The walls were adorned with more portraits of seemingly ordinary people. The floor was wooden, but they walked along a red carpet which ran down the center.

"May I have your name?" Ariel asked the munchkin.

The munchkin turned to smile at the angel. "I am honored Your Grace would inquire," she said. "I am called Nora, Mistress of the House."

"It is very nice to meet you Mistress Nora," Ariel said.

"And you, Your Grace," Nora replied.

"So are you in charge of all of the munchkins?" Peter asked.

"I have command of the house, yes," she answered, "but

that command is for the service of Bishop Nicholas. I serve at his good pleasure."

Strom frowned. "Do you not tire of being a servant?" he asked Nora.

The munchkin stopped in her tracks, causing those following her to stop as well. She turned to face the dwarf with a bewildered expression on her face. "Why would I ever tire of serving?" she asked.

Strom gruffed. "Well, I certainly would not want to spend my life as a slave to another."

"The King of all Kings, the Lord of the Universe, Christ Jesus, Himself, came not to be served but to serve others. Yet you think you are above serving others, Master dwarf?"

Strom hesitated. "Well, I didn't mean that I was above it," he said sheepishly.

"Good," Nora replied sharply before spinning on her heel to once again lead the group along the hall. "Because those who wish to be great must first learn to serve humbly."

Nora soon stopped in front of a room and opened the door. "This will be your room, Master dwarf," she said to Strom.

Strom nodded and mumbled his thanks as he stepped inside. He closed the door abruptly. Nora frowned, but turned and continued walking along the hall. She soon stopped in front of another door.

"This will be your room, young Master," she said to Peter as she opened the door.

"Thank you," Peter smiled as he stepped through the door followed by Ariel and Nora. "Wow!" he exclaimed. The bedroom was enormous, easily as large as the entire first floor of the rectory where he and his mother lived with Father Joe and Ms. Naomi. The floor of the room was covered with plush white carpet, and the walls were decorated in red, green, and gold wallpaper that consisted of lines crisscrossing one another to form diamonds. Against the near wall was a large fireplace with flames already crackling and warming the room. Upon the other walls hung large portraits, but not of ordinary people. These portraits were of men and women, girls and boys, dressed in shining armor, wielding shields and swords. Some rode on horseback. Some stood beside angels. Others smiled as if posing for a photograph.

In the center of the room stood a king-sized, four-poster bed, with sheer curtains hanging from the posts. Euripides leapt from Peter's shoulder with an excited squeal, hurried across the floor and scurried up the leg of the bed. He climbed all of the way up one of the four posts and then turned and faced Peter and the others. He spread his arms out wide before allowing himself to fall backward. He landed on the soft mattress and sank so low that Peter lost sight of him.

Peter rushed to the bedside to make sure his friend was all right. He was relieved to see a smiling Euripides lying on his back staring up at Peter. "It's a feather mattress!" Euripides shouted with glee. "It's the softest thing I've ever felt, Peter. You have to try it."

Peter nodded and pulled himself up onto the high bed, immediately sinking down into the feather mattress. "It's like sleeping on a cloud!" Peter exclaimed excitedly.

Nora chuckled. "I take it you approve of your room, Master Peter?" she said.

"Oh yes," he said happily. "Thank you."

"Excellent," Nora said. She then clapped her hands and another smaller door on the right wall opened. Two munchkin men stepped out, dressed in fine suits with short pants and high stockings, reminding Peter of the suits Benjamin Franklin wore. "A hot bath has been prepared for you. And when you are finished, some clothes for sleeping are in the wardrobe," Nora explained as she pointed to the large mahogany wardrobe cabinet set against the left wall. She then nodded to the two munchkins standing at attention by the door to the bathroom. "These two will serve you in anyway you require. Give them your clothes, and they will have them laundered and ready again for you before you leave. If you need anything else, simply ring that bell." Peter looked to see that she was pointing to a small silver bell resting atop his bedside table.

"Yes, ma'am," he said. "Thank you."

Nora then turned to Ariel. "If Your Grace will follow me, I will show you to your apartment."

Ariel shook her head. "I am grateful, but I have no need to sleep, Mistress Nora," she said. "I will remain vigilant throughout the night."

"Oh," Nora said somewhat surprised and dismayed. "But we had a team of munchkins eager to serve you. A bath has been drawn, and your armor should be polished."

Ariel nodded with a sigh, not wanting to disappoint the munchkins. "Very well, Mistress Nora, lead the way." She then turned to Peter. "I shall return after my bath." Peter suddenly looked nervous. He turned to glance through the giant windows at the darkness outside.

"But what if a shedom comes to kill me again?" he asked.

Ariel walked over to him and placed a comforting hand on his shoulder. "I doubt even the bravest of shedom would dare attack you inside these walls," she said. "I will not be gone long. You will be safe I assure you."

Peter nodded, but it was clear that he was still scared.

Nora made a suggestion. "I tell you what, Master Peter," she began. "I will send one of the Bishop's finest knights to guard you. How does that sound?"

Peter perked up immediately. "Okay," he said.

"Excellent," Nora replied. "In the meantime, why don't you go ahead and take a bath. Dilbert and Gilbert will be here with you," she said motioning to the two munchkins standing at attention on either side of the bathroom door.

"All right," Peter said and slid off the bed.

Nora led Ariel out of the room, closing the door behind them as Peter walked into the bathroom, followed by Euripides who had leapt from the bed to hurry across the soft carpeted floor.

The bathroom was magnificent with a large gilded mirror, marble sinks with golden faucets, and an enormous marble tub in the center of the room as big as the king-sized bed. The tub was filled with warm water and a mountain of white bubbles. Peter and Euripides smiled at one another and Peter hurried to strip off his clothes while Euripides rushed up the steps to the side of the tub and leapt off the edge, disappearing into the bubbles with a splash. Peter finally pulled off his last sock and joined his friend in the warm water. Peter bathed himself as Dilbert (or was it Gilbert) set a pair of soft pajamas and slippers on a cushioned stool and collected Peter's dirty clothes to be washed.

Peter and Euripides played in the tub for a long while with Peter using the suds to make a fluffy white beard for himself while pretending to be Saint Nicholas. Euripides laid on his back paddling around the tub, forming tunnels through the mountain of bubbles.

"This is so much better than the cold baths in the little wooden bucket Mistress Griselda gives me once a month back home," Euripides said. "We should stay here forever!"

"I can't," Peter frowned. "I have to find the Amulet of

AN ELVISH KNIGHT

Eternity so that I can save my mother."

Suddenly Peter heard a tapping on the bedroom door.

"I'll answer it, Master Peter," said Gilbert (or was it Dilbert) from outside of the bathroom. Peter heard the bedroom door open and then heard voices. A moment later one of the munchkins appeared at the door to the bathroom. "Sir Palamedes has arrived, Master Peter," he announced.

Peter looked at Euripides wide-eyed. He had never met a real-life knight before and was very excited to do so. Peter climbed out of the sudsy water grabbing a nearby towel and quickly dried himself off. His hair was still fairly damp when he pulled on the pajamas, placed his glasses on his face, and slipped the slippers onto his feet. Peter rushed into the bedroom expecting to find a tall and dashing knight in shining armor. Instead he was surprised to find a small elf dressed in chain mail and a tunic of blue and gold checkers. His large pointy ears stuck out from beneath his shining silver helmet and a flowing blue cape was clasped around his neck by a silver stag's head.

The elvish knight greeted Peter with a flourishing bow. "It is a great pleasure and deep honor to guard someone as noble as yourself, Master Peter," the knight said.

Peter returned the bow. "Thank you," he said. "And you are Sir Palamedes?"

"Yes, young Master," the knight replied.

"Are you really a knight?" Peter asked.

Palamedes drew his sword and slashed it through the air as if fighting some invisible foe. "I am not just any knight," Palamedes said. "I am the knight who captured the famed Questing Beast!"

"What's a questing beast?" Peter asked.

"It is a fierce and repulsive creature, with the head of a

serpent, the body of a leopard, and hooves like a deer."

Peter climbed up on top of his feather bed, situating himself to get comfortable while watching Palamedes. Euripides joined Peter, lying down on one of the soft feather pillows. "Could you tell me how you caught him?" Peter asked excitedly.

"Of course," Sir Palamedes said with another flourishing bow. "It was a dark night and I..." he began but was interrupted when the door to the bedroom opened, and Ariel stepped inside. Peter slid down from the bed and stared at her. He had never seen anyone so beautiful in his life.

Ariel no longer wore her armor, but rather a soft, white sleeveless gown which fell to her bare feet. Her golden hair hung loosely in ringlets framing her perfect face. She carried no sword, but smiled gently at Peter.

"You're beautiful," Peter said.

"Thank you, sir," the angel replied with a slight curtsy. She then turned to Palamedes. "And who is your friend?"

"Oh," Peter said, having temporarily forgotten anyone but Ariel existed. "This is Sir Palamedes."

The small elvish knight bowed so low that his head nearly touched the floor. "It is the greatest honor to meet you, Your Grace," he said. And then, unable to reach her hand, the knight placed a kiss on the tip of her big toe.

"What a perfect gentleman," Ariel, smiled. "Thank you, Sir Palamedes. The honor is mine."

"Sir Palamedes was just about to tell me about the time he caught the questing beast," Peter said excitedly.

"Is that right?" Ariel asked as she crossed the room and lifted Peter up onto his bed.

"Yeah," Peter said. "It's got a snake's head and the body of a leopard!"

AN ELVISH KNIGHT

"Sounds terrifying," Ariel smiled.

"It is, Your Grace," Sir Palamedes agreed.

"Perhaps another time," Ariel said. She then turned to Peter. "Right now it's time to get some sleep."

"But I want to hear the story," Peter whined.

"Not now," Ariel said firmly. "We've had a long day today, and will have another one tomorrow. You need rest."

"All right," Peter moped as he laid back onto the feather bed. Euripides was already asleep, curled up on the feather pillow beside Peter's.

Ariel pulled the covers up, tucking Peter in, before leaning over and kissing him gently on the forehead. "I'll see you after lightrise," she said. Peter nodded. Ariel then turned to Sir Palamedes. "Would you mind watching him a little longer, while I go and speak with Nicholas?" she asked.

"It would be my great honor, Your Grace," Palamedes replied.

Ariel waved her hand through the air, and all of the candles suddenly blew out. The only light remaining in the room came from the flickering fireplace. "I will not be long," she said, before turning and gliding from the room. Peter watched as the door closed shut, but couldn't keep his eyes open any longer. Soon he had drifted off to sleep for some much needed rest.

CHAPTER TWELVE
GIFTS

"Time to rise and shine," a voice said and Peter opened his eyes to light streaming in through the windows. He rolled over and rubbed his eyes before sitting up, almost expecting to see Ms. Naomi greeting him, eager to tell her his dream about angels, dwarfs, elves and Santa Claus. Instead, he saw Ariel, bathed in the morning light and smiling brightly at him. She no longer wore a soft gown, but was once again clothed in her white dress and armor.

"Good morning," Peter said as he returned her smile.

"How did you sleep?" Ariel asked.

"Great!" Peter exclaimed through a yawn as he stretched his arms high in the air.

"Wonderful," Ariel replied. "Get dressed. We've got a lot to do today before darkfall." Peter nodded and then pushed back the covers and swung his feet over the side of the bed to land on the floor. "And wake up Euripides," Ariel chuckled.

Peter turned back to the bed to find the small gopher still

curled up atop the soft feather pillow. He tapped Euripides with a finger. "Euripides, time to get up," he said.

"No, no, Master Grifeth, not yet," the small gopher said as he turned away from Peter.

"Euripides!" Peter shouted, causing the gopher to jerk his head up in bed and glance around the room, startled. When he saw Peter's smiling face, he relaxed.

"Oh, it's you," he said. "I was having the most wonderful dream."

"It's time to wake up," Peter told him.

"Okay," Euripides yawned as he stretched out his body.

Peter glanced about the room. "Where is Sir Palamedes?" he asked Ariel.

"I relieved him of his guard duty," Ariel replied. "Now get dressed and then come to the Great Hall for breakfast and your outfitting."

"Yes, ma'am," Peter nodded and Ariel swept out of the room closing the door behind her.

"Breakfast!" shouted Euripides excitedly. "Hurry up Peter. I'm starving." Peter pulled off his pajamas, leaving them in a pile on the floor, and found his own clothes, folded neatly atop a small chest, presumably cleaned and left there by either Gilbert or Dilbert. Peter got dressed quickly, crossed the room to the door, and pulled it open. Euripides hurried out of the room with Peter close behind, heading for the Great Hall and hoping Santa Claus served cookies and candy canes for breakfast.

When they arrived, they found Nicholas, Ariel, and Strom waiting for them at the table. Sir Palamedes was there, too, standing atop a buffet, watching the room like a hawk. Peter waved at the elf, who responded with a bow. Peter pulled out a chair and plopped down as Euripides climbed up on the table beside him.

"Well, it's about time," Strom gruffed at Peter.

Nicholas laughed at that. "Apparently, Master Strom is not a morning person."

"Sorry, Your Excellency," Strom apologized and Peter could tell that he meant it. "I'm just hungry."

"Well then, let's eat." Nicholas rang a small, silver bell, and soon a stream of munchkins marched into the hall, each carrying a covered platter of hot food. After thanking God for the food, Nicholas, Peter, Strom, and Euripides were soon digging in. Peter was excited to have waffles covered with bananas, strawberries, and a delicious chocolate sauce, an egg and two strips of bacon. He washed it all down with a tall glass of freshly-squeezed orange juice.

When they had finished eating, Strom sat back in his chair and rubbed his full belly. "Where do you get all of this amazing food up here on the mountain peak?" he asked Nicholas.

"Our most generous Lord provides," Nicholas smiled without further explanation. "Now if everyone is ready, why don't we move to the sitting room?"

Soon the group was once again sitting in red velvet wing backed chairs by the fire, with Nicholas and Strom puffing away on pipes while Euripides curled up on the rug, attempting to take an after breakfast nap. Nicholas watched Peter for a long while as the boy kept glancing nervously at the floor.

"I've been prayerfully considering what you need for your holy quest. I've asked the Lord to show me, and He has done just that," Nicholas said between puffs of smoke. "Are you ready?"

Peter nodded eagerly. "Yes, sir," he said as he bounced up and down in his chair with anticipation. The boy's excitement amused Nicholas.

"Very well," the old man said and then set down his pipe and reached into the great red bag beside his chair. He pulled out a small cloak that matched the color of the bag. "Here you are," Nicholas said and tossed the cloak to Peter.

"What's this?" Peter asked.

"It's a cloak, boy," Strom laughed as he blew smoke from his nostrils. Peter picked it up to find what appeared to him to be a cape with a hood. "Cloaks are wonderful in the cold or the rain."

"Yes, quite wonderful," Nicholas smiled, "but this one is special."

"How?" Peter asked.

"Hold it in front of the fire," Nicholas smiled.

Peter slid down from his chair and walked to the fire, holding the cloak up. The cloak suddenly changed from the red color of the bag to colors that matched the flames in the fireplace. "Whoa!" Peter exclaimed.

Nicholas laughed. "Now put it on and go and stand by the wall," Nicholas instructed.

Peter did as he was told. He placed the cloak over his shoulders, clasping it in the middle with silver doves. He then pulled the hood over his head and walked over to the wall.

"Turn around," Nicholas said, and Peter obeyed.

"He's disappeared!" Strom exclaimed, clearly baffled.

"No," Nicholas smiled as he rose from his chair. He walked over to Peter and grabbed the edge of his cloak waving it. Strom could then see waves in the green and gold pattern. Like some chameleon, the cloak had changed to look exactly like the wallpaper.

"Incredible," Strom said.

"It's called a concealing cloak, and it will come in quite

handy, I assure you," Nicholas said.

"That's cool," Peter smiled.

"And that's not all, my boy," Nicholas said. He returned to his chair and motioned for Peter to sit as well. Then Nicholas reached down into his bag and pulled out a long wooden staff.

"What's that?" Peter asked.

"This is a walking stick," Nicholas smiled broadly.

"Okay," Peter said, clearly unimpressed.

"You don't like it?" Nicholas asked.

"In the boy's defense, the stick is a bit of a letdown after the concealing cloak, Your Excellency," Strom explained.

"Ah, but this is no ordinary walking stick," Nicholas told them. "Ariel, would you mind?" he asked.

"Not at all," Ariel replied before rising from her chair and moving to the center of the room. She drew her sword and removed her shield from the sling between her wings.

Nicholas held the staff up. "Stick, attack the angel!"

The staff flew out of his hand and across the room, toward Ariel. Ariel readied herself in a fighting stance. The staff swung at her as if being wielded by someone. Ariel blocked the blow with her shield. The staff swung again, and again Ariel blocked it.

"Stick, stop and return!" Nicholas commanded and the miraculous staff stopped attacking Ariel and flew back across the room into Nicholas' outstretched hand. He then tossed it to Peter.

Peter caught the staff and stared at it wide-eyed. "That's so cool!" Peter said. "Stick, attack Strom!" he commanded, and the stick flew from his hand to slam into the dwarf's head.

"Hey!" Strom shouted.

"Stick, stop and return!" Nicholas shouted before the stick could do any more damage. It flew to Nicholas' hand once again. Nicholas fixed Peter with a sour glare. "This is not a toy, Peter," he scolded. "You can seriously hurt someone with it."

"I'm sorry," Peter said.

"It's not me who you should be apologizing to," Nicholas said.

Peter turned to Strom. "I'm sorry, Strom, I didn't mean to hurt you."

Strom nodded. "It's all right," he said as he rubbed the bump on his head. "You're just a boy. What could you possibly know about miraculous sticks?"

Nicholas fixed his gaze on Peter. "Are you sure you're ready for this?" he asked.

Peter nodded. "Yes, sir," he replied. "I'll be really careful from now on."

"All right," Nicholas relented and tossed the stick to him. "Now there is one more gift." Nicholas opened his bag and reached inside, pulling out a pair of armored boots. He held them up to show them to everyone. "These, Peter, are the Boots of the Gospel of Peace."

"Wow," Peter said as he admired them. "What do they do?"

"Well, you wear them on your feet," Nicholas explained. "Come, put them on."

Peter nodded and rushed across the floor, ripping his own shoes off without even bothering to untie them and then slipping the boots over his feet. They were a lot lighter than he thought they would be.

"Run around the room in them," Nicholas prompted.

"Yes, sir," Peter said and then began to jog around the room. "They feel good," he said as if he were trying out shoes at the store with his mother.

CHAPTER TWELVE

"Run as fast as you can," Nicholas instructed him.

Peter obeyed, running as quickly as he could toward the far wall. The boots took off, and Peter suddenly found himself running at blinding speed. In fact, he was running so fast that he couldn't stop before he hit the wall, but instead of slamming into it as he expected, he ran straight up it. He then sprinted across the ceiling and down the far wall to finally stop beside Ariel's chair.

Peter stood still, panting heavily while staring at everyone with an expression of fear mixed with shock. His expression slowly turned to one of excitement, and he took off again, running straight up the wall, across the ceiling and back down the far wall once more.

"Haha!" laughed Nicholas. "Let's see those se'irim catch you now."

"Those are amazing gifts!" Ariel exclaimed. "What do you say?" she asked Peter. The boy smiled and rushed to Nicholas' chair and threw his arms around the old man.

"Thank you!" he said.

Nicholas smiled cheerily at the hug and patted Peter on the back. "You're most welcome, my boy." He then looked down at Peter. "And let's not forget to thank the one who is really responsible for all the gifts you get." Peter looked at him quizzically and Nicholas pointed toward the sky.

"Oh, yeah!" Peter said. "Thank you, God!"

"Very good, Peter," Nicholas said as he released him and Peter walked back to his chair and sat down. Nicholas then turned his attention to Strom. "I think I have something in here for you, my dwarven friend."

"Me?" Strom asked as his eyes lit up. He'd never received a gift from Santa Claus before. In fact, he'd never received a gift from anyone before.

GIFTS

"Oh yes," Nicholas said as he dug around in his bag. "The Lord was quite pleased with your change of heart, Strom, and wanted to give you something." Nicholas seemed to be having a hard time finding it, however. Finally, his hand clenched it. "Aha!" he shouted. "Here it is." Strom watched with anticipation as Nicholas pulled out a large green emerald. He tossed the precious gem through the air, and Strom caught it.

Strom stared at the shiny stone, glistening in the firelight. It was as big as his fist. He'd never seen an emerald that big before. In fact, he didn't know emeralds existed that were as big as the one he held in his hands. Not only was it big, it was completely flawless. Strom didn't speak for a long time, but when he did he said: "It's the most beautiful thing I've ever seen. I will treasure it always." But then he stopped. He looked up at Nicholas and then Ariel and then Peter.

"I can't," Strom said as he held the emerald out for Nicholas to take back. "I can't take this. I will love it too much. I will value this stone above everything else, even over God Himself. I must not tempt myself."

"You cannot return a gift of the Lord," Nicholas said.

Strom sighed in frustration but then had an idea. "I'll give it to Peter," he said. He turned to the boy. "Peter, take it. You can take it safely, as you do not value wealth over all else."

"Really?" Peter asked. "You want me to have it?"

"I do," Strom said.

Peter slipped down from his chair and took the gem from Strom. "Thank you Strom," he said. He stared at the sparkling gemstone. It was so big and pretty. Peter imagined he could sell it and have enough money to buy him and his mom a house once she got better. Maybe enough would even be left over that he could afford to attend the private Christian school where a lot of his friends from church went.

CHAPTER TWELVE

Peter slipped the stone into his pocket.

Nicholas smiled at the dwarf. "Well done, Master Strom," he said. "Because your heart has truly changed and you have turned from greedily seeking the treasures of the world, I have something else for you." Nicholas reached into his bag once again and this time pulled out a long-handled war hammer. He held it out to Strom who slid down from his chair and crossed over to Nicholas with wide eyes. He accepted the hammer, and could not believe its weight.

"It's so light," Strom said.

Nicholas nodded. "Yet it will crush anything. Nothing can stand in its way. You can burst through a stone wall with one swing."

Strom gasped. "Thank you, Your Excellency!" he exclaimed and then turned his eyes heavenward. "And thanks be to God Almighty!"

"Amen!" Ariel exclaimed in response.

By this time, Euripides had slipped across the room to stand by Nicholas' chair, his small pink nose sniffing the big red bag. "Is there anything in there for me?" he asked.

"Hm," said Nicholas. "Let me see." He opened his bag once again and peered inside. "Ah, yes," Nicholas smiled. He pulled out a small, green hat with red feather in it that reminded Peter of Robin Hood's. Nicholas then placed it on top of the gopher's head.

Euripides stood up on his hind legs and adjusted the hat on his head. "How do I look?" he asked.

"Very dashing," Ariel smiled.

"Really?" Euripides asked.

"Definitely," Ariel said.

"It does look quite nice on you, Euripides, but that is not the reason I gave it to you," Nicholas said.

"It's not?" Euripides asked.

"No," Nicholas said. "If you are going to go on an adventure with such large people and fight such enormous monsters as se'irim there is a real concern that you will get stepped on. Perhaps even by a friend on accident." Euripides nodded his agreement.

Nicholas turned to Strom. "Master Strom, take your new hammer and smash Euripides."

"What?" Euripides asked in panic.

"It's all right, Euripides," Nicholas said. "Trust me."

"Are you sure about this?" Strom asked.

"Of course," Nicholas said. "The Lord has assured me that the hat will protect him."

"If you say so," Strom said and stepped over to Euripides, raised the hammer and let it fall.

Sure enough, the hammer was stopped by what appeared to Peter to be some kind of force field.

"Whew," Euripides said in relief.

"That's unbelievable! It's like some impenetrable glass ceiling is above his head." Strom said.

"Not just above his head. He's protected on all sides, as long as he is wearing the hat," Nicholas assured them.

Strom smiled. "So if I hit him from behind like this..." Strom swung the hammer like a golf club, slamming into Euripides' force field. The field stopped the blow, but Euripides went flying through the air. He slammed into the wall (or at least his force field did) before bouncing off and hitting the ceiling and falling back to the ground, where Ariel reached out and caught the little gopher before he landed.

"Ouch," Strom said. "Is he all right?"

Ariel brought the gopher close to her face to examine him. Euripides stared back at her and then suddenly reached forward and gave her a kiss. Ariel threw back her head and laughed. "He's fine," she said.

Nicholas shook his head. "We had better be going," he said. "I want to get you on your way before the next darkfall."

"Good idea," Ariel replied.

"So where are the tunnels to go back down the mountain?" Peter asked.

Nicholas smiled at him. "We're not taking the tunnels."

Soon Nicholas, Peter, Ariel, Strom, Euripides, and Sir Palamedes were situated in Nicholas' red sleigh. Peter was giddy with excitement. He did not know anyone who didn't want to ride in a sleigh with Santa Claus. Nicholas cracked the reins, and the eight reindeer began to move. The reindeer galloped as quickly as they could toward the side of the mountain.

"Where's the road?" Strom asked, concern ringing in his voice.

"Roads?" Nicholas chuckled. "Where we're going, we don't need roads!"

The reindeer galloped faster and faster toward the side of the mountain.

"Wait!" Strom shouted. "Stop, stop!" But it was too late for the reindeer to stop. Instead they ran right over the cliff and Peter, Strom and Euripides screamed in terror. But they did not fall. The reindeer, sleigh, and everyone in it flew through the air. As the wind blew his brown hair, Peter gazed over the side of the sleigh at the land of Evermore far below. He couldn't believe he was actually flying in Santa Claus' sleigh. It was something every kid had dreamed of. How did he get this lucky?

GIFTS

The reindeer flew down lower and lower coming in for a landing in the green grasses of a meadow at the base of the mountain. Strom rushed out of the sleigh as quickly as he could. "I'm never going in that thing again if I can help it," he said. "Munchkins and elves may fly, but dwarfs most certainly do not!"

"Very well, my friend," Nicholas said.

Peter threw his arms around Nicholas' neck in a giant hug. "Thank you for everything," he whispered.

"You are most welcome, my boy," Nicholas smiled. Peter climbed out and joined his friends on the ground.

"Your Excellency," came Sir Palamedes' voice.

"Yes, Sir Palamedes?" Nicholas asked.

"If it pleases you, I would very much like to accompany young Master Peter on his quest."

"Oh?" Nicholas asked.

"Yes, Your Excellency. It is dangerous, and he could certainly use another experienced sword."

Nicholas turned to Ariel. "What say you?" he asked the angel.

"We would be honored if Sir Palamedes accompanied us," Ariel replied.

"Very well, Sir Knight," Nicholas smiled. "I shall see you when you return."

"Thank you, Your Excellency," Palamedes replied and then hopped down from the sleigh to stand on the grass beside Ariel. "And thank you, Your Grace."

Nicholas smiled at his friends. "The Lord be with you," he said.

"And with your spirit," the others replied in unison.

Then Nicholas snapped the reins and the reindeer began to gallop once more. "On Dasher, on Dancer, on Prancer, and

CHAPTER TWELVE

Vixen! On Comet, on Cupid, on Donner, and Nehemiah!" with that the reindeer rose into the air carrying Saint Nicholas and his sleigh back up to the top of the mountain.

"Nehemiah?" Peter asked. "I thought the last reindeer was Blitzen."

Ariel shook her head. "No, the writer of the poem just needed a name to rhyme. The eighth reindeer has always been called Nehemiah."

Ariel turned to her small party. "Are we ready?" she asked.

The others nodded, and once again they started out on their quest.

CHAPTER THIRTEEN
RUN!

Ariel led the way along the rocky, hilly path away from the mountain. Peter wished that Nicholas had flown them further, but Strom was glad he had not. Strom was accustomed to climbing over rocky ground, but the dwarf's stomach could not have taken much more flying or he would have become sick.

Peter glanced down at Sir Palamedes who was traversing the ground with ease. Peter was impressed that such a small creature as an elf seemed to climb hills and rocks more easily than he could. It just went to show Peter that he could not judge a person by his size. Euripides preferred to ride on Peter's shoulder but would occasionally leap down and sprint to the top of the hill to see what was ahead before scurrying back up Peter's leg to reclaim his perch upon the boy's shoulder.

"The gopher travels in style," Palamedes laughed.

Peter nodded with a chuckle. "It does get old to have him breathing in my ear all of the time though."

CHAPTER THIRTEEN

Euripides was offended. "Well, if that's the way you feel about it, then I'll just climb down and walk myself."

"Yes, gopher," Palamedes called. "Come down here so that I can throw a saddle and harness on you, and you can carry me."

Euripides stared at Palamedes for a long moment, unsure if the elvish knight was being serious or not. He decided not to risk it. "I think I'll just stay up here with Peter," he said.

As they hiked along, Ariel kept glancing at the sky as if she feared the darkness might fall unexpectedly any second. Her wariness did not go unnoticed by Strom, who brought up the rear while carrying his large war hammer slung over his shoulder.

"Where do you intend to spend darkfall tonight, Your Grace?" the dwarf asked. "Certainly not here in the open."

"Not if I can help it," Ariel replied. "If we can make it over the river, we should be safe in giant country."

"Giant country?" Peter asked excitedly. "You mean there are real giants here?"

Palamedes laughed. "You are all giants to me," he reminded Peter.

Ariel turned to smile at Palamedes before answering Peter's question. "Yes, Peter, there are real giants in Evermore," she told him.

"Enormous creatures," Strom added. "Some as tall as a tree!"

"Really?" Peter asked in disbelief.

Palamedes laughed again. "Everyone is as tall as a tree, my red-bearded friend. It just depends on how tall the tree is."

Strom shot the elf a dirty look. "You know what I mean," he gruffed.

"In any event, the giants are large enough that se'irim

generally steer clear of them if they can help it," Ariel explained.

"But they are friendly to humans?" Peter asked. "I mean, they don't eat little boys like in the fairy tales?"

"Well, not one as scrawny as you," Strom smiled wickedly. "They'd want to fatten you up first."

Ariel frowned at Strom as the dwarf began to laugh. "You're going to scare him," she said and then turned to Peter. "Don't worry, the giants won't eat you."

"But your gopher is another story entirely," Palamedes added with a laugh.

Euripides gasped. "I don't want to go to giant country," he said.

"Have no fear, Euripides," Ariel smiled reassuringly. "I won't let anyone eat you."

"Thank you, Your Grace!" Euripides exclaimed gratefully.

"I can carry you away if I need to," Peter told the gopher. "No giant can catch me in these boots. No one can."

"Is that right?" Ariel asked, a spark of amusement in her voice.

"Sure it is," Peter told her. "You saw how fast I ran."

"So you are the fastest person in Evermore?" Strom asked.

"Do you think you're faster?" Peter fired back. "Wanna race?"

Strom shook his head with a chuckle.

"How about you, Palamedes?" Peter asked. Ariel spoke up before Palamedes had a chance to answer.

"I shall accept the challenge," she said.

"You?" Peter asked. Ariel nodded. "Sure," he said.

"All right," Ariel replied as she stopped walking. "How about to those stones and back." Peter followed her gaze to a large outcropping of rocks jutting ten feet into the air about a hundred yards away.

"Okay," he agreed before lifting Euripides off his shoulder and setting the gopher gently on the ground next to him. "Do you want to take off your armor or anything?" Peter suggested.

"No, I think I'll be all right," Ariel replied.

"Well, don't use that as an excuse when you lose," Peter smirked arrogantly.

"I'll remember not to," Ariel laughed. She then turned to the dwarf. "Kindly give us the signal to begin, Master Strom."

"Very well," Strom said as he stepped up beside the two of them. Palamedes and Euripides hurried up to the top of a large boulder to have a better view.

"Ready?" Strom asked, and both Peter and Ariel nodded. "Run!" Strom shouted.

Peter took off at a sprint, running as fast as he could. It was incredibly fast, too. Faster than any man. Faster than any horse. But not faster than an angel.

Ariel waited until Peter was about halfway to the stone outcropping before she even started. She wanted to give him a head start. She zipped past him—nearly knocking him off of his feet in the process—to the rocks and back before Peter had taken ten more steps. Peter came to a stop and turned around to look at Ariel standing beside Strom, hands on her hips, waiting for him to complete the race.

"How in the world did you do that?" Peter shouted to her.

Ariel threw back her head and laughed. "That was just a little jog," she shouted back. "Wait until I really get going."

Peter began to jog back toward them.

Suddenly Ariel, Strom, and Palamedes froze as the low rumbling of a horn blared through the air.

"What was that?" Peter asked as he rejoined his friends.

"Hush!" Ariel snapped as she scanned the hills, rocks, and

mountains.

"It can't be," Strom mumbled as he scanned the sky. "It's too early. The light is fully out."

The horn blasted again. "They are getting very bold to come out in the light," Palamedes said, and in a flash, his sword was in his hand. Ariel drew hers as well.

"I don't know where it's coming from," she said as she spun in circles searching for the source of the sound. Soon they had their answer.

"There!" Strom shouted as he pointed back toward the mountain.

The others turned to see what Strom was pointing at, and Peter felt his heart leap into his throat. Hundreds, if not thousands of se'irim poured from hidden caves and caverns in the mountain and surrounding hills. All of them were charging toward Peter and his friends as quickly as they could.

"We're going to die!" Euripides shouted as he scurried back up Peter's leg to the top of the boy's head, clinging to his hair for safety.

"Ouch!" Peter shouted. "Don't pull my hair!" he told the terrified gopher.

"Peter, run!" Ariel shouted. Peter obeyed, ignoring the gopher perched atop his head and running as fast as he could toward a path through the stone outcropping. Ariel turned to the others. "We have to get across the river! Go!"

Strom and Palamedes nodded their understanding, then turned and ran away after Peter and Euripides. Ariel stood her ground, sword and shield gripped firmly in her hands. If she could hold the se'irim off long enough, Peter and the others might get away. She stared at the mass of giant red monsters charging toward her as she whispered a prayer. "Lord, please give me the strength to hold these devils back long enough for the others to escape. And if it be Your will, oh Holy God, please guard and protect Peter and his friends and guide them to safety on the other side of the river." Ariel released a breath. "Amen," she said as she twirled her sword round in her hand, waiting for the se'irim.

Meanwhile, Peter ran as fast as he could, his miraculous boots carrying him to the rock outcropping in a flash. His heart was thumping quickly in his chest as he approached the path between two giant stones protruding from the earth.

"Look out!" Euripides shouted at Peter from atop the boy's head. Giant boulders began falling from the top of the stones blocking Peter's path and he skidded to a stop as monstrous se'irim appeared. The creatures had been waiting to spring their trap. Se'irim suddenly appeared from all around him preventing Peter from fleeing. He spun round and round as the beasts closed in, drool dripping from their pointy fangs and terrifying weapons gripped in their clawed hands. "What are we going to do?" Euripides shouted in panic as his claws dug into Peter's scalp.

"Ow!" Peter shouted as he reached up to pull Euripides from his head with his left hand. It had to be his left hand because he held his staff his right hand. "The staff!" Peter shouted as he suddenly remembered the gift Nicholas had given him. "Stick, attack the se'irim!"

The staff flew from Peter's hand and began to swing wildly at the se'irim, dancing from creature to creature. The shock of being attacked by a flying staff momentarily halted the red skinned beasts. The staff zipped back and forth quickly, fighting as many of the se'irim as it could. It effectively delayed the monsters long enough for Sir Palamedes and Strom to reach them and break through the circle of beasts surrounding Peter.

RUN!

Strom slammed his mighty war hammer into the back of one of the se'irim, sending the creature flying all the way to the other side of the circle of red devils and slamming into another. Palamedes sliced the calf of one of the monsters with his tiny sword, sending the se'irim falling to the ground with a howl of pain. The tiny elf then leapt up the legs of another, hurried up to its shoulder and brought his sword down in the middle of the creature's head, poking through its skull and killing the monster instantly. As the se'irim fell to the ground dead, Palamedes leapt from its head toward another of the devils, stabbing it right between the eyes.

As valiantly as Palamedes and Strom fought, however, they were vastly outnumbered. Even the miraculous staff couldn't save Peter forever. One of the beasts charged toward the boy, its giant spiked mace held high over its horned head. Peter turned to run, but in his panic tripped over his own boots, falling to the ground. As he hit the ground, Euripides fell from his grip and quickly ran away, toward the safety of Strom and his war hammer.

Strom glanced up to see the se'irim about to smash Peter under the weight of its giant mace. He knew he could not reach them in time to save his friend, but then noticed Euripides sprinting toward him. "Hold on gopher!" Strom shouted before swinging his hammer like a golf club, and smashing into Euripides' miraculous force ball. The gopher— force field and all—flew back toward the se'irim charging toward Peter.

Euripides' force ball struck the se'irim right between the eyes and then—like a pinball—bounced off and hit another in the nose, and then bounced off and smashed into the jaw of another. Before Euripides and his miraculous force ball were finished ten se'irim had been knocked to the ground.

CHAPTER THIRTEEN

Euripides fell down beside Peter. He tried to stand, but his head was dizzy and his legs wobbly and he ended up falling over. Strom threw back his head with boisterous laughter and proclaimed: "The Lord's mighty hand is truly at work today!"

But there were still a score of se'irim to deal with. "Peter, run away!" Strom shouted as the boy pushed himself to his feet.

"The path's blocked!" Peter replied.

Strom's eyes rose to see the boulders blocking the way with se'irim standing atop them ready to stop anyone who attempted to climb over. "Leave it to me, boy!" Strom shouted and then released a mighty battle cry as he charged past Peter and up the hill to the boulders blocking Peter's path. When the dwarf reached the boulders he swung his war hammer with all of his strength, slamming it into the rocks, crushing them and sending the broken pieces—and the se'irim on top of them—flying away into the valley below.

Peter was about to dash through the newly cleared path when he was suddenly snatched up from behind by a se'irim's massive red claw.

"Oh no, you don't!" Euripides shouted and leapt onto the beast's leg, sinking his long teeth into the creature's skin. The se'irim screamed in pain as it kicked Euripides away.

"Help!" Peter shouted. "Ariel!"

The angel stood a hundred yards away, watching as the horde of red devils charged toward her. She readied herself as they were almost upon her when she suddenly heard Peter cry out. "Help! Ariel!" She turned to see Strom and Palamedes fighting desperately against overwhelming numbers as a se'irim carried Peter away.

Ariel was gone in the blink of eye. She covered the distance before any of the se'irim had a chance to react. With sword

RUN!

flashing, Ariel cut down all of the remaining se'irim and caught Peter in her arms before he fell to the ground. She set him upright on his feet.

"Thank you," Peter exclaimed as he wrapped his arms around her.

"That's why the Lord sent me," she smiled. She then took him by the hand and led Peter and the others to the top of the hill between the two giant stones. "There's the river!" she said as they reached the crest of the hill. Peter peered down into the valley at a small river with a stone bridge extending over it. Peter guessed the bridge was only a couple of hundred yards away. "Hurry!" Ariel commanded. "I'll hold the se'irim here."

"I don't want to leave you!" Peter argued.

"Go!" Ariel commanded and Peter relented.

"Stick return!" he shouted and after the staff was safely back in his hand he dashed away down the hill.

"Thank you, Your Grace!" Strom said as he scooped up Euripides and carried the gopher at a sprint down the hill toward the bridge.

"You are the finest warrior I have ever seen," Palamedes informed Ariel before hurrying after the others.

Ariel watched Peter and his friends flee before turning back toward the mass of se'irim charging toward her up the little hill. She positioned herself in the path in front of the giant stones. The se'irim would get caught in a bottleneck here, giving her a chance. Sure, she was stronger and certainly faster than the red-skinned devils, but with their massive numbers, they would eventually overwhelm her.

The first of the monsters reached her a few breaths later, and Ariel dispatched him quickly. She spun and took down the next two, but more pressed in. Ariel fought as hard as she could, and se'irim after se'irim fell at her feet. She glanced over her shoulder to see Peter safely on the other side of the bridge, waving his friends over as they sprinted across. Time to go. Ariel darted away and in a flash stood beside Peter and the others.

"Ariel!" Peter shouted excitedly and threw his arms around her waist once again.

"I'm all right," Ariel assured him as she returned his embrace. There was a thunder of hooves, and everyone looked up to see a massive army of se'irim galloping down the hill toward them. The creatures slowed as they reached the banks of the river, and Ariel, Strom, and Palamedes stared at them defiantly. The se'irim stood on the riverbank staring at the water but not wanting to go in.

"They're scared of water," Ariel explained. "If I can hold the bridge long enough..." she began, but Strom didn't wait for her to finish. He raised his mighty hammer and swung downward crushing the bridge and collapsing it into the river.

The se'irim howled and screamed in anger and frustration. Strom chuckled at them.

"Well done, master Dwarf!" Palamedes exclaimed as Peter patted him on the back.

"Yeah come get us now, you big ugly goats!" Euripides shouted across the river at the devils on the far banks. "Have a little swim."

But the excitement was short lived as the sky suddenly began to darken. A great shadow fell over the land from behind the army of se'irim. "No!" Ariel shouted. "It's too soon!" She fell to her knees. "Lord, if it be Your will, please help Your servants!" But the light continued to be pushed back by the darkness.

As the shadow fell down the hillside, Ariel saw shedom stepping out of the darkness. She gasped. The shedom released terrifying shrieks that cut the air and began urging the se'irim forward. The se'irim decided that they were more frightened of the wrath of the shedom than the water and began walking into the river. Ariel knew there were too many of the devils to fight, especially once the shadow reached them, and the shedom crossed the river as well.

"Make for the trees!" Ariel shouted to her companions as she pointed to a stand of trees seemingly out of place in the distance. They ran quickly with the se'irim close on their trail. The small group reached the trees and Ariel turned to see the shadow had been halted at the river. With their side of the river still bathed in light, the shedom would not cross, giving them a chance to survive. Not much of a chance, but a chance none-the-less.

"Get ready!" Ariel shouted as the se'irim galloped toward them, releasing terrifying howls. Peter swallowed hard but held his staff at the ready.

Then something amazing happened. Just before the se'irim reached the stand of trees, the trees themselves came to life. Giant clubs, swords, and axes swept forward, cutting through the horde of se'irim. Peter looked about frantically at the fighting trees and suddenly realized they were not trees at all. Instead, they were men disguised as trees, wearing amazingly realistic camouflage. But the men were as tall as trees, and Peter gasped as he realized what they were.

"Giants!" Euripides cheered.

Yes, an army of giants had been waiting in the field, completely still and hidden, with camouflaged cloaks and branches making them appear to be trees. They waited for the last possible second to attack the se'irim and when they did, the se'irim army was devastated. Some of the se'irim made it through the line of giants, however, desperately trying to kill

Peter. One was about to cut the boy down with its deadly two-headed battle axe when a normal-sized man stepped forward and slammed the shaft of a bow across the monsters' face. The man was dressed as a tree just like the giants, but he was no taller than Ariel.

The man drew an arrow from a quiver slung over his back, notched it, pulled back the bowstring, and released it. The arrow hit the se'irim right between the eyes.

"Thank you!" Peter shouted to the man.

"Don't mention it!" the man said as he turned around. When Peter saw his face, he realized he wasn't a man at all. He was as tall as a man, but his face was young like Peter's. He was just a boy. A giant boy. "I'm Orion!" the giant boy said. "What's your name?"

"Peter Puckett," Peter smiled.

"Nice to meet you, Peter Puckett," Orion replied before drawing another arrow from his quiver and turning and shooting it at the se'irim. The red devils were now retreating, running full speed back to the river. Even the shedom who stood on its banks could not convince them to keep fighting the giants.

The shedom shrieked and cursed, but they could not cross the river as there was full light on that side. "We won!" Peter shouted excitedly, finally feeling safe. "They're running away."

"Indeed they are, lad!" Strom said happily. "Always good to go to battle with giants on your side!"

But the shedom were not quite done yet. One snatched a spear from a retreating se'irim, reared back and threw it like a javelin. The intent was to kill Peter. That had been the demons' mission from the start. The spear's flight was perfectly on target. Peter didn't even see it. He was too busy celebrating the victory. At the last moment, he glanced up to

RUN!

see the spear falling toward him, and his breath caught in his throat.

"Peter!" Strom shouted and leapt forward pushing Peter out of the way. The spear missed Peter, but not Strom. The dwarf felt it pierce his back, and he fell to the ground. Ariel rushed toward him, dropping to her knees beside his still body.

"Why did he do that?" Peter cried as tears poured down his cheeks.

Ariel looked at the boy. "Because he loves you. And there is no greater love than a man who lays down his life for his friends."

CHAPTER FOURTEEN
LAND OF THE GIANTS

Peter thought the giant's village looked like something he'd once seen when his dad had taken him to a renaissance fair, except the buildings were much, much larger. The furniture was much larger as well, and Peter had to climb up into a chair before he could sit down in it.

Peter and his friends were taken to the home of Grunder Tewk, the father of the boy giant Orion, and the leader of the band of giants who had rescued them. The house was small and tidy. Small for giants at least. Mistress Tewk, Grunder's wife, was quite excited to get visitors, especially a Messenger of the Lord. She was also eager to assist Strom with his injuries, promising that no dwarf had ever died in her house, and she did not plan on having one die there today. Peter wanted to ask how many nearly dead dwarfs had been brought to the Tewk home, but thought better of it.

The se'irim's spear had impaled Strom, but—by the grace of God—the dwarf had survived. Mistress Tewk quickly cleared off the dining table, transforming it into an operating table. With Ariel assisting, she had removed the spear and wrapped a white bandage around the dwarf to stop the bleeding. Strom was moved from the dining table to Orion's bed where he could get some rest.

While Strom rested, Grunder took Peter, Ariel, Palamedes, and Euripides to meet with the Town Council. Peter stood beside Ariel feeling quite small in a room full of giants, and he couldn't even imagine how tiny Palamedes and Euripides must feel. The council met in the Common House which was a building anyone in the town could use and was frequently used for events such as receptions and meetings—particularly, council meetings.

The five elders on the council all sat in large chairs at the front of the Common House. The three men had long white beards that ran all the way to the floor, and the two women wore their gray hair pulled back into buns atop their heads. All five council members stared at Peter and his friends with stern and inquisitive looks on their faces.

"Why have you brought the se'irim into our lands, Your Grace?" one of the elders asked Ariel in a gruff and demanding voice.

The angel shook her head back and forth. "We did not bring them, Your Honor," Ariel said. "They chased us and we fled here."

"And why were they chasing you?" inquired another of the five elders.

"Because they serve the Dark One," Ariel replied. "As everyone in this room knows."

"You are not the first angel to visit our little valley, Your Grace," a third elder informed her, "but you are the first to be chased here by a thousand se'irim. We would like to know why the devils are after you."

Ariel let her head drop. "They are not after me, Your Honor," Ariel explained. "They are after the boy," she said as she pointed to Peter. A gasp filled the room.

"Why would the red devils brave the light and water to chase a boy?" Grunder asked.

Ariel looked up at the giant and then back at the council. "Because Peter is on a mission for the Lord Almighty." Another gasp filled the room.

"Himself?" asked someone else in the room.

"Yes," Ariel said. There was muttering and talk throughout the Common House.

"Silence!" one of the Elders demanded and a hush quickly fell throughout the house. "What is this mission, Your Grace?"

Ariel turned to Peter. "Why don't you tell them, Peter?" Ariel suggested.

Peter was nervous. These giants were enormous and grumpy. They could squish him under their boots if they wanted. Nevertheless, he nodded to Ariel and cleared his throat as he stepped forward. "Um, well, Your Honor, because my mother is sick," Peter said. "And she is going to die." Peter heard some of the women giants sigh in sadness for this boy who could lose his mother. "And, um, God said that if I get this amulet it would save her."

"The Amulet of Eternity," Ariel said.

"And where is this amulet?" one of the Elders asked.

"Down deep past the waters of the Leviathan in the Realm of Goblins," Ariel said.

Murmurs spread throughout the house.

"Quiet!" shouted one of the Elders. He then turned to Grunder. "Sir Grunder do you have a question?"

"Yes, Your Honor," Grunder replied. "Why would the Lord Almighty send such a small boy on a dangerous quest? Is his father too much of a coward?"

There was agreement throughout the room, until they were silenced by a stern word from Ariel. "The Lord chooses whom the Lord chooses," she snapped. "And who are you, Grunder Tewk—and who are you, Elders—to question the decisions of the Lord Almighty?"

Grunder bowed his massive head under Ariel's gaze. "I meant no disrespect to the Lord," he said.

"Just to young Peter here and his father?" Ariel asked. Grunder did not answer. Ariel turned to Peter. "Tell them why your father isn't on the quest."

Tears built up in Peter's eyes. "My father is dead," he said before breaking down and weeping into his hands.

"Was he sick, too?" asked someone in the crowd, worried that the illness might be contagious.

"Did you bring a plague to our village?" asked another who clearly feared the same.

"No," Peter said as he wiped his eyes and shook his head. "My father was killed in the war."

Suddenly, the room burst into raucous weeping and gnashing of teeth. Grunder Tewk felt ashamed for calling the boy's father a coward. He approached Peter and lowered himself to one knee. Then he leaned over and placed a giant hand on Peter's tiny shoulder. "Please accept my deepest sympathies and my sincerest apologies for insulting your father's good name."

Peter nodded. "It's okay," he said.

Grunder then stood. "We must give them shelter during the darkfall," he told the Council. The elders briefly discussed it amongst themselves before turning back to the room.

CHAPTER FOURTEEN

"Yes, we shall shelter them during the darkfall, and at lightrise, we shall send a party to escort them through our country to the edge of the Shadow Wood."

A loud cheer filled the room, and Peter turned to see Orion sitting on a chair, dangling his legs and smiling broadly at him.

"But we shall take them no further," another elder said, and Peter thought his voice sounded ominous indeed.

Darkness had fallen, and Peter sat on the edge of Orion's bed talking to Strom. The dwarf was sore and spoke in a raspy voice, but Ariel assured Peter that his friend would pull through all right. "What's it feel like to get stabbed with a spear?" Peter asked.

"It hurts, boy," Strom replied in a rough voice. "It hurts badly."

"Well, thank you, Strom," Peter said softly. "You saved my life."

Strom smiled and reached out and patted Peter's arm. "I just paid back the favor," he said dismissively. Peter nodded. "But," Strom continued. "I do not think I will be up for accompanying you on the remainder of your quest to find the Amulet of Eternity."

Peter's head dropped. That was sad news. He'd grown to like Strom, grumpiness and all, but at least the dwarf would survive and would be well taken care of by Mistress Tewk.

The door opened, and Mistress Tewk stuck her enormous head into the room. "Master Strom needs his rest, young Peter," she said.

Peter nodded. "Yes, ma'am," he replied. Mistress Tewk smiled as her head disappeared from the doorway. Peter stood from the bed and made his way to the door. He stopped when he reached it and looked back at his friend. "I'll say good-bye to you before we leave in the morning," he said.

Strom nodded. "I would appreciate that," the dwarf said and then after a slight pause added, "my friend."

Peter smiled and stepped out of the room, closing the door behind him. When Peter stepped into the common room he found Orion staring at him. "How is the dwarf?" he asked softly.

"He will survive," Peter replied. "Thank you for asking."

"Good," Orion said cheerfully. "Wanna go for a walk?"

"Sure," Peter said.

A toothy grin spread across Orion's face. "Let's go," he said.

"Where do you think you are going?" came Mistress Tewk's voice as she fixed Orion with a stern gaze.

"I was just going to show Peter the town," Orion replied.

Mistress Tewk peeked out of the window. "Looks like darkness has fallen," she said. "The shedom are after Peter. Perhaps you should stay indoors tonight."

Grunder suddenly spoke up. "Oh, let the boys have a walk about," he said. "Half the men in town are standing guard out there. A bloody shedom would be daft to attack here tonight." He then remembered Ariel and turned to her, softening his tone. "That is, if Your Grace thinks it's all right."

Ariel turned to Peter to see the boy mouth the word "please." She then turned back to Grunder and his wife. "I think it will be all right," she said. "I'll step outside and keep them in my sight."

A smile spread across Mistress Tewk's face. Knowing the angel would be keeping an eye on the two boys made her feel much better. "Well, if Your Grace thinks it's all right, who am I to argue?" She then turned to Orion, and her tone became firm and commanding. "But you had better not leave the town."

"We won't," he promised.

"And take your bow and sword with you. Just in case," Grunder told his son.

"Yes, sir," Orion replied and turned from Peter to retrieve his bow, sword, and quiver of arrows.

"I'll take my staff, too," Peter said thoughtfully.

"Good idea," Ariel agreed.

Peter found his staff and cloak leaning against the wall, not far from the hearth. He glanced down to see Euripides curled up in a ball in front of the fire. "Euripides, you wanna come for a walk with me and Orion?" he asked.

Euripides lifted his head slightly to glance at Peter. "Out there in the dark?" he asked. "No thank you."

"All right," Peter chuckled. He glanced around to see if he could find Sir Palamedes but did not see the small elvish knight anywhere. He threw his cloak over his shoulders, lifted his staff, and joined Orion at the door. The young giant led Peter out of the house and Ariel followed behind. Just as they were stepping into the darkness, something dropped from the roof in front of them. Peter glanced down to see Sir Palamedes in a fighting stance, his tiny sword drawn.

"Who goes there?" he demanded.

"Sir Palamedes, it's me, Peter," Peter said.

"Peter who?" Palamedes asked, pretending not to know his friend as he pointed his sword menacingly at the pair of them.

"Peter Puckett," Peter said.

Palamedes stared at him for a moment as he rubbed his chin thoughtfully. "The name does sound familiar," the small knight said before looking past Peter and Orion at Ariel standing silently behind them, smiling at the elf's game. "And you do have a Messenger of the Lord with you. I suppose I will let you pass."

Orion chuckled. "You're a funny elf," he said.

"Were you up on the roof?" Peter asked Palamedes.

"Yes, of course," the elf replied as if there were anywhere else he might have been. "It's an excellent vantage point to spot incoming enemies."

Peter and Orion both turned to look up at the roof of the house, which being a house for giants, was considerably higher than a roof on a house for humans. "How did someone as small as you get up there?" Orion asked.

"How?" Palamedes smiled. "Like this!" he cried and leapt into the air, bouncing off Peter's leg and landing on top of Orion's head before springing upward and grabbing hold of the edge of the roof, pulling himself up. He then leaned over and waved at the two boys.

Orion and Peter laughed. So did Ariel. "Well done, Sir Palamedes!" Ariel exclaimed.

"I wish I had an elf," Orion frowned as if Palamedes were Peter's pet instead of his friend.

"They're awesome!" Peter beamed.

"All right, you two," Ariel said gently. "If you want to walk around get going. I'll stay near the house but will keep an eye on you."

"Thanks, Ariel," Peter smiled.

"Yes, thank you, Your Grace," Orion said with a bow. He then turned to Peter. "C'mon, let's go."

Peter nodded excitedly and Orion led him away. The town was surrounded by a wall of enormous posts, similar to the wall that surrounded the dwarven village, but taller. The wall was not quite as tall as an adult giant, however, and the guards standing around the wall could see over, watching the darkness in case an attack of se'irim or shedom came.

"How old are you?" Peter asked Orion.

"What do you mean?" Orion asked in reply.

"I mean, what's your age?" Peter said.

Orion tilted his head and gave Peter a quizzical look. "I don't understand."

"Like, I'm ten years old," Peter said. "How old are you?"

"Oh," Orion smiled, suddenly understanding, or at least thinking he understood. "I don't know how tall a year is, but I'm over six feet tall."

"No," Peter stopped and stared at the giant as he shook his head in frustration. "I'm not asking how tall you are, I'm asking how old you are."

"I'm not old," Orion laughed. "I'm young. I'm not even seven feet tall yet. When I'm old, I'll probably be as big as me Da—he's over twelve feet tall—and I'll have a long white beard."

Peter sighed. "That's not what I mean," he said. "When is your birthday?"

"What's a birthday?" Orion asked.

"The day you were born," Peter said.

"Oh," Orion laughed. "I don't know. I don't remember anything about the day I was born. I was too small to remember, I guess. But me Ma says that I was plenty big for her liking. Says I cried a lot too. Screamed all through the darkness and light, she says. But I don't remember." Orion turned and looked out at the darkness in the sky. "Ma says the dark didn't last as long back then. And she says when she was just a wee little girl, that there was hardly any darkness at all."

"I wonder why," Peter frowned. He didn't like the dark, especially in Evermore, where he assumed it was always full of shedom and se'irim.

"Me Da says it's because the Dark Lord is taking over, and if he's not stopped, he will soon push out all of us good, light lovin' folk."

"Aw," Peter frowned. "That's terrible."

Orion nodded. "Yes, it is." He then drew his sword. "But he won't get rid of us giants without a fight, I can promise you that!" Peter smiled at his new friend's confidence. Orion slid his sword back into its sheath and then looked down at Peter. "Your da was a warrior?"

Peter nodded. "Yes," he said. "He was a Marine."

"Is that like a knight?" Orion asked.

"Kinda," Peter replied.

"What war was he in?" Orion asked. "Me Da fought in the Great Ogre and Giant War and the Second Ogre and Giant War. He was also involved in The Battle at Troll Bridge."

Peter shook his head. "It's a war back where I come from. You wouldn't have heard of it."

"Oh," Orion said. "Was he fighting ogres?"

"No," Peter said.

"Trolls?"

"No," Peter said.

"Red devils and shadow demons?" he asked referring to the names commonly used for se'irim and shedom among giants.

"No, he was fighting other men," Peter said.

Orion looked at him quizzically. "But he's a man," Orion said, and Peter nodded. "Why would a man go to war with other men?"

"I don't know," Peter replied honestly. "Because they were bad men. Don't you have bad giants?"

Orion nodded. "Of course. But we banish them, never to return." Orion looked down at the ground. "Me Da says that there are more bad giants now than there used to be. It's the

175

darkness, he says. The more darkness in the world, the more evil us giants become."

Peter nodded. "There is a lot of darkness where I come from," he said. But Peter wasn't speaking of the darkness in the sky, but rather of the darkness in men's hearts. Peter was suddenly saddened by the darkness growing stronger in Evermore, and he silently prayed that God would bring light back to this land and to his own.

Strom lay in Orion's room, listening to the door open and close as Peter and Orion returned to the house to get some rest before the next day's journey. As the house went dark with everyone going to sleep (Peter and Orion sleeping in the common room), Strom stared at the ceiling, hurting. It wasn't the pain from his spear wound that was bothering him, though that did hurt a lot. It was his heart that hurt. His heart was breaking. Tears began to roll down his cheeks onto the red whiskers on his face.

Strom wanted to ask God for help because he realized that only God could do what Strom needed. But Strom also knew how wicked he was. He knew he was a sinful dwarf, a terribly sinful dwarf. He had cheated other dwarfs, lied, and even stolen from time to time—and worst of all, he never even cared that he had done those wicked things. He had only ever cared about himself and his treasure. Oh, that treasure! Strom had loved his treasure more than anything, and it was the treasure that drove him to sin and wickedness. But now that he was far away from the treasure, he realized how stupid it had been to love rocks, no matter how colorful and shiny they were and no matter what wonderful things he could trade them for.

LAND OF THE GIANTS

But Strom's heart was changing. He didn't want treasure anymore. Not the shiny rocks type of treasure anyway. He wanted the type of treasure the angel Ariel had talked about: treasure in Heaven. But most of all, right now, he wanted to continue on the quest with Peter. He wanted desperately to help his new friend save his mother.

"Lord," Strom whispered in the darkness as he prayed to God. "I know I've been a wicked dwarf. A terrible, wicked dwarf. I've hurt so many people. I've always been selfish, never caring about anyone else. I don't deserve any good things from You." He sniffed as the tears came more quickly.

"But Lord, I am so very sorry for what I've done," he said, and he meant it. Strom's change of heart was real. He felt warm inside, instead of the coldness he normally felt. "They say You are generous and merciful and forgiving. Please forgive me, Lord. Please forgive me. I don't want to be a wicked dwarf anymore. I want to be a good dwarf."

Strom wiped his eyes and nose with the sleeve of his shirt. "Most of all Lord, I want to help Peter. No one has ever been nice to me before, Lord. Peter helped me when he didn't have to. He saved me from certain death when he could have just run away. I know he's just a little boy, but he's the first real friend I've ever had."

Strom swallowed as he got to the point of his prayer. "Lord, if you are willing, could you please heal me?" he asked. "Not for me. Heal me for Peter so that I can help him on his quest. To do what he has to do, he will need all of the help he can get. So please, Lord God, please make me better, so that I can help my friend on his quest to save his mother."

Strom lay silently in the dark for a long moment not knowing what else to do or to say. He finally just whispered "Amen," and closed his eyes to sleep, leaving everything in

CHAPTER FOURTEEN

God's hands.

CHAPTER FIFTEEN
THE SHADOW WOOD

Peter awoke at lightrise to find Orion, Grunder and Sir Palamedes already sitting down to breakfast at the giant table. He turned over and saw Euripides still curled up in a furry little ball in front of the fireplace.

"Euripides," Peter said. "It's time to wake up—we have a long journey ahead of us." The gopher slowly lifted his head, blinking in the light.

"Already?" he whined.

"Yes," Peter said as he pushed himself up and walked over to his furry little friend. "Now come on, Mistress Tewk already has breakfast ready."

Peter bent down and lifted Euripides up off the rug in front of the fireplace and petted him like a cat. He carried the gopher over to the table, set Euripides on top of a giant chair, and then climbed up himself. He lifted Euripides onto the table where Mistress Tewk had set out a small breakfast for each of them on a large plate. Well, it was a small breakfast by giant standards, but was not small at all by Peter's standards. Peter had to stand on the chair to reach the giant table, but he still managed to wolf down his breakfast. When he was done, he thanked Mistress Tewk and leapt down from atop the chair.

As he landed on the wood floor he looked up to see Strom standing in the middle of the room holding his war hammer and smiling at him. "Strom!" Peter exclaimed. "You're better!"

"Yes, I am, lad!" Strom smiled. "Thanks be to our great Lord who heard my cries and healed me in the night."

"The Lord does not always answer our prayers exactly as we want Him to," Ariel explained, "but if our hearts are pure, and our prayers conform to His will, He will answer them." Peter nodded. He'd had a lot of recent experience with answered prayers.

"So you'll be joining us?" Peter asked.

"I wouldn't miss it, lad," Strom smiled, and Peter rushed over to the dwarf and threw his arms around him in a big hug, which took Strom a bit off guard. The dwarf just stood uncomfortably, not really knowing what to do, but then he finally returned Peter's embrace. He was surprised to find it made him feel warm inside. Peter released Strom and turned to see the others readying for the journey.

"Get your things, Peter," Grunder said. "It's time to go."

The entire town turned out to see Peter and his party leave. There was lots of waving and cheering—and even a little crying—mainly from the sweet mothers who prayed their boys loved them as much as Peter loved his own mother.

"The Lord be with you!" one of the elders shouted out to them.

"And with your spirit," the party responded in unison.

Peter, Ariel, Strom, Sir Palamedes, Euripides, and an escort of ten giants—including Grunder and Orion—left the town and set out for the Shadow Wood, hoping to make it there well before darkfall.

"Why do they call it the Shadow Wood?" Peter asked as they walked along.

"Because the Wood is darkness itself," Sir Palamedes answered as he strolled beside Peter. As usual, Euripides was riding along on Peter's shoulder.

"I don't like the sound of that," Peter said.

"Nor should you, boy," Strom agreed as he walked on Peter's other side. "'Tis a vile and wicked place full of all manner of dangers and temptations of every sort."

"Then why are we going there?" Peter asked.

"Because you have to pass through it to get to your destination," Ariel explained.

"Do se'irim live there?" Peter asked.

"Worse than se'irim live there, boy," Strom said ominously. "Much worse."

"Like shedom?" Peter asked as a shiver danced up his spine.

"Even worse than shedom," Palamedes said.

"What could possibly be worse than shedom?" Peter asked.

"The Fallen," Grunder said without turning around. He marched along several yards in front of Peter and the others, Orion by his side.

"What are the Fallen?" Peter asked.

"Fallen angels, Peter," Ariel told him.

"Fallen angels?" Peter asked. "You mean like Lucifer?" Father Joe had told Peter the story of how the angel Lucifer had been jealous of God and led an army of angels in rebellion. God had cast Lucifer and those who followed him out of Heaven.

CHAPTER FIFTEEN

Ariel glanced around with a hand on the hilt of her sword as if the devil himself might appear at any moment. "Yes, him and his army," she said. "But I'd prefer we not say his name. And in point of fact, the Fallen can appear anywhere the Lord permits them to. There is no better chance of running into one in the Shadow Wood than there is right here in the open."

Strom swallowed hard as he glanced about, gripping his war hammer tightly in both hands. It hadn't occurred to him until just that moment that if the shedom and the se'irim were after Peter, then much worse things wanted him, too. He briefly regretted coming on this quest, but then scolded himself for such a selfish thought. Peter was just a boy being pursued by dark forces—very dark forces. He needed all the help he could get.

"Have you ever seen the Fallen?" Peter asked Ariel.

Ariel looked down at the ground with sadness. "I knew every one of them," she replied. "Lucifer was the most beautiful of all the angels. He shone like precious stones in the fire. But his pride drove him to evil and he was cast out of Heaven along with his army. They are no longer the angels they once were. They have been twisted by pride and wickedness."

"How did pride and wickedness twist them?" Peter asked.

"Sin turns you into a creature of darkness, Peter," Ariel explained. "With mankind, the effects of sin are hidden away. Humans turn dark on the inside, which is even more dangerous because it is harder to see who has embraced the darkness and who serves the light. But with angels, sin disfigures our very appearance. We become dark and demonic."

"Terrifying creatures," Palamedes said.

"Well I don't want to see any fallen angels," Euripides

asserted.

"Me either," Peter agreed.

"Nor do I, gopher," Strom said.

"Don't worry, I'll shoot them with my bow," Orion boasted as he turned around to grin broadly at his new friends.

"Hold your tongue, boy," Grunder scolded his son. "They would tear you apart. Do not go around boastfully challenging them, lest you call attention to yourself."

"Your father is wise, Orion," Ariel agreed. "You should listen to him. Do not scoff at those you do not understand. For even the Archangel Michael, the mightiest angel in all of Heaven's Armies would not be so bold as to scoff at the devil."

"Yes, Your Grace," Orion replied sheepishly.

"But don't be fooled by appearances," Ariel cautioned. "The devil can masquerade as an angel of light."

"Then how can I know the good from the bad?" Peter asked.

"You know them by their deeds," Ariel said. "Those who try to convince you to do evil or turn against God are themselves evil. No godly human or angel of light would ever try to get you to sin. And none would ever speak ill of the Lord."

Peter nodded.

When they were about halfway to the Shadow Wood the party took a break to rest and eat. Strom unslung the satchel of food that the giants had given them from his shoulder, and distributed bread and cheese to Peter, Euripides, Palamedes, and himself. He then wrapped the remaining food back up and slipped it inside the satchel. Everyone was nervous about entering the Shadow Wood and they ate in silence. When they were finished Grunder signaled it was time to move again and they set out once more.

They had walked for what seemed to Peter to be an eternity when he heard Grunder's booming voice. "We're almost there," the giant informed them as he noticed the two scouts he'd sent ahead on top of a hill signaling them. When Peter and the others reached the scouts atop the hill, they gazed down into the valley below, and Peter saw an enormous forest of black and terrifying trees.

"That's the Shadow Wood?" Peter asked, terrified to go anywhere near it, much less into it. "It's so big."

"Yes," Ariel agreed. "It will be quite a journey to get through it."

"This is as far as we go, Your Grace," Grunder said. "We will watch you from here to make sure you make it into the Wood without incident, but we will not go any further unless necessary, and we certainly are not traveling into that forest."

"I understand, Sir Grunder," Ariel said. "We greatly appreciate all that you and your people have done for us."

Peter was sad. He had desperately wanted the giants to come with them into the dark and scary Shadow Wood. He also didn't want to leave his new friend Orion.

Peter turned to Orion. "It was nice meeting you, Orion," he said.

"It was nice meeting you, too, Peter, and I hope to see you again someday."

Peter smiled. "Count on it." Peter then threw his arms around Orion and gave the boy giant a giant hug. He then turned and walked down the hill after Ariel and the others. "Good-bye," he waved.

"Don't step on any trolls," Orion said causing Peter to laugh.

"The Lord be with you, Peter," Grunder said.

THE SHADOW WOOD

"And with your spirit," Peter replied with a smile before trotting down the hill to catch up with Ariel. Ariel led the now much smaller party down into the valley and to the edge of the wood. There she and the others stopped and stared into the darkness.

The Shadow Wood looked even creepier up close than it did from the top of the hill. Peter glanced over his shoulder to see the giants still watching them, waiting for them to enter the woods as Master Grunder had promised they would. He turned back toward the trees and took a few steps forward until he was right beside Ariel. Peter reached up and took hold of the angel's hand.

"I'm scared, Ariel," he said.

She nodded. "I know you are, Peter," Ariel replied.

"But I'll be brave, because I know you'll protect me," he said.

Ariel fought back the urge to cry. She truly loved this little boy and his sweet heart. She turned toward him and lowered herself to her knees in the dirt so that she could peer into his eyes. "Your guardian angel may not enter the Shadow Wood with you, Peter," she said.

"What?" Peter asked as he began to tremble. He wanted to cry. How could he step into that darkness without Ariel?

"But the Lord will watch over you."

"I can't do it without you, Ariel," Peter said.

"Do you want to save your mother?" Ariel asked. Peter nodded. "Then you have to do this. Following the Lord is not always easy. In fact, sometimes it is very difficult. But in the end, it is worth it."

"Why can't you come?" Peter asked.

"Because you don't need me. Christ is all you need."

"But where is he?" Peter asked as he looked around. He

would certainly be willing to walk into the woods if he could hold Jesus' hand, but he didn't see Him anywhere.

"Do you see that lighted path?" Ariel asked as she pointed toward the woods. Peter turned to see a small path through the darkness of the trees that was lit up as if in open sunshine. No darkness or shadow fell upon it at all.

"Yes," Peter told her.

"It is illuminated by the Light of Christ. If you stay on that path and do not wander off, nothing in those woods can harm you."

"Nothing?" Peter asked as he turned back toward her.

Ariel shook her head. "Absolutely nothing. I promise. As long as you do not deviate from the path, you will be perfectly safe."

"But what if I get off of it?" Peter asked.

"Don't," Ariel said sharply.

"But what if I do?"

"Then find it again and get back on it as quickly as you can," Ariel said.

"What if I get lost?" Peter asked with tears in his eyes. "How can I find it again?"

Ariel tapped his chest with her finger. "Just follow your heart, Peter," she said. "If you truly seek Christ in your heart, you will find Him."

"I wish I had someone else to go with me," Peter said. He was shaking with fear and Ariel pulled him into a tight embrace.

"I said your guardian angel may not enter the woods with you," she said. "I didn't say your other friends couldn't."

"Really?" he asked and then turned to see Strom, Euripides, and Sir Palamedes watching him. Peter pushed back his glasses and wiped the tears from his eyes before replacing them on his nose. "Will you guys come with me?" Peter asked in a weak and cracking voice.

"Ha!" Strom laughed. "Do you think the Lord God healed me so that I could let you go off into this dark forest alone?"

Peter smiled as he shook his head. "No," he said.

"Of course, I'll come with you, lad!" Strom stepped up beside Peter and slapped him on the shoulder. "A thousand se'irim could not keep me away."

Peter then turned to Sir Palamedes. "An elvish knight does not fear the dark," the elf said. "You have my sword, young Master Peter."

"What about you, Euripides?" Peter asked the gopher who now stood all alone on the grass. Euripides looked down at the ground, nervously.

"I'd like to Peter, but it's so scary in there," Euripides said. "I think I'm going to stay with Ariel."

Peter frowned. He was sad but he understood. He wouldn't want to go into the woods either if he didn't have to. He turned back to Ariel and threw his arms around her once again. She squeezed him tight and kissed him on his cheek. "I love you," she whispered into his ear.

"I love you, too," Peter said and then pulled away as he wiped a tear from his eye. He turned to Strom and Palamedes. "I guess we had better go on," he said. Strom nodded.

"If it pleases you, Peter, I shall lead the way," Palamedes said.

"Yes," Peter replied. "It would please me very much, thank you."

"And I shall guard the rear," Strom said. "We shall keep you safely in the middle."

Peter turned and smiled at the dwarf. "Thank you, Strom." The three took a deep breath and then stepped toward the wood.

"The Lord be with you," Ariel told them.

"And with your spirit," Peter, Strom, and Palamedes replied.

Peter glanced back at the hill and waved one last good-bye to Orion and the other giants before disappearing into the tree line.

Euripides watched them go and then scurried up to stand next to Ariel's boot. "I wanted to go with him," he cried. "It's just so scary. But what if something happens?"

Ariel said nothing.

"He needs me!" Euripides said. "If something happens to him and I wasn't there to help him, I'd never forgive myself!"

"Well, then," Ariel said. "I think you know what you have to do."

Euripides nodded, and took a deep breath summoning all of his courage. "Peter, wait! I'm coming!" Euripides shouted as he dashed into the woods.

CHAPTER SIXTEEN
THE LIGHTED PATH

The woods surrounding them were dark and scary, but the path was well lit and free of any roots or stones or anything else that might trip them up. "Stay on the path," Peter mumbled under his breath. "Just stay on the path. We'll be through the woods soon."

Suddenly, they heard a blood-curdling shriek pierce the air and Peter, Strom, and Palamedes all froze, scanning the darkness around them. Peter turned to look at Strom and then turned back to Palamedes. "What was that?" he asked.

"Are you sure you want to know?" Palamedes asked.

"No," Peter said.

"I didn't think so," the elf replied. "Come on." Palamedes once again began walking along the path, following the light set out in front of them.

There was another shriek, but this time they did not stop, but kept on walking. "Just ignore it," Strom suggested. "Keep to the path, and the darkness will not harm us."

"Right," Peter said. "Stay in the light, and I'll be fine."

Then another sound startled them.

"Peter!" came a cry from behind. Strom spun around quickly and raised his mighty hammer. He relaxed when he saw it was just the gopher coming to join them.

"Euripides, you came!" Peter exclaimed excitedly as the rodent scurried up his leg to perch himself once again on the boy's shoulder.

"Of course I came!" Euripides snapped as if the matter were ever in question. "What would happen if you got yourself locked in a se'irim's cage again? Who would rescue you?"

Peter threw back his head and laughed. "Well I certainly feel better with you here with us, Euripides," Peter said. And he truly did. It always feels nice to have friends with you when you go through dark times.

"Let's go," Palamedes suggested and then led the way along the path. The next sound Peter heard was a howl that split the air and he glanced into the darkness to see those wolf creatures that Ariel had called "night stalkers" that had attacked him back at the church. At least four of the fiends ran parallel with the path, slipping through the shadows, far enough away that they were not an immediate threat, but close enough that they were terrifying.

Peter heard a hoot and turned to see a white owl flapping its wings as it came down to land on the branch of a black and twisted tree. "A snow owl," Peter smiled at the bird as he saw it staring back at him.

Strom grunted. "Owls are a bad omen," he snorted.

"Many dark creatures inhabit these woods," Palamedes reminded them. "But none can stand up to the power of Christ. No matter how big and scary, or how evil, the Light of

Christ will defeat them all."

"I wish Christ were here with us," Euripides quivered as he scanned the darkness around them and trembled with each terrifying sound that emanated from it.

"Ariel told me that Jesus is always with us," Peter reminded the gopher. "And my friend Father Joe told me the same thing."

"Who is Father Joe?" Euripides asked, happy to divert his attention away from the creatures in the shadows.

"He's a priest. I live with him and his wife, Ms. Naomi," Peter said. "They've been taking care of me and my mom while my mom is sick."

"A wise priest indeed," Strom commented.

"Truly," Palamedes agreed. "How else could there be a lighted path through a wood so evil and dark, except by the wonderful Light of Christ?"

"We must not stray from it," Strom said, "but even if you do, Christ has not abandoned you. He will still be there, watching you."

That gave Peter great comfort. He liked the idea that Jesus was always watching him. He needed that comfort now as the shrieks that once seemed far off now sounded closer. He looked out into the shadows and noticed the night stalkers were also moving closer and closer to the path, watching Peter and his friends with eerie eyes. Euripides clung tightly to Peter's hair, and Peter kept having to ask him not to pull on it too hard because it hurt. "Sorry," Euripides would say, but it was not long before the gopher was pulling it once again.

"The wolves do not worry me," Strom said as if sensing Peter's and Euripides' fear. Peter decided not to ask Strom what *did* worry him. He didn't want to think about it. He just wanted to get through the woods safely, find the Amulet of

Eternity, and get back home as quickly as he could to save his mother.

"Father Joe always says I should talk to God when I am afraid," Peter said, as much to himself as to the others.

"Speaking to the Lord is always a good idea," Palamedes agreed. "When I am afraid, I also find that it helps to recite Holy Scripture," Peter could not imagine the elvish knight ever being afraid.

"Would you mind reciting some out loud?" Euripides asked.

"Not at all, my furry little friend," Palamedes smiled. The knight cleared his throat and began to recite the twenty-third Psalm. "The Lord is my shepherd; I shall not want. He maketh me lie down in green pastures; he leadeth me beside the still waters.

"He restoreth my soul; he leadeth me in the paths of righteousness for his name's sake.

"Yea, though I walk through the valley of the shadow of death, I will fear no evil: for thou art with me; thy rod and thy staff they comfort me.

"Thou preparest a table before me in the presence of mine enemies: thou anointest my head with oil; my cup runneth over.

"Surely goodness and mercy shall follow me all the days of my life; and I will dwell in the house of the Lord for ever."

"That's beautiful," Strom said, his voice softer than normal.

Peter smiled. He agreed. The words Palamedes had quoted had definitely been comforting. "Who wrote that?" Peter asked.

"King David, when he was beset by his enemies. But he always trusted the Lord," Palamedes explained.

"David," Peter said. "Was that the same David that

defeated the giant Goliath?"

"Indeed it was, young Peter," Palamedes replied.

Peter remembered the story. Before he was king, when he was just a young boy like Peter, David had been a shepherd who watched over sheep, protecting them from wolves and lions. One day his nation of Israel went to war with their enemies, the Philistines. The Philistines' greatest warrior was a ten foot tall giant named Goliath. Goliath challenged Israel's greatest warrior to a duel, but none of the Israelite soldiers had been brave enough to fight him because he was so big and scary.

David trusted that the Lord would protect him from the giant, and although grown men—including David's own older brothers—had been too afraid to fight the giant, the young boy David accepted Goliath's challenge. David didn't even wear armor or carry a sword. Instead, he marched onto the field of battle with nothing but a sling and some stones. It was the same sling David used to hurl rocks at wolves and lions when they tried to eat his sheep.

Goliath was insulted that the Israelites would send a boy to fight him, so he cursed David and told the boy he would feed him to the birds. But David still showed no fear, for he trusted God would get him through. David shouted to Goliath, "You come to me with a sword, and with a spear, and with a shield—but I come to you in the name of the Lord of hosts, the God of the armies of Israel, whom you have defied!" David knew that God was far stronger than any sword, or spear or shield, even in the hands of a giant like Goliath. So David placed a stone in his sling, spun it around, and released it. God's hand guided the stone to hit Goliath between the eyes, killing the giant.

Peter smiled as he remembered the story of David and

Goliath. If the boy David, the smallest of all his brothers, could trust in God enough to face a giant ready to kill him and feed him to the birds, then Peter could trust God to get him through the scary dark woods.

Peter was suddenly snapped out of his thoughts by a new sound in the woods. It was a grunt, but not like the grunt of a man. This reminded Peter of the grunt of a bear mixed with the snort of a bull. Peter, Strom, and Palamedes all froze and turned to their left to stare into the shadows. There Peter saw something moving. It wasn't a night stalker as it was much too large. Was it a se'irim? The thing moved closer and Peter could tell that it was leaning forward onto its knuckles like a gorilla.

"A bugbear," Strom whispered, and Peter could hear the fear in his voice.

Peter swallowed hard as the creature snorted again and then raised itself onto its hind legs, its gigantic arms stretched into the air as it released a deep and terrifying roar. The bugbear then dropped back onto all fours and began to charge toward them. As it got closer, Peter could see its pointy ears and matted fur, its giant menacing eyes, and its bottom teeth protruding upward from its bottom jaw. The ground shook as the bugbear thundered nearer and nearer to them.

"It's going to crush us!" Euripides screamed as the creature charged them.

"Stay on the path," Strom reminded them, but never-the-less held his mighty hammer at the ready.

The bugbear charged closer and closer! "We can't stop it!" Euripides shouted. The bugbear released another terrifying roar, and Peter realized its mouth was big enough to gobble him up whole. Euripides could stand it no more. He leapt from Peter's shoulder and ran as fast as he could off the path and into the darkness of the woods.

"Euripides, come back!" Peter shouted. He dashed into the darkness after his friend.

"Peter, no!" Palamedes screamed. "Stay on the path!" But it was too late, Peter had disappeared into the woods chasing the gopher. Palamedes glanced at Strom and saw the dwarf sigh, but then nod. They were both thinking the same thing. Even though neither wanted to leave the safety of the path, they had to follow after Peter and Euripides.

Dashing from the safety of the path, Strom and Palamedes were vulnerable to the bugbear and soon felt the giant beast's hot breath on the back of their necks. Strom glanced over his shoulder to see the monster opening its large mouth to gobble the dwarf up. Strom released a scream of terror, but before the bugbear was able to eat him, Palamedes leapt upon the creature's back stabbing it repeatedly with his tiny sword.

The creature howled in pain, but did not stop charging. The beast turned and snapped at Palamedes with its massive jaws as the small elf danced away before slicing the monster again. The bugbear tried to swat at Palamedes as it ran, but was not quick enough to catch the tiny knight. Finally, and perhaps by pure luck, the bugbear managed to hit Palamedes with its massive hand, knocking the elf off its back and into the darkness of the forest floor.

Happy to rid itself of the pest, the bugbear turned its attention back to chasing the dwarf. However, just as its head swung back around, it saw Strom waiting for it, his mighty hammer held high. The bugbear did not have time to stop or change course before Strom struck him with all of his might. The power of the miraculous hammer sent the bugbear flying high into the sky and out of sight.

Strom stood still watching the monster fly away. He

glanced down at his hammer glad he'd given away that emerald. The shiny rock, no matter how big, would have been useless to him on this quest. The hammer had come in handy many times already. His thoughts then turned to the elvish knight. "Sir Palamedes!" Strom shouted in the darkness as he retraced his footsteps hoping to find his companion. "Palamedes, are you all right?"

"Over here!" Strom heard a small voice shout and rushed to find Palamedes brushing leaves from his cape. The knight smiled up at Strom. "You certainly gave that beast what for!" he laughed.

"Well, if you had not attacked it, I would have surely been eaten," Strom smiled at his little friend.

"We make a good team, Master dwarf!" Palamedes said.

"Indeed we do, Sir elf!" Strom laughed. "Now, we should go and find our other friends before something worse than that bugbear finds them."

Palamedes nodded. "Lead the way," he said and watched Strom turn and step in the direction he hoped Peter and Euripides had gone, when suddenly a net flew out of the darkness ensnaring Strom. Palamedes leapt forward to free his friend, but was quickly caught in a net of his own. Palamedes struggled against the net as he was lifted into the air. He stopped when he saw his captors. Palamedes swallowed hard when he realized they had been captured by some of the most wicked creatures in Evermore—men.

CHAPTER SEVENTEEN
VANITY FAIR

Peter rushed through the darkness in a desperate attempt to catch Euripides and take him back to the lighted path. Unfortunately, he had lost sight of the gopher. Fear began to overwhelm Peter when he realized that he was all alone in the darkness surrounded by evil creatures that wanted to kill or even eat him.

Peter stopped running to listen. Fortunately, he could no longer hear the bugbear chasing after him, but he had no idea where he was or how to get back to the lighted path. "Euripides!" Peter called in the darkness. He heard no response. "Strom, Sir Palamedes!" This time he did hear a response, but it wasn't what he was hoping for. Instead of his friends, Peter heard a howl. The night stalkers! Peter stopped shouting, fearful it would likely draw the wrong sort of attention to himself.

Peter's heart was racing, and his breathing was heavy as panic began to set in. How had Ariel told him to find the lighted path if he lost it? "Follow my heart," he whispered to himself. He tried to listen to what his heart was telling him, but the only thing he heard from it was beating like a bass drum inside his chest. He was too scared and panicked to follow his heart. Peter could not think of the light because all he could think about were the monsters that lurked in the darkness ready to devour him.

HOOT! Peter jumped, startled when he heard the owl. He scanned the treetops and saw it sitting on a tree branch, its white feathers almost gleaming in the darkness. Strom was right, owls were a bad omen! The last time he'd seen that owl it was followed by the bugbear. Was the monster close behind the white bird again? Peter heard a rustle in the bushes in front of him. It seemed too small to be a bugbear, but that didn't mean it wasn't a night stalker or something equally terrifying.

Peter gripped his staff and readied to fight whatever it was, when—to his great relief—Euripides appeared from the bushes. "Peter!" the small gopher shouted excitedly.

Peter breathed a sigh of relief and lowered his staff. "Euripides, you scared me!" he snapped at his friend.

"I'm sorry Peter," the rodent replied.

"And why did you run off like that?" Peter demanded. "We're supposed to stay on the lighted path! Now we're lost in the darkness."

"I know, Peter, but that bugbear was so terrifying!" the gopher replied. "I thought he was going to kill us all."

"Well, now we're in real trouble," Peter said.

HOOT!

Peter glanced up at the owl as it stared back at them.

"It's going to eat me," Euripides said.

HOOT! HOOT!

Suddenly, Peter heard a rustle in the bushes behind them and gasped when he saw two night stalkers step out, walking on their hind legs. The beasts stared at Peter and Euripides as a low growl emanated from their snarling lips.

"Stick, attack!" Peter shouted, and his staff flew from his hands, darting past the black trees and swinging at one of the night stalkers, knocking it down before assaulting the other. It began to bang the creature on top of its head incessantly, until the beast dropped to all fours and hurried away. The staff then turned back to the first as the creature was pushing itself back to its feet. The night stalker did not wait around to be attacked again, however, and fled after its companion.

"Stick, stop and return!" Peter shouted and the staff returned to his hand.

"That got'em!" Euripides exclaimed happily.

But then there was more movement in the bushes.

HOOT!

Peter looked at the owl again. "We should go!" he told Euripides as a tingle danced up his spine. Euripides agreed, and they rushed through the darkness once more without really knowing where they were going. Peter let his boots carry him quickly away, terrified that at any moment he would be set upon by wolves, or bugbears, or worse.

As Peter ran, he thought he saw light ahead, peeking through the darkness of the woods. As he got closer the light became a soft glow, then a brighter glow. "Look!" Peter shouted. "There is light up ahead!"

"Is it the path?" Euripides asked.

"I don't know," Peter replied, but when he reached it, he realized it was not the path at all. Instead, the woods ended in a green meadow. Beyond the meadow, Peter saw a small city and in the center of the city was a castle. "We must have made it through the woods!" Peter exclaimed excitedly.

They emerged from the dark trees into the light, crossing the bright green meadow before stepping onto cobblestone streets which led into the small city. The buildings were all made of wood or stone. The city was full of little shops with small signs announcing their goods hanging above their doors. However, the city itself appeared empty of people. Peter noticed no one, not a man or a woman, not a boy or a girl. He didn't even see a cat or a dog.

"It's a ghost town," Peter said causing Euripides to tremble.

"I'm afraid of ghosts," Euripides told him as he clung to Peter's hair once more.

"I didn't mean there are actual ghosts," Peter explained. "A ghost town is simply a town that's deserted."

Euripides glanced around. He didn't see anybody either, but then something caught his ear. "I hear music!" the gopher exclaimed.

Peter stopped and listened. "Yeah, I hear it, too," he said. "Where's it coming from?"

"That way!" Euripides shouted as he pointed toward the castle. Peter glanced up and saw guards stationed on the castle walls. The town wasn't deserted after all. Peter began walking toward the castle, but suddenly stopped as he remembered his other friends.

"I wonder where Strom and Sir Palamedes are," Peter said.

"Maybe they are already inside the castle," Euripides suggested.

Peter hoped so. He didn't know where else to look. Besides, he was getting hungry, so he decided he would look for them inside the castle. Peter jogged toward the castle and as he got nearer he noticed people entering and leaving through the open gate. Above the gate was a large banner that proclaimed "The Vanity Fair Today." Guards in chain mail armor, covered in black tunics emblazoned with a red dragon stood guard at the gate. However, they didn't challenge anyone entering the castle grounds.

Peter strolled past the guards with Euripides perched upon his shoulder and inside found a festival taking place in the castle courtyard. "Welcome to the Vanity Fair!" shouted a man in a boisterous voice as he leaned forward, offering Peter an apple on a stick. "Have a candied apple."

"Thank you," Peter said with a smile, as he accepted the apple. It was shiny and red and he was quite hungry. He bit into it, but found it to be very hard on his teeth.

"I will take care of it for you, Peter," Euripides offered. "Gophers have very strong teeth, you know."

Peter smiled. "All right," he said as he handed the apple to Euripides. "Just don't get any stuck in my hair." But Euripides had already dug in.

Peter continued walking through the fair as crowds pushed around him to get a look at the wares for sale, like mirrors, makeup, perfumes, jewelry and fine clothing. Peter noticed fortune tellers, a man eating fire, and a pair of jugglers. Artists painted stunning portraits of beautiful people in the finest clothes Peter had ever seen. His stomach growled when he noticed children stuffing their faces with cookies and cakes. He was about to try and find something to eat when Euripides spoke into his ear.

"Let's find the music," the gopher suggested eagerly.

"Okay," Peter smiled. Food could wait. He weaved his way through the crowd, feeling somewhat under-dressed compared to everyone else. Even the children wore suits of colorful silk, and the air was so thick with perfume that he could barely breath. Soon, Peter found a stage where a small munchkin dressed as a clown danced as a merriment band played lively songs. He looked tired, like he had been dancing for a very long time. The crowd of people were booing angrily.

"Poor little guy," Euripides said. "He just doesn't have the gift of dance."

"The crowd isn't being very nice to him," Peter commented.

"Well, they expect good dancing, not whatever it is that munchkin is trying to do." Before Peter could stop him, Euripides had leapt from his shoulder and hurried beneath the feet of the crowd to jump onto the stage. The gopher began to dance, shaking his chubby hips back and forth and spinning and leaping into the air. The crowd cheered, and someone yanked the munchkin from the stage. Euripides had the spotlight all to himself, and he loved every moment of it.

Soon the song ended, and Euripides bowed to the crowd, as people tossed flowers onto the stage for him. "Thank you!" Euripides smiled grandly.

"Hey Euripides, let's go somewhere else!" Peter called, and the gopher turned to join him, but was stopped when the crowd chanted "dance, dance, dance," summoning Euripides back. More and more people joined the audience, eager to watch the dancing gopher. Euripides had never had a crowd this big before, and he didn't want to leave. He wanted to dance. But most of all he wanted their cheers and adoration.

"You go ahead, Peter," Euripides smiled. "I'll catch up later."

Peter chuckled. "All right, but don't get lost in the crowd," he cautioned. Euripides waved Peter's concerns away and the merriment band began to play once again. Euripides started to dance as Peter wandered off to see if he could find something to eat.

VANITY FAIR

Peter saw a woman selling pastries and a man selling turkey legs, but he soon remembered he didn't have any money. Well nothing except his giant emerald. He certainly didn't want to trade something so valuable for a single turkey leg. As he stood pondering what to do, a woman grabbed him and spun him around to face her. Peter had never seen a woman in so much makeup. Her face was a soft white with green and purple eyeshadow, pink cheeks, and ruby red lips. Her appearance startled him at first, but then caused him to chuckle when he realized how much she resembled a clown.

"Aren't you just the most handsome man I've ever seen?" the woman asked.

"Me?" Peter asked in reply.

The woman laughed. "Darla, come and see this one!" she shouted. Another woman, whom Peter presumed was Darla, joined them and bent over to look at Peter. She was just as extravagantly painted as the first one. "Wow, he really is quite handsome."

"My mom tells me I take after my dad," Peter said.

"Well, I would certainly love to meet your dad," Darla giggled. "Denise, don't you think he should enter the handsomest man contest?"

Denise smiled broadly. "That's an excellent idea!" she exclaimed.

"But not in these clothes!" Darla said.

"Oh, no!" Denise agreed. "Our handsome little man needs much finer clothes than this!"

"What's your name, handsome?" Darla asked.

"It's Peter," he replied as he pushed his glasses up closer to his face. "Peter Puckett."

"It's very nice to meet you, Peter Puckett," Denise smiled. She then took him by the hand and pulled him away. They were soon in a shop in the little city just outside the gates of the castle, and Peter was seated in a tall blue velvet chair.

"Master Giorgio makes the most magnificent clothes in the entire realm!" Denise explained.

"He will certainly know how to dress you for the contest!" Darla agreed.

A moment later, a plump man with an impressive mustache entered the room from behind a great curtain, followed by a trio of young boys who appeared to be just slightly older than Peter. The man wore a red and white striped suit that Peter thought made him look a bit like a chubby candy cane. "Ah, Denise, Darla, my sweets!" the man said as he kissed each of the women on the cheek. "What have you brought me?"

"Master, look at this," Darla smiled and stepped out of the way for Master Giorgio to see Peter.

"Ah!" Giorgio exclaimed. "Exquisite!" He looked Peter up and down. "You are not from around here or I would certainly have known you before."

"No, sir, I'm not," Peter admitted.

"You must be the most popular boy in your city!" Master Giorgio exclaimed.

"Actually, I don't have a lot a friends," Peter confessed.

"What?" everyone in the room gasped.

"Well, here, my young Lord, you will be worshiped!" Master Giorgio smiled. He then clapped his hands and the trio of young apprentices stepped forward. "Remove the young lord's clothes."

"What?" Peter asked surprised by that command.

"We can't very well dress you in new clothes while you are wearing the old ones now can we?" Master Giorgio asked.

"I suppose not," Peter said as he stood from the chair. One of the trio began to pull Peter's shirt over his head. "Wait a second!" Peter shouted as he pulled his shirt back down. "I'm not getting undressed here in front of everyone!"

"Why not?" Darla asked him. "We don't mind!"

"*I* mind!" Peter said gruffly.

"Very well," Master Giorgio frowned. "Take him to the back while we pick out a suit for him."

The trio of apprentices led Peter to the back of the shop to a small dressing room. He was soon undressed with his clothes lying in a heap on the floor. Master Giorgio brought Peter a suit of fine blue and silver silk. Peter's eyes went wide. It was very beautiful and the softest material he had ever felt. Peter pulled the suit on and admired himself in the mirror. His new suit made him look really regal. In fact, he looked better than he had thought. He always thought of himself as kind of nerdy looking, but as he gazed at his reflection he realized Darla and Denise were correct. He really was quite handsome.

He stepped out of the dressing room, and Darla and Denise fell all over themselves singing his praises. "Never have I seen a handsomer man," Darla smiled, batting her enormous eyelashes.

"He is a grand lord indeed," Denise agreed.

"Except those boots!" Giorgio exclaimed.

Peter looked down to see the boots Nicholas had given him. "What's wrong with my boots?" Peter asked.

"They are fine, I suppose, for one who walks everywhere," Giorgio said. "But you are a lord, carried in carriages, the halls of your castle covered in rose petals!"

Peter thought that last bit sounded weird. "But I like these boots. They were a gift from…" he began but was cut off.

"You may put them back on afterward," Darla suggested.

"Well…" Peter said hesitantly, "…I guess. If they will be safe."

CHAPTER SEVENTEEN

"Of course," Giorgio replied. "We will keep everything safe for you here. When you are done you may change once again." He then turned to the trio and snapped his fingers. One immediately left to fetch some silk slippers while another knelt down and removed Peter's boots. Soon they had the new slippers on Peter's feet.

"We should go, or we'll miss it," Denise said.

"Oh yes, we must hurry!" Darla agreed. They began to hustle Peter out of the shop.

"Wait, my cloak and staff!" Peter exclaimed.

"They will be here with your clothes when you return," Giorgio assured him.

Peter nodded and allowed himself to be pulled from the shop by Darla and Denise. Once they were out of sight, Giorgio took Peter's clothes, boots, cloak, and staff and put them all into a sack. He then dropped the sack into a trash bin outside his shop. He frowned at the staff which was too long to fit all of the way inside and so the top was protruding. Giorgio sighed, realizing there was nothing he could do about it. He stepped back inside his shop to have one of the trio empty the bin. A moment later, a white owl fluttered down and landed on top of the staff.

CHAPTER EIGHTEEN
THE BEAUTIFUL PRINCESS

The stage was already filling with dashing and handsome young men all dressed in their very finest clothes. Darla and Denise ushered Peter onto the stage beside the others and then hurried into the crowd to watch their young protégé. An older man in a suit of garnet colored silk, stepped in front of the line of young men.

"Ladies and gentlemen," the older man began in a booming voice. "Welcome to Vanity Fair's handsomest man contest!" The large crowd erupted with applause and cheering! "Look at all of these deliciously handsome young men!" The host shouted above the crowd. "Who will you crown the winner?"

Names were called out from various persons in the crowd, and Darla and Denise shouted "Peter!" as loudly as they could manage. Peter waved to them, and they blew kisses in return. Peter was really enjoying himself. He'd never been popular before, and certainly no one except his mom and Ms. Naomi and a couple of the older ladies at church had ever called him handsome.

"Remember," the older man shouted above the crowd, "the winner gets the great honor of receiving a kiss from Her Most Royal Highness, Princess Jezebel, herself!" At this point the crowd cheered so loudly that Peter was forced to cover his ears.

A princess! Peter's excitement rose to a new level. He peered down the line at the other young men on the stage. His vain pride began to grow. These other men were handsome, sure, but they were not nearly as handsome as he was. He smiled to himself, confidently hopeful that he would win the kiss from the princess.

"As you no doubt remember, we shall choose the winner by the cheering of the crowd," the host announced. "Whoever receives the loudest cheers shall be named the winner and receive the precious kiss!" He then began with the first young man—a tall, dark-haired and muscular boy. The crowd cheered loudly and Peter fumed with envy. The next was a blond young man who Peter thought resembled a plastic toy doll. The crowd cheered even louder.

Why did they think these boys were handsome? Peter's jealousy grew as each young man received loud cheers. Peter became increasingly irritated. He wanted to win! He wanted to win more than he'd ever wanted to win anything before in his life. And he deserved it! None of these other boys were nearly as handsome as he was!

The host stepped in front of Peter and turned to the crowd. "And who thinks our last young man is the handsomest?" he shouted. The crowd went nuts. It was by far the loudest. Even the other contestants were shouting and cheering for Peter. "We have a winner!" the host shouted as he took hold of Peter's hand and raised it high above his head. "What is your name, my young lord?"

"Peter Puckett," Peter replied.

"Lord Peter Puckett, everyone!" the man announced and the crowd began to chant "Peter! Peter! Peter!"

Peter beamed proudly as he was led to the center of the stage and all of the other contestants were ushered off so that they would not share the spotlight with him. Peter gazed into the crowd and saw Darla and Denise there, clapping excitedly. He waved to them, and both women nearly fainted.

Suddenly, the crowd parted as silence fell over it. Peter watched as a golden throne appeared, being carried through the crowd by four muscular men. A girl in a deep purple dress sat upon the throne, a regally aloof expression on her face. Everyone in the crowd lowered themselves to their knees as the throne passed. Peter assumed the young woman was Princess Jezebel. As the throne neared the stage, he was able to get a better view of her. She had dark hair of a deep mahogany color, which was crowned with a glistening diamond encrusted tiara. Her large, almond-shaped eyes turned upward and were dark like her hair.

Her throne soon reached the stage, and the Princess rose. The host dropped to one knee and pulled Peter down with him. Princess Jezebel stepped down from the throne and onto the stage and Peter noticed she was wearing soft purple slippers to match her dress, with bright red rubies at the tip of their toes.

Princess Jezebel stepped lightly onto the stage and glided more than walked to stand before the kneeling Peter. She let her gaze drop down to him. "You may rise, Lord Peter," she said in an alluring voice that beckoned him to her and made him want to follow her. Peter rose to his feet and turned his head upward to look into her eyes.

CHAPTER EIGHTEEN

Peter was surprised to discover that despite her violet eyeshadow, pink blush and ruby red lips, the Princess did not appear to be much older than him. But she was beautiful, like the girls he'd seen on television. She was possibly the most beautiful girl he had ever seen, and was certainly more beautiful than any of the girls at his school.

"I'd hoped you would win," she whispered with an inviting smile and Peter blushed as she leaned forward and placed a soft kiss upon his cheek. The crowd went wild, hooting and hollering, cheering and clapping. Peter glanced down to see Darla and Denise wiping tears from their eyes like proud mothers.

Princess Jezebel slipped her hand over his, intertwining their fingers. "Would you join me at the joust?" she asked softly. Peter swallowed nervously, too excited to even get words out through his lips. He managed a nod and the Princess smiled with delight. "Fabulous!" she squealed happily and then turned around and began gliding back to her throne, pulling Peter along with her. She stepped off the stage and onto the throne, urging Peter to step on as well. He did so and as she sat gracefully, she pointed to the empty space at her feet. "Sit there," she said and Peter obeyed. The crowd once again lowered themselves to their knees as the Princess and Peter were carried away.

From a distance, Euripides noticed Peter on the throne being carried away with the Princess. He had grown tired from dancing so long and decided to rejoin his friend. "It has been a lot of fun, but I must be going!" he shouted over the music to the crowd and was about to leap off of the stage and chase after Peter when he was snatched up by the scruff of his neck as a sharp knife was placed to his throat. "Dance," the wielder of the knife growled.

THE BEAUTIFUL PRINCESS

***

Peter enjoyed watching everyone kneel as he and the princess were carried through the Fair. He glanced up at her, still amazed at how fortunate he was to have won a kiss from a real-life princess. Not only was she a princess, but she was the most beautiful girl Peter had ever seen. And she clearly liked him because she had invited him to ride on her throne with her to see a joust.

Peter was super excited about the joust! He'd never seen a real joust before, but what little boy doesn't want to see actual knights in armor jousting? In fact, Peter—like most boys—had often dreamed of being a knight. These weren't tiny elvish knights either, but men—men in armor on horseback.

The throne came to a halt at a grandstand and Princess Jezebel stood regally before stepping over Peter and off the throne. She beckoned Peter to follow her as she led him to a small box where sat a ruggedly handsome man in a black doublet fastened with shiny gold buttons. The man had a clean-shaven face and a head full of wavy golden brown hair. He was surrounded by courtiers who paid little attention to the joust as their attention was fully on him and they stared at him adoringly.

"Father," Jezebel said and the man turned to see her standing before him with Peter just behind her.

"Ah, my darling, you've brought a friend," the man said with a welcoming smile.

"Yes, Father," Jezebel said. "May I present Lord Peter of Puckett." She then turned to Peter. "And this is my father, King Apollyon."

"It's nice to meet you, sir," Peter said causing the king's eyebrows to rise up on his head.

CHAPTER EIGHTEEN

"Your Majesty," Jezebel prompted him.

"Excuse, me, I meant, it's nice to meet you, Your Majesty," Peter said correcting himself.

The King's smile broadened into a laugh. "And it is nice to meet you too, Lord Peter," he said. "Won't you join us?"

Peter turned to Jezebel to see her smiling at him and nodding her head vigorously. "Yes, thank you, Your Majesty," Peter said. Jezebel took Peter by the hand and led him up to her father. The king shooed the two courtiers to his right away so that Jezebel and Peter could take their seats. Jezebel kissed her father gently on the cheek and then sat down. She motioned for Peter to sit down beside her. Suddenly, trumpets blared and Peter's attention was drawn to the jousting field before them.

"Your Royal Majesty!" shouted a man in a large red tunic standing in the center of the green field. "Your Royal Highness, My Lords and Ladies! For your pleasure and entertainment we have two of the finest knights in all of Evermore! Sir Azul the Green and Sir Verde the Blue!"

Peter saw two knights astride horses on opposite sides of the field and smiled at their colorful armor. Sir Azul was decked out in green armor from head to toe. Even the hair of his horse was dyed green. Sir Verde wore nothing but blue armor and sat astride a blue horse.

The man in the center of the field bowed low at the waist and then hurried from the field. King Apollyon rose to his feet. "Let the joust begin!" he shouted. The crowd cheered loudly as the two knights took their lances from nearby pages and awaited the trumpet to sound. When the trumpet blared, the colorful knights urged their mounts forward in a thunderous charge, each desiring to knock the other from his horse.

THE BEAUTIFUL PRINCESS

Sir Azul the Green was thrust from his saddle and fell to the ground with a thud. Sir Verde the Blue turned his horse and dismounted, drawing his sword as Sir Azul pushed himself to his feet. Sir Azul drew his sword as well and the two knights met in the middle of the field, their swords clanging together in combat.

Princess Jezebel clapped her hands excitedly. She turned to see Peter grinning from ear-to-ear as he watched the sword fight. She leaned over and whispered in his ear. "Isn't it thrilling to see men fight each other in mortal combat simply for your entertainment?"

Peter nodded, but then remembered what "mortal combat" meant. He turned to Jezebel. "You mean they are fighting to the death?" he asked.

She turned to see deep concern on his face. "Of course not," she smiled reassuringly. "It's just a show." Suddenly a squeal of pain arose from the field, and the crowd went wild with applause. Peter tried to turn his head to see what had happened, but Jezebel placed a hand on his cheek and kept him facing her. "I'm starving," she said. "Would you like to get something to eat?"

At the mention of food, Peter felt his stomach rumble. He *was* hungry. "Yes," he said with a nod.

Jezebel turned to her father. "We're ready to eat," she said.

"When my daughter is ready to eat, she is ready to eat," the King mused. "Let us retire to the castle."

The table in the Great Hall was even larger and more impressive than the one at Nicholas' house and it was covered in desserts. Cakes, pies, cookies, candies, éclairs, ice cream, brownies, puddings, Turkish delight and more filled the enormous table. Peter had never seen so much food before in his life. He imagined there were enough desserts to give his entire school an upset stomach.

Jezebel had started eating from a plate filled by her servant as soon as she had sat down. The princess had two servants attending her at the table. One was a pretty young girl who appeared just a bit younger than Jezebel herself, with soft white skin and yellow hair tied back into a ponytail. The other had dark eyes and skin, and her hair was cropped close. Both servants wore dresses as white as snow. Peter was assigned two boy servants. One had red hair and freckles and the other was short and squat. The servants stood behind him as he ate.

King Apollyon sat at the head of the long table with Jezebel to his right and Peter to his left. No one else sat at the table, though there was enough sweets to feed everyone who had attended the joust. When Jezebel wanted something new, she snapped her fingers, and one of the girls behind her would fetch it for her. Peter, who was unused to being served, reached for his own food until Jezebel corrected him.

"Let the servants do it," she said. "That's what they are here for—to serve."

Peter nodded. "Sorry," he said as he remembered how Ariel and Nicholas had explained that serving others was a blessing. He turned to the freckled faced boy behind him. "Could you please get me a chocolate chip cookie?" he asked nicely.

Jezebel giggled. "No, silly," she smiled. "That's how you would ask someone equal to your station to get something for you. But servants are nothing. We are everything. They live to serve us because they are beneath us. Watch." She snapped her fingers. The little blond girl handed her a cookie.

"How did she know what you wanted?" Peter asked.

Jezebel smiled. "A good servant learns to anticipate your every need and desire."

"Oh, okay," Peter said.

Apollyon sensed Peter was uncomfortable with the conversation and decided to steer it in a different direction. "So, Lord Peter, what brings you to my lands?"

Peter swallowed a piece of cookie and then wiped his mouth with his sleeve. He cringed when he realized what he was doing and quickly snatched a napkin to use instead, eliciting an amused smile from the king.

"I am on a quest, Your Majesty," Peter said.

"How exciting," Jezebel smiled gaily. "What kind of quest?"

"I am going to recover the Amulet of Eternity," Peter said.

Apollyon stared at him in awe. "The Amulet of Eternity?" he asked. "Whatever for?"

"The angel Ariel said it would save my mother's life," Peter told him.

"An angel told you that, did she?" Apollyon asked with a smirk.

"Yes," Peter said. "Why?"

"Oh, no reason," Apollyon smiled. "But how do you propose to get the amulet? Is it not held in the Realm of Goblins?"

"Yes, Your Majesty," Peter said.

"And will you not have to swim through the seas of the Leviathan to reach the Realm of Goblins?"

"Yes, Your Majesty," Peter said.

"That sounds extremely dangerous for a little boy," Apollyon said.

Peter nodded.

"Aren't you scared?" the king asked.

CHAPTER EIGHTEEN

"Yes, Your Majesty. I'm very scared," Peter admitted. "But Ariel says if I trust the Lord, He will protect me."

"Which lord is that?" Apollyon asked.

Peter looked up at the King slightly bewildered. He did not realize there was more than one Lord. "Jesus Christ," he said.

"Oh," Apollyon chuckled. "Of course, this is all his doing."

Peter frowned. "What do you mean?" Peter asked.

The king sighed. "Jesus and his father always like to make things more difficult than they have to be."

Peter tilted his head to the side in confusion. "How so?" he asked.

"Didn't you ever wonder why Jesus had to die on the cross?" Apollyon asked.

Peter shrugged. "To save us from our sins," he said.

"Yes, the Scriptures say that he was a sacrifice that his own father demanded in order to forgive the world of its sins, right?" Apollyon asked.

"Right," Peter agreed.

"But why couldn't God have just forgiven the world?" the King asked. "Why make Jesus suffer so much?"

Peter shrugged. "I dunno," he said.

"Because he likes to make people do unnecessary things— hard, dangerous, deadly things—for no reason at all. Just to get his kicks. He's what adults would call a sadist."

That didn't sound right to Peter. God loved His Son. God loved Peter. God wouldn't do that. There had to be a reason that Jesus was sacrificed, and just because Peter didn't know the answer didn't mean it didn't exist.

"I'll have to ask Ariel or Father Joe about that," he said. "They know a lot more than I do."

"No need," Apollyon said with a wave of his hand. He

didn't want Peter asking anyone about what he was saying. He wanted Peter to trust *him*. "I can prove it to you."

"How?" Peter asked.

"Come with me," Apollyon smiled as he rose from the table. Peter rose as well. Jezebel started to rise but her father waved her back down. "You finish your sweets, my darling, I'm just going to show Peter something." Jezebel smiled and nodded. She snapped her fingers and one of her servants cut her a slice of pie.

Apollyon led Peter from the Great Hall down a dimly lit corridor and into the Throne Room. The room was twice the size of the Great Hall with tapestries depicting valiant battles lining the walls. Apollyon ascended the steps to his throne, a high-backed golden chair with dark red cushions. He turned and sat down, before smiling at Peter who stood below staring up at him.

"What if I told you I could get the Amulet of Eternity for you, without you having to brave the Leviathan or the goblins?" Apollyon asked.

"How could you do that?" Peter asked, not wanting to get his hopes up.

Apollyon threw back his head and laughed. "How? My boy, I already have the amulet," he said.

Peter stared at him for a long moment. "How did you get it?" Peter asked.

"Does it matter?" Apollyon asked.

Peter supposed not. "And you'll let me have it?" Peter asked. "To save my mother?"

"Yes," Apollyon smiled. "And your so-called 'Lord Jesus' could have done the same thing, but he wanted to see you suffer. In fact, he doesn't need the amulet at all. He could have just healed your mother—made her well again—but he didn't!" Peter could tell Apollyon was getting angry. "No, he wanted a little boy to risk his life! For what? So he could enjoy making you play his sinister little game, that's why!"

Apollyon calmed himself. "But I will give it to you, and all I ask in return is that you remain here as one of my knights."

Peter smiled. "A knight?" he said. "Me?"

"Yes, you, Peter," Apollyon smiled.

"But what about my mom?" Peter asked.

Apollyon laughed. "Do you think I would not allow your mother to join you? She can live in the castle as well, Peter."

"Really, we can live here in the castle?" Peter was getting excited.

"Yes, of course. Jezebel is fond of you. You could live with us and one day maybe you and she could be wed." Peter blushed. "You will have everything you've ever wanted. Your mother will be safe, and you'll have all the friends you could ever want. In fact, they will worship you. What do you say?"

Peter tried hard to think of a reason not to do it. It seemed too easy, but perhaps the king was right. "I'd like to talk to Ariel first," Peter said.

"Ariel?" Apollyon smirked. "She's as wicked as Jesus, playing her little games with you. Making you go into the Shadow Wood by yourself. She lied when she said she couldn't come in, Peter. Angels can enter this wood too!"

This wood? Peter suddenly realized that he was still in the Shadow Wood. He hadn't actually escaped it like he and Euripides had thought. Where was Euripides anyway? Then another thought crossed Peter's mind. A sinister thought. "How did you know what Ariel told me?"

Apollyon smiled and stood. "It doesn't matter, Peter," he said. He then looked past Peter, at something lurking in the shadows. The king beckoned that something to him. Peter turned and what he saw caused him to gasp. Stepping out of the shadows was a terrifying creature. It was taller than Peter—about the size of a short man—with pointy ears that looked like bats wings and a pointy nose like that of a witch. It had hairless skin that was a green so dark it nearly looked black, and it had glowing yellow eyes and terrifyingly jagged teeth. Peter realized instantly that the creature was a goblin.

The goblin carried a small silver box in its clawed fingers. It sneered and hissed at Peter as it crept past him to approach Apollyon. The goblin climbed the stairs to the throne and knelt before the king, presenting him with the silver box. Apollyon accepted the box and then looked down at Peter.

"Here it is, Peter," the king said. "The Amulet of Eternity is inside this box. I will give it to you without you having to sneak past the Leviathan or face a horde of goblins." He pointed to the goblin still on its knees. "Trust me when I tell you, you do not want to run into these guys in the dark caverns. They are so wicked and evil they make se'irim look like puppy dogs."

Peter stared at the silver box as Apollyon held it out to him. He did want it. He wanted it more than anything. He wanted to save his mother, and he wanted to do it without having to face Leviathan or the goblins, especially now that he'd seen a goblin.

"I'll give it to you," Apollyon said. "And all you have to do is kneel down at my feet and swear your allegiance to me."

Suddenly, Peter remembered a story that he'd learned in Sunday school about Jesus being tempted in the wilderness. The devil came and told Jesus he would give Him the whole world if Jesus just bowed down and worshiped him.

Peter shook his head. "N-no, thank you, Y-Your Majesty," Peter stammered. He was starting to tremble.

CHAPTER EIGHTEEN

Apollyon sighed. "Very well," he said before turning to the goblin. "Put this back."

"Yes, Sire," the goblin hissed as it accepted the silver box.

"I-I g-greatly appreciate your hospitality, Your Majesty, b-but I think should b-be going now," Peter said and was about to turn and walk out of the throne room, when suddenly Apollyon was beside him in a flash. He snatched Peter up by the arm.

"Oh you'll be going now, will you?" the king hissed as his eyes glowed red, and Peter noticed rows of sharp teeth lining his mouth. "You'll be going all right! To the dungeon!" Apollyon dragged Peter from the throne room, down and down and down stone steps until he finally reached the bottom. There he pulled Peter into the cold wet dungeon dimly lit with a few flickering torches. Peter noticed rows and rows of prison cells.

"Peter!" he heard and turned to see Strom locked up in a cell, and Sir Palamedes on a nearby table trapped in what appeared to be a small animal cage.

"Praise the Lord you are all right!" Palamedes said.

Apollyon threw back his head and cackled. "Oh you are far from all right!" he hissed as he shoved Peter. "This is your last chance, boy! At darkfall, I will throw you and your friends into the fire if you do not bow down and worship me right now!" Peter began to cry. "Worship me!" Apollyon shrieked.

"No!" Peter shot back. He didn't know where he had summoned that courage from, but he knew he would not worship this demon.

"Then soon you shall die," Apollyon sneered and dragged him to a cell, opened it, tossed Peter inside, and slammed the door shut with a clang. He then spun on his heel and stormed away, back up the stone steps, and out of the dungeon.

THE BEAUTIFUL PRINCESS

Peter curled up in a ball and wept. He could vaguely make out words from his friends in a nearby cell, but wasn't paying any attention. He was scared and upset. Why had he left the path? Why had he been so foolish as to fall for everyone's flattery. His pride would cost him his life! He should have returned to the Light of Jesus, but now there was no way out.

But wait, maybe there was. Maybe Jezebel would save him. If he could somehow get a message to her. She probably didn't know he was down here. She liked him, didn't she? Or was she just feeding his vanity as well?

Peter wept and wept. He wanted to pray and ask Jesus for help, but he'd gotten himself into such a mess, he didn't think Jesus would care to help him. He'd been too wicked—much too wicked. So instead of praying and asking Jesus to forgive him, Peter laid on the floor of the cell weeping.

CHAPTER NINETEEN
THE KING OF SALEM

Euripides was still dancing. He didn't have much choice in the matter, as the alternative was death. Exhausted, he now understood why the munchkin he first saw had been dancing so badly. Who knows how long that poor creature had been forced to dance! Euripides had begun his dancing routine with great flourish, drawing the cheers of the crowd. It had inflated his vain pride and he had reveled in it. Euripides had always wanted that sort of attention—to be a real star with real crowds—but now he was paying the price. He didn't know if he would ever be allowed to stop dancing. He knew he'd eventually collapse from exhaustion and wondered if he would be killed then or simply swept off the stage.

His dancing was not very entertaining anymore, and the crowd had turned hostile. They had started out throwing tomatoes at him. Tomatoes probably didn't feel good when they hit you, but Euripides assumed they were better than a shoe. Or worse, a horseshoe. No fewer than two iron horseshoes had already been flung at him. Luckily, he had been quick enough to dodge them, but he was not quick enough to avoid the squash. The large yellow gourd had been flung at him by a mean old woman in the third row, and when it slammed into Euripides, it hit him so hard that he fell off the stage to land in the grass behind. At least, that's what it looked like. In truth, Euripides' miraculous hat had protected him, and he only pretended to collapse.

The small gopher lay there for a long while until the crowd got tired of waiting and urged the munchkin back onto the stage—against the little man's wishes, of course. While the munchkin took Euripides' place, a big burly man—assuming the gopher was dead—picked him up to toss him outside the castle gates. As he carried the gopher, however, Euripides suddenly opened his eyes and bit the man in the hand with his very large teeth.

"Ow!" the man shouted in pain, but released Euripides. Euripides scurried away as quickly as his little legs would carry him, dodging peddlers and customers alike. He had seen Peter disappear into the castle with persons of apparent importance and hoped they could help him. He hurried through the open gate of the castle and past the guards.

"Hey!" one of the guards shouted.

"What was that?" asked the other.

"A badger?"

"I think it was a gopher."

"Too fast to be a gopher."

By the time the guards stopped arguing over what Euripides was and actually went after the small rodent, Euripides had made it into the kitchen. "Peter!" he shouted. "Peter!" Finding no one in the kitchen but a scullery maid who paid him little mind, Euripides set out toward the Great

CHAPTER NINETEEN

Hall. When he reached it, he found Jezebel throwing pies at her servant girls. She laughed hysterically as she hurled pies at them. The servants were not dodging the pies as one might expect. Instead, each girl made sure the pie found her face. Basically, they were not getting hit in the face with the pies, but were rather hitting the pies with their faces.

Euripides recognized Jezebel as the girl Peter had gone into the castle with and hurried over to her. "Excuse me, m'Lady," Euripides said with a flourishing bow.

Jezebel stopped throwing pies to look down at the small brown gopher at her feet. "How did you get in here?" she asked.

"I was simply…" he began, but Jezebel interrupted him.

"Hey, you're that dancing gopher, aren't you?" she asked excitedly.

"Yes, I am, and I'm looking for…" Euripides began, but was once again interrupted.

"Dance for me," Jezebel commanded.

"M'Lady," he began to protest.

"It's 'Your Royal Highness'!" Jezebel snapped. "I am the princess!"

"My apologies, Your Royal Highness," Euripides said with a bow. "I have never performed for royalty before, and it would be a great honor to dance for you, but…"

"Of course, it would," Jezebel laughed. "There is no greater honor than serving and pleasing me." She turned to her servant girls. "Is there?"

"No, Your Royal Highness," the girls insisted as they bowed low before Jezebel, their pie-covered faces pressed against the stone floor.

Jezebel suddenly noticed the mess of pies (that she had caused) everywhere. The mess infuriated her. "Clean this place up immediately!" she screamed.

"Yes, Your Royal Highness!" the servants said as they hurried to obey.

"And if I find any pie on the floor, you'll be licking it up!" She then turned to Euripides. "Well?" she demanded.

"Well what, Your Royal Highness?" the gopher asked.

"Dance for my pleasure," she insisted.

"Yes, Your Highness," Euripides said and then began to dance, shaking his hips back and forth and twirling through the air. Jezebel laughed and clapped her hands.

"Wonderful!" she smiled. "I'm going to keep you. You will dance for me whenever I desire!"

"Of course, Your Highness, but may I ask what happened to my friend Peter?"

"Peter?" Jezebel repeated. "I don't really know. He's with my father, I suppose."

At that precise moment, Apollyon re-entered the Great Hall. "What is that?" he asked in disgust as he pointed to the small rodent.

Jezebel smiled excitedly. "He's a dancing gopher," she said. "Isn't he splendid? He's a friend of Peter's."

"Is that right?" Apollyon asked.

"Yes," Jezebel replied. "He's looking for him."

"Oh," Apollyon smiled. "Well, I will take you to him."

"Thank you, Your Majesty!" Euripides exclaimed as he stopped dancing, so tired that he nearly fell over.

Peter had calmed himself with the help of his friends Strom and Palamedes. He now sat up, leaning his back against the iron bars of the cell. He'd wiped the tears from his eyes and listened as Strom attempted to formulate a plan to get them out of the dungeon before Apollyon had them all executed. Palamedes just listened. He seemed confident and showed no fear.

"If the Lord wants to release us, He shall," Palamedes had explained. "And if He doesn't, He won't. The only thing we can do is pray and wait patiently."

But Peter knew the Lord was probably too mad at him to help. He decided that unless Jezebel discovered he was down here and rescued him, the only hope Peter and the others had was Euripides. But how would Euripides even discover they were in the castle, much less the dungeon? It seemed like a very long shot and Peter hung his head in despair. But then he heard something. Something familiar. It sounded like the scurrying little feet of Euripides. Could it be? Peter stood up and walked to the front of the cell, watching the entrance to the dungeon.

"Peter?" he heard Euripides' little voice call just before he saw his friend hurry into the room.

"Euripides!" Peter shouted excitedly. The gopher turned to see Peter and the others inside the dungeon cells.

"What are you doing in there?" Euripides asked.

"King Apollyon captured us!" Peter explained. "He's not a good man, he's evil and…" but then Peter stopped cold as he watched Apollyon step into the dungeon.

Euripides turned to look up at the king just as Apollyon reached down and scooped him up by the scruff of the neck. "Aha!" Apollyon shouted excitedly. He strode across the dungeon and tossed Euripides in a small cage used to trap rats. He then turned to Peter. "Tomorrow after your execution, I think I shall feast on gopher stew!" he cackled.

"Please, don't!" Peter shouted.

"Oh, you don't want me to eat your little friend?" Apollyon

sneered. "You can save him, Peter. You know how, don't you?" Peter nodded. "Say it."

"If I bow down and worship you," Peter said as he fought back tears.

"Yes," Apollyon smiled wickedly. "Bow down low to the ground, worship me as your god and I will let you and your friends go free. It's so simple."

Peter didn't know what else to do. He didn't want to worship this wicked king, but he didn't want Euripides to be eaten either and he certainly didn't want to be executed. Peter felt as though he had no other choice. Tears streamed down his cheeks as he began to lower himself to his knees.

"Yes," Apollyon smiled wickedly. "All the way down."

Suddenly, a memory popped into Peter's mind. It was his father's funeral. Peter was crying. His mother was crying. Her friends were crying. But one of his father's best friends was not crying. He stood stiff in his crisp blue uniform, white gloves and white hat, his face firm. The Marine turned to Peter and gave him a smile and a wink. After the funeral he had come and spoken to Peter. He told Peter that it was all right to be sad that he had lost his father, but he should be happy for him, too.

"Why?" Peter had asked.

"Because your dad was a brave man who died for what he believed in. We all have to die sometime, Peter, and some people will tell you that the lucky ones are those who live to be old and die quietly in their beds. But I think the lucky ones are those who God allows the honor of dying while fighting for what's right. And that's exactly what your father did. He's up in Heaven watching you, Peter, even now, to see if you will have the courage to fight the good fight, too."

Peter stopped just before his knee hit the stones of the

dungeon cell. "No!" Peter shouted as he thrust out his chin defiantly. His dad would be disappointed to see him bow down before this demon king. If Apollyon wanted to kill him and his friends, so be it. He would not worship him. Then words came out of his mouth that were completely unnatural for him. "The Lord God Almighty rebuke you!" he spat.

Apollyon's face suddenly turned white with fear, but the fear soon evaporated into rage. "You will die!" he shrieked and rushed from the dungeon.

"Well done, Peter!" came Strom's booming voice.

"That will teach the wicked king. We are not his slaves! We serve the Lord Almighty!" Palamedes said.

"I'm glad you didn't worship him, Peter," Euripides said from his little cage. "But I do wish there was some way we could escape. I don't want to be eaten." The gopher began to cry. "It's all my fault," he said.

"How is it your fault?" Peter asked.

"Had I not left the lighted path, we would have never ended up here."

Peter nodded. "But if I had trusted Jesus instead of leaving his light to chase after you, we wouldn't be here either."

"Strom and I could say the same," Palamedes confessed.

"Yes, but if I had not given into vanity and been seduced by fine clothes, a cheering crowd, and the approval of a pretty princess, I would never have been thrown into this cell," Peter explained. "I left the boots, staff, and cloak Nicholas had given me behind for some shiny new silk clothes."

"It was just as much my fault for seeking vain glory, dancing on a stage in front of a cheering crowd," Euripides admitted.

"Pride," came a voice from the darkness of the cell next to Peter's. He saw a man sitting in the shadows and Peter was surprised he had not noticed him before.

"What did you say?" Peter asked.

"I said 'pride.' Pride is a terrible sin. It caused the fall of the devil and the fall of man. It seems it has ensnared you as well," the man explained.

"He's right," Peter said as he slumped down onto the floor. "My pride got me trapped here."

"Mine, too," Euripides agreed.

"You should try praying," the man said. "Ask God to forgive your foolish pride. Ask him to rescue you."

Peter shook his head. "God won't listen to me," he said as he began to sob, laying his head in his arms. "I'm a wicked little monster."

The man stood, walked over to the door of his cell and opened it. He stepped out of his cell and over to Peter's. "All mankind is wicked, Peter Puckett," the man said. "It takes true humility to admit how wicked you are."

Peter looked up, lifted his glasses to wipe the tears from his eyes and then settled them back down on his nose to peer at the man. The man was tall—over six feet—and was very handsome in his violet colored suit and long blood-red cape. He had golden skin and shiny brown hair that fell below his ears. His beard and mustache were well kept and his piercing blue eyes penetrated Peter down to his soul.

Peter also realized that the man had somehow managed to escape his cell. "Who are you?" Peter asked.

The man smiled. "I am Melchizedek, King of Salem and High Priest to the Lord God Almighty!"

"What are you doing in this dungeon?" Strom asked from the other cell.

"Rescuing you, of course," Melchizedek smiled. He then turned to Peter. "You may not pray for your own safety, Peter, but others pray for you all the time. And God is answering their prayers."

"Who?" Peter asked.

"Who? Father Joseph and Ms. Naomi. Of course, Ariel does. And I do."

"Really?" Peter asked. "How do you even know me?"

Melchizedek smiled. "I know everyone, Peter." He then opened the door to Peter's cell without even having a key. "And I knew you would not worship Apollyon." Peter scrambled to his feet as Melchizedek released Strom, Palamedes, and Euripides. Strom and Palamedes recovered their weapons and then joined Melchizedek. "Let's hurry!"

Melchizedek led the way up the stone steps ascending from the dungeon. They somehow avoided all of the guards and slipped out of the castle and back into the fair. Melchizedek led them quickly through the crowd, while trying not to call too much attention to themselves. It didn't work.

"Halt!" came a shout, and all of them turned around to see a squad of armed soldiers charging after them from the castle.

"Run!" Melchizedek shouted. The small party pushed their way through the fair and out the gates into the town. They hurried through the streets of the town to the grassy meadow on its edge. "We've got to get you back to the woods!" They sprinted across the meadow and when they reached the woods, Melchizedek turned to face the charging soldiers. "Go back to the path," he told Peter and the others. "I'll deal with Apollyon's men."

"Deal with them?" Strom asked. "How? You don't even have a sword."

Melchizedek smiled. "I have the sword of God's Holy Word!" he said and reached his hand to his mouth and pulled a long shining blade from his throat, as if he were a circus performer.

"How did you do that?" Euripides asked.

"No time!" Melchizedek shouted. "Hurry!"

"But how do we find the path?" Peter asked, the concern ringing in his voice.

"Christ will lead you," Melchizedek told him. "Just follow your heart!"

Peter nodded, took a deep breath, and stepped into the woods.

"I will stay and fight with you!" Palamedes declared to Melchizedek.

"I thank you for your courage, my elvish friend, but Peter needs you more than I!"

"As you command, Your Majesty!" Palamedes said with a flourishing bow. He then followed Peter and the others into the woods. Before he disappeared, however, Palamedes glanced back to see Melchizedek charging the squad of soldiers with his sword drawn. Then Palamedes noticed a white owl flapping its wings as it flew over the field toward the woods chasing Peter and the others.

CHAPTER TWENTY
THE CHAPEL ON THE HILL

Peter ran as fast as he could, which wasn't as fast as before because he was no longer wearing his miraculous boots. Nor did he have his cloak or staff, but he did have his life, and Peter desperately wanted to keep it. Euripides was riding on Peter's shoulder as normal and Strom was right on his heels. Peter hoped that Palamedes was not too far behind the dwarf.

Peter wasn't sure if he was running in the right direction to find the lighted path, but he was trusting God to lead him there. He was beginning to learn to let go and let the Lord take care of him. After all, how many times had Peter thought he was going to die only to be saved at the last minute? Peter was terrified of the darkness of the woods but tried to suppress that fear as he ran. What good would being afraid do him anyway? As he ran, he saw movements in the shadows to his right and left. Then he heard something fluttering above his head.

HOOT! HOOT!

THE CHAPEL ON THE HILL

Peter glanced up to see the white owl above them. *Wicked omen!* Just as the thought left his mind, night stalkers leapt out of the shadows on both sides, growling fiercely as they charged toward Peter on all fours, their white fangs glistening in the darkness. Peter screamed in terror as the beast on his left pounced. Its jaws were so close to Peter's face that Peter could smell the dog breath, but just before they clamped down, Strom slammed the creature with his mighty hammer. The beast sailed off into the darkness with an agonizing yelp!

The wolf on Peter's right came in for the kill next. Strom had no time to turn and hit it before it took Peter down. But to Peter's great surprise, Euripides leapt from his shoulder and met the wolf in midair, chomping down on the beast's ear with his sharp teeth. The night stalker yelped in pain as it violently shook its head, tossing Euripides into the leaves of the forest floor. The night stalker bared its wolf-like fangs and was about to pounce on Euripides when Sir Palamedes appeared out of nowhere, sword drawn, and positioned himself between the night stalker and the small gopher. The wolf leapt at the elf, but it didn't stand a chance. The small knight used his sword to make short work of the beast and the night stalker collapsed dead in a heap.

Peter rushed to Euripides and found him lying completely still. Peter scooped the gopher up into his arms. "Euripides!" he exclaimed, afraid his friend was dead.

The gopher peaked through the slits in his eyes. "Is it gone?" he asked Peter.

Peter smiled at the gopher who had played opossum. "Yes, Sir Palamedes took care of the night stalker."

Euripides lifted his head to look at the small knight. "Thank you, Sir Palamedes," the gopher said with relief in his voice.

CHAPTER TWENTY

Palamedes gave the gopher a flourishing bow. "My pleasure, my brave friend," he smiled.

"You saved my life again," Peter told Euripides. "You are the bravest gopher I have ever met."

Euripides smiled. "Really?"

"Yes!" Peter exclaimed.

HOOT! HOOT!

"We should hurry before that wicked owl calls more of its fiendish friends to attack us!" Strom suggested.

Peter glanced up at the owl perched in the top branches of a tree and nodded. "Let's go," he said. He placed Euripides back on top of his shoulder and once again began to sprint through the dark woods as fast as he could. Strom and Palamedes followed close behind. Peter suddenly stopped in his tracks causing Strom to run into him, knocking him forward.

"What in the…?" Strom began, but then glanced up to see what had caused Peter to halt. Standing in the woods not twenty feet in front of them was a black figure, in a black cloak, holding a black sword. "Shedom," Strom whispered through dry lips. The demon began walking toward Peter and his friends taking slow and deliberate steps. It clearly sought to terrify them before it killed them. Demons always get a thrill out of terrifying their victims.

"Get behind us!" Palamedes instructed Peter as he and Strom moved to the front. The elf knew that they could not outrun the shedom because it could reappear anywhere darkness existed, and in the Shadow Wood, they were surrounded by darkness.

Peter shivered, terrified of the demon moving toward them. He didn't think Strom and Palamedes could possibly defeat a shedom, and without his staff or other weapon, he was useless in a fight. He wished Ariel were there to save them. Tears began to build in his eyes. Then he remembered what Ariel had said when he asked why she couldn't come. "Because you don't need me," Ariel had told him. "Christ is all you need."

Suddenly Peter realized why Ariel was not allowed to accompany him into the woods. Jesus wanted Peter and his friends to depend on Him to save them. Having his guardian angel there allowed Peter to depend completely on Ariel without realizing it was the Lord Jesus Christ who had sent her to guard him in the first place.

Peter wiped the tears from his eyes as he watched the shedom move closer and closer. "All I need is Christ," Peter whispered to himself as he lowered himself to his knees to pray. "Please Lord, save me and my friends from the darkness. I trust in You!"

The shedom raised its sword just before it reached Palamedes and Strom who both readied for the attack.

"Oh merciful Lord, guide us to safety with Your Holy Light!" Peter said but was unsure where those words had come from. He did not normally talk like that. But it didn't matter. Before the shedom could drop its dark blade, a brilliant light engulfed Peter and his friends. The shedom shrieked in anger as it could not enter the light to harm Peter.

Peter then noticed that the light formed a path, starting with them and stretching out into the darkness cutting through the forest. Peter smiled. He had never needed to find the path. He simply had to trust in Christ and the Lord would show him the path through the darkness.

"Aha!" Strom shouted excitedly.

"Praise Jesus!" Sir Palamedes smiled.

"Let's hurry!" Peter cried as he began to run along the illuminated path. The shedom shrieked again, but this time no one feared it. Jesus was protecting them, and they all realized it. Euripides stuck his tongue out at the demon as they ran away.

It was not long before the Light of Christ led them out of the darkness of the Shadow Wood. Peter laughed excitedly as he and his friends stepped from the tree line and into a well lit field at the base of the hill. He turned to see the others laughing with glee as well.

"I thought our goose was cooked for sure," Strom said. "But the Lord delivered us again and again."

Peter nodded. "I've learned Jesus can always save me, even when it looks like it's impossible."

Sir Palamedes nodded. "And that, my young friend, is one of the most valuable lessons you could ever learn," he smiled.

HOOT! HOOT!

All eyes turned skyward to see the white owl soaring out of the tree line and fluttering down toward them. Strom and Palamedes raised their weapons, expecting the bird to attack, but instead there was a flash of light blinding them and when they could see again Ariel stood where the owl had been.

"Ariel!" Peter cried and rushed to the angel wrapping his arms around her. She returned his embrace. "It was you," he said. "You were the white owl."

"Yes, Peter," she smiled. "I was watching over you."

"But you said you couldn't go into the woods," Peter insisted.

"No, I said your guardian angel could not enter the woods with you," she smiled. "The point was for you to learn to depend on the Lord instead of me. You didn't realize I was there and so you never depended on me. You learned to trust the Lord, and you survived."

Peter frowned and dropped his head in shame. "But I left

the path," he said. "And I was vain and prideful. I just cared about attention and these pretty clothes." He looked down at his silk clothes, but they were no longer pretty. In fact, they looked like the rags of a beggar—torn, dirty, and ratty. "What happened?" he asked.

Ariel frowned. "The treasures we think we have in the world are mere rags," she explained. "True treasures come from God."

Peter nodded his understanding. "But I left my gifts behind," he said angry at himself. "I can't believe I was so stupid to leave them."

Ariel laughed. "Gifts from the Holy Spirit are not so easily parted with," she smiled. She reached behind her wings and produced his staff, cloak, boots, and even his old clothes.

Peter shouted with glee! "Thank you, Ariel!" he exclaimed.

She handed them to him. "You are going to fall sometimes, Peter, but when you do, you need to turn back to Jesus. Ask His forgiveness and start following Him again. That's exactly what you did." Peter smiled. "Now change quickly, I fear darkfall is almost upon us."

Ariel turned away from him to survey the horizon as Peter stripped off his rags and put his old clothes back on, including his boots and cloak. Then, with staff in hand, he was ready to go. "We must hurry," Ariel said, realizing the light was beginning to fade. "There is a chapel at the top of the next hill. We will be safe there."

Ariel led the way with Peter and the others following close behind. Peter wore his miraculous boots that could propel him forward at incredible speeds, but he didn't want to outrun his friends. As they crested the first hill, a large shadow began to fall over the land!

"Darkfall!" Strom shouted frantically. He heard a

thunderous sound behind him and turned to see a hundred se'irim, emboldened by the darkness, emerging from the Shadow Wood to give chase.

Peter and the others sprinted down the hill and began to ascend the second. Peter could see the small chapel at the top of the hill, but knew they would not reach it before the shadow reached them. Ariel must have realized it as well, for she turned to Peter and shouted, "Peter, run as fast as you can!"

Peter nodded before darting off toward the chapel, his miraculous boots carrying him and Euripides way ahead of the others. He just had to make it inside of the chapel and he would be safe. He was so close now. Almost there. But the shadow overtook him and drenched the entire hill in darkness.

"Look out!" Euripides shouted directly into his ear as a shedom suddenly appeared from the shadow between Peter and the chapel. Peter skidded to a stop as the shedom drew its long black blade from its sheath. Peter changed directions, running parallel with the chapel and hoping to swing around behind it. The shedom, however, vanished into the darkness and reappeared right in front of Peter again.

"It rides the darkness!" Euripides told him. "We can't outrun it!"

"Stick, attack the shedom!" Peter shouted and his staff flew from his hand toward the shadow demon. The shedom raised its jagged black blade to defend itself from the staff. While it was distracted, Peter turned and ran back in the other direction, heading toward the chapel's entrance. Unfortunately, another shedom appeared right in front of him. Peter had no weapons to fight, but he wasn't out of tricks.

Peter snatched Euripides off his shoulder and pulled him close to his body. He then threw the hood of his cloak up over his head and curled up into a ball, seemingly disappearing into the darkness. The shedom hissed as it searched for the boy, swinging its sword wildly. The blade moved closer and closer to Peter and was just about to strike him when it was suddenly stopped with a thunderous clang.

Peter peeked out from behind his cloak to see Ariel had arrived in a flash to do combat with the shedom. The demon shrieked at the angel before turning its sword to swing at her. The two blades clanged again and then Ariel went on the offensive. The shedom backed up as Ariel got the upperhand. But then the demon's comrade joined the fight. Ignoring the staff that kept hitting him in the helmet, the shedom leapt at Ariel. The angel raised her shield to block the blow just in time.

Ariel then spread her wings wide and she shone so brightly with light that she momentarily blinded both demons. She flapped her magnificent wings and rose up into the air. "She can fly again," Peter whispered excitedly to Euripides. "The Lord has finally healed her wing."

The two shedom screeched at her, but she was beyond their reach. As they leapt into the air trying to reach her, Strom and Palamedes caught up with them and attacked. The shedom quickly turned to defend themselves, and when they did Ariel dove back to the ground, slicing each of the demons with her sword, causing both to burn up in a bright light.

Peter's staff dropped to the ground, and he stood and rushed toward it, scooping it up with his hand. Ariel landed back on top of the hill as Palamedes and Strom bowed gracefully to her. She smiled, but then her attention turned to the horde of se'irim charging up the hill toward them. "Get inside quickly," she commanded and they rushed to obey. Strom reached the door first and swung it open allowing Peter, Euripides, Palamedes, and Ariel to enter before closing the door behind them.

The chapel was simple, but pretty. There were no stained glass windows or ornate portraits, but there was a marble altar with a golden crucifix suspended from the ceiling above it, depicting Jesus dying on the cross. Behind the altar was a large golden door encrusted with shimmering jewels. It looked just like the door Peter and Ariel had gone through when they entered Evermore.

Palamedes ran to the window and peered out at the se'irim that surrounded the chapel howling and snorting, with anger that their prey was safe inside the chapel. "They are everywhere," the knight exclaimed.

"This is holy ground—they may not enter," Ariel explained. "We are safe as long as we stay inside. They will disperse at lightrise."

"I thought you said some demons can enter a church," Peter reminded Ariel.

Ariel nodded. "Yes," she said. "But they will have no reason to after you and I leave."

"You and Peter?" Strom asked in confusion.

Ariel glanced down at him. "Yes, Master dwarf. Peter and I have come to our destination and it is time we left Evermore."

"Leave?" Euripides shouted. "You're leaving?"

"Yes, Euripides," Ariel said. "And I am afraid the three of you must remain here."

Euripides began to cry. "But I want to stay with Peter," he said.

This caused Peter to cry, too. "Can't Euripides come with us?" he asked. "He can live with me."

"Yeah!" Euripides agreed.

"I'm afraid not, Peter. Euripides must stay in Evermore

with the others," Ariel said. "Now say your good-byes."

Peter nodded as he wiped the tears from his eyes. He stepped over to Strom who was fighting back tears himself. "Thank you for all of your help, Master Strom," Peter said.

"No, my boy, thank you!" Strom threw his arms around Peter and pulled the boy into a tight squeeze before releasing him.

Peter then stepped over to Sir Palamedes. "You are the bravest elf I have ever known," he said.

Palamedes nodded. "That is because I am the bravest elf to ever live," he smiled. "The next time I see you, I will finally tell you the tale of how I captured the Questing Beast."

"I'd like that," Peter smiled and then bent down and hugged the tiny knight.

Finally, Peter stepped over to Euripides. The gopher was crying. Peter scooped him up into his arms and squeezed him tight. "I'm going to miss you most of all," he whispered in his ear.

"Will you ever come back?" Euripides asked.

"Perhaps," Ariel said gently. "If the Lord wills it."

Peter placed a kiss on Euripides' furry cheek and then set the gopher on the ground. He turned to Ariel.

"Are you ready?" she asked. Peter nodded. "Good." She then looked past him at the others. "It was an honor to meet you three. Remember to always trust in the Lord and seek His will instead of your own."

"Yes, Your Grace," Strom, Palamedes, and Euripides said as they bowed at the waist.

"Do you still have the key?" Ariel asked and Peter nodded. The giant key still hung from a golden chain around his neck and Peter pulled it out from under his shirt. "Open the door."

Peter crossed the chapel, walked past the altar, and inserted

CHAPTER TWENTY

the key into the door. He turned it, and the door opened.

"Peter!" Strom called, and Peter turned around to face him. "The Lord be with you."

Peter smiled at his friend. "And with your spirit," he said. Then he and Ariel stepped through the door, leaving Evermore behind.

CHAPTER TWENTY-ONE
THE MERMAID'S KISS

Peter stepped through the door and into a small church. The church had no stain glass windows, nor were there any pews. In fact, besides the modest altar and large crucifix hanging on the wall, one might not even realize it was a church at all. The church was inside of a strip mall in an abandoned dollar store, with large glass windows in the front and rows of metal folding chairs facing the altar, where the congregation sat. Peter smiled. He recognized the church immediately.

Holy Spirit on the Sea was a small church in Southern California that he and his parents had attended when his father was stationed at Camp Pendleton. He and Ariel had crossed the length of the United States in their journey through Evermore, from the East Coast to the West Coast. The church was in the cozy beach community where Peter's family had rented an apartment—the same apartment that he and his mother were living in when his father went to war and never came home. Peter's smile turned to a frown. The last time he had been in this church had been at a memorial for his father.

Peter stepped past the altar, crossed between the folding chairs, and stood in front of the large glass front. It was dark outside, but the parking lot was illuminated by street lamps. Still, Peter could see the Pacific Ocean just on the other side of the street. He knew the pier was nearby. His parents used to take him for walks there when he was little. Those were such happy times, before his father had been killed and his mother had become sick.

Peter began to cry. He felt ill, like he wanted to throw up. He turned around to face Ariel who stood just in front of the altar, watching him. "Why did you bring me here?" he asked. The angel flashed a sympathetic smile as she walked over to him, placing her arms around him and pulling him close to her. He hugged her tight as he wept.

"I brought you here because this was the closest door to where you need to go next," Ariel explained as she knelt down and wiped tears from his face. "But I do not think this is a coincidence. In fact, what humans often call coincidences are really the Lord's work. And the Lord is hard at work with you, Peter."

Peter sniffed and wiped his nose with the sleeve of his shirt. "So, where do we go now?" he asked.

Ariel shook her head. "*We* do not go anywhere," she told him. "I am staying here in the church until you return. But you must walk down to the pier and jump off the end into the water. You will swim down deep into the depths of the sea, through the waters of the Leviathan."

A look of horror washed over Peter's face. "You mean I have to swim in the ocean alone?" he asked. "I'm not supposed to ever swim without an adult."

Ariel smiled. "And that is an excellent rule to follow. But

just this once, the Lord wants you to jump in without an adult."

"All alone?" he asked.

"You will not be alone, Peter," Ariel said. "The Lord will be with you."

"Will you be there again, like last time, disguised as a fish or something?"

Ariel frowned. "Not this time, Peter," she told him. "I really cannot leave the church until you return. But I would not be surprised if the Lord sent others to help you on your journey."

Peter turned and looked back out through the window at the ocean. "What am I supposed to do after I swim past the Leviathan?" he asked.

"You must enter the Realm of Goblins," she explained. "And there you will find the Amulet of Eternity."

The thought of entering the Realm of Goblins was even more terrifying than jumping off the pier and evading the Leviathan. Peter remembered how scary the goblin he'd seen with Apollyon was. The mere thought of the wicked creature sent a chill up Peter's spine and he began to tremble.

"I'm too scared," he said.

Ariel placed a finger on his cheek and turned his head back to face her. "You have already faced shedom, se'irim, a bugbear, night stalkers, and Apollyon himself, one of the devil's top princes." she said. "You are extremely brave."

"But I didn't do those things alone. You were there, and Strom, and Euripides, and Sir Palamedes."

Ariel nodded. "And Jesus," she smiled. "Don't forget that Jesus and His Holy Spirit were there as well. Though you did not see Them, They were always there, watching us and protecting us from harm. If you continue to have faith in

245

God, He will not leave you alone."

"Promise?" Peter asked.

Ariel smiled and pulled him back into an embrace. "I promise, Peter," she said. "There is nothing in the entire universe which I am more sure of." She pulled away again and peered deeply into his eyes. "Trust in the Lord, and He will guide you and protect you, and save your mother as well."

Peter nodded. He did not want to do this. He was more terrified than he'd ever been in his entire life, but he had to, to save his mother.

"Are you ready?" Ariel asked.

"I guess so," Peter shrugged.

"Let's pray together," she smiled and he nodded as he squeezed his eyes closed. "Holy Lord, please watch over Your servant, Peter, as he begins this very dangerous quest. He is doing Your holy will, oh Lord, and we trust that You will guide and protect him throughout his mission. All these things we ask in the name of the Father, the Son, and the Holy Spirit."

"Amen," Peter said. He felt better. The prayer helped.

Ariel rose and stepped over to the door, turning the latch and unlocking it. She pushed the door open. "You have everything you need?" she asked him.

Peter nodded. "I have my staff, my cloak, my boots," he said and then looked up at her with a smile. "And I have the Lord."

Ariel kissed him on top of the head. "Good, boy," she smiled. "Be careful and have faith."

"I will," Peter replied and then stepped through the doorway into the parking lot.

"The Lord be with you," Ariel said.

"And with your spirit," Peter replied. He then turned and walked across the parking lot toward the beach as Ariel watched him go. Peter exited the parking lot, looking both ways before crossing the street. It was late and the street was empty, so he quickly dashed across, then down a small hill, past a couple of houses, across a railroad track and onto the beach.

Peter saw the pier to his right and made his way there as quickly as he could. He stepped onto the pier, and when he did, he noticed a homeless man asleep, curled up with a thin blanket covering him. The sound of Peter's footsteps must have jarred the man awake, because he sat up and looked at Peter.

He was an older black man, with gray in his beard and temples. He wore a red USMC hat, and beside him was a small piece of worn cardboard with the words "Homeless vet please help," scrawled in black marker. Peter's eyes met the old man's, and the man flashed a friendly smile at him.

"You're out pretty late, young man," the old Marine said.

Peter nodded. "Yes, sir," he replied. "I'm sorry, but I have to hurry."

"Okay, I won't hold you up, but could you spare a few dollars so I can get me some breakfast in the morning?"

Peter frowned. He looked at this poor old Marine Corps veteran and wanted to help. His dad was a Marine after all. Peter felt such pity for him, but he hadn't brought any money with him. "I'm sorry, I don't have any," he told the man.

"That's all right," the old man said and started to lie back down. Suddenly, Peter remembered the emerald in his pocket that Strom had given him. He pulled it from his pocket and looked at it. It was beautiful. He had planned on selling it to buy a house for him and his mother, but as he looked at the homeless man sleeping on the pier, his heart filled with compassion. He didn't need this emerald. He would have his mother, and that would be good enough.

CHAPTER TWENTY-ONE

"I do have this," he said, and the homeless man sat up again. Peter stepped over to the man and handed him the giant emerald.

"Is this real?" the man asked as he peered at the shiny green gem.

"I think so," Peter replied.

"This must be worth a fortune," the man said. He looked up and his eyes met Peter's. Peter saw tears there. Tears of joy and relief. "Thank you, young man," he said. "You are truly building up treasure in Heaven that will neither rust nor spoil," the man said and then lay back down, curling up with his emerald.

Peter continued past the homeless veteran and along the pier until he finally came to the end. He climbed up on the rail and peered over at the waves rolling by beneath him. A cool wind blew past. Peter knew the water would be cold. The Pacific Ocean near Southern California was cold even during the summer, and so Peter expected it to be miserably cold tonight. But the cold was the least of his worries. He suddenly had a fear that sharks were waiting just below to gobble him up. Then he remembered the Leviathan. He sighed. *I can't do this*, he thought.

Peter shook the thought from his head. He had to do it. If he didn't, his mother would surely die. He had to have faith that Jesus Christ would watch over him. Peter slowly climbed on top of the rail and swung his legs over the edge, allowing his feet to dangle. He sat there for a long time trying to build up the courage. Then he squeezed his eyes tight. "Lord, please give me the faith and courage to do Your will," he prayed. When he opened his eyes he felt much better.

"Here goes," he said and leapt over the side into the cold water with a splash. Peter sank quickly, weighed down by his clothes and boots. In fact, he forgot all about the sharks and even the Leviathan as he began to fear he would drown instead. Then something moved nearby and he remembered the sharks. He panicked as it swam toward him. But when the creature's face stopped right in front of Peter's, he realized it was not a shark at all, but a dolphin.

The dolphin squealed something and then swam around Peter and underneath his arm. Peter suddenly realized what the dolphin wanted him to do. He grabbed hold of the dolphin's dorsal fin and the dolphin swished its tail, diving deep into the blackness of the ocean and pulling Peter along with it.

Peter rode the dolphin deeper and deeper, amazed that the ocean was this deep here by the pier. It seemed to go on forever. In fact, Peter was quickly running out of air and was beginning to panic when the dolphin suddenly stopped swimming. Peter let go of its fin, and the dolphin hurried away. Then Peter saw something else. A girl was swimming toward him. No, it wasn't a girl. It was a mermaid.

The mermaid smiled as she brought her face close to his, her dark hair dancing in the water all around her. She then reached up and took hold of the back of his head. To Peter's surprise, she pulled his head toward her own and pressed her lips to his. The mermaid was kissing him. She forced his mouth open, and Peter felt air rush into his mouth and then into his lungs. She wasn't kissing him. She was helping him breathe.

The mermaid pulled away again, and took him by the hand. "My name is Amatheia," she said. Then Peter realized she hadn't said anything at all because her lips had not moved. Instead, Peter had heard the voice in his head.

"I'm Peter," he said inside his mind, and the mermaid

beamed.

"Come on, Peter," Amatheia replied. "We must hurry before the Leviathan catches us out here in the open." She swished her tail and swam deeper into the ocean. Just as Peter was beginning to run out of air again, Amatheia turned and pressed her lips to his, filling his lungs with oxygen once more. He was starting to enjoy swimming with a mermaid.

"The Lord sent me to find you, Peter," came Amatheia's voice in his head, "to guide you to the entrance to the Realm of the Goblins." She turned her head to gaze at him as she swam. "You must have a lot of courage."

Peter smiled. "Not really," he thought. "But I have learned to have faith."

Amatheia pulled him into a cavern near the ocean floor. They swam into the darkness until they finally popped out in a cave that formed some kind of bubble underwater. Peter took a deep breath filling his lungs with air.

"Are you all right?" Amatheia asked. This time her lips did move.

"Yes, I'm okay," Peter replied.

The mermaid guided him to the edge of the little pool where he took hold of some rocks and pulled himself out of the water. He turned around to look at Amatheia. "Is this how the goblins get in and out?" he asked, thinking the one he saw did not look very aquatic.

"No," she laughed. "They have another way. This is a back entrance, one they do not normally worry about, because it is guarded by the Leviathan."

Peter nodded and stood up. "Thank you, Amatheia, for all of your help."

"I will wait for you here, Peter, and help you back to the surface."

Peter smiled gratefully, very glad to hear that.

"Thank you," he said. "I'll be as quick as I can." He turned to walk into the cave.

"May the Lord be with you," the mermaid said.

"And with your spirit," Peter replied. He found a tunnel and entered it, praying that God would guide him to the Amulet of Eternity.

CHAPTER TWENTY-TWO
THE REALM OF GOBLINS

Peter felt his way along the cold stone walls of the tunnel. It was pitch black and he could not see anything. He tripped and stumbled, falling to the hard rocks and banging his knee. "Ouch!" he cried as the pain shot through him. This trek was slow and dangerous, and Peter wished that he had Euripides to guide him in the darkness. Or even better, the power to light the tunnel like Ariel had illuminated the tunnels in Evermore. Suddenly it struck Peter, that Ariel did not have the power to do that. In fact, Ariel had no power at all. All of her power actually came from God. If God would illuminate the tunnels in Evermore, why would He not illuminate them here?

Peter rolled over onto his knees. "Lord," he prayed. "Please light this tunnel, so that I can find my way through it. You are the light of the world, Lord, and I need that light now, desperately."

Peter used his staff to push himself back to his feet and as he did so a thought flashed through his mind. Ariel had slammed her sword down on the stone floor to illuminate the tunnels in Evermore. He should do that here. He raised his staff above his head, and then, while having faith that the Lord would answer his prayer, he slammed the staff down against the rocks. But nothing happened. Peter sighed. Why wasn't God answering his prayer? Peter sat down in the dark. He was so confused. Father Joe said God would always answer prayers.

Peter slammed the staff against the floor again. "C'mon light up!" he said, but nothing happened, and he wondered what was going on. Was God really not going to answer him? He slammed his staff against the floor one more time, and when nothing happened he got angry. He was about to shout, to scream at God, but then he realized, God *had* answered his prayer.

Peter sat down in the dark, ashamed of himself for getting angry at God. Who was he to get angry at the creator of the universe? He was treating God like He was a genie in a bottle. He acted as though God were the servant, when in reality, Peter was God's servant. God had answered Peter's prayer, just as Father Joe had promised He would. Peter just didn't like the answer. In this long journey to save his mother, this was the first time God had answered Peter with a flat "No."

Peter pushed himself back to his feet and felt along the cold stone walls, moving slowly as not to fall. It took a long time, feeling around in the darkness of the tunnel, but Peter eventually saw light up ahead. He crept up to the light, noticing that it poured through a hole in a stone wall in front of him. He got down on his hands and knees and stuck his head close to the hole so that he could see out. What he saw was a large cavernous room with torches lining the walls, throwing dancing shadows everywhere.

CHAPTER TWENTY-TWO

Then Peter heard the scratchy voices of goblins talking not far away. He moved closer to the hole and could see two of the disgusting creatures standing just a few feet from him, holding long spears as if on guard. Peter suddenly realized why God had refused to grant his prayer to light the tunnel. The goblin guards would have noticed the light and been alerted that he was there. Peter scolded himself again. He had to remember that God, not he, always knew what was best. Peter watched the goblins who were too busy chatting to notice him.

"Why are we even here?" one of the goblins asked.

"Because His Highness doesn't want the boy to get through," said the other.

The first goblin laughed a scratchy cackle. "How would a human boy swim past the Leviathan and get in here?" it asked its friend.

"I don't know," the second admitted with a snicker. "Seems to me the Leviathan would have had itself a tasty treat."

"Oh yes, I don't think the Leviathan likes anything better than little boy," cackled the first.

"Except maybe little girl!" exclaimed the second and they both laughed so hard they doubled over while holding their bellies. Peter acted quickly, seizing the opportunity to scurry out of the hole and into the large cavernous room. He attempted to sneak past the goblins and out of the room, but one of them suddenly spotted him.

"Hey!" it screeched. "Halt!" The other turned around and saw Peter as well. Both pointed their spears at him. But Peter had no intention of halting.

"Stick, attack the goblins!" he commanded and the staff leapt from his hand slamming the first atop its skull and sending the creature to the stone floor. It then swung at the second goblin, but the goblin blocked it with its spear.

"Stop that!" the goblin hissed at the stick, but the stick did not stop. In fact it kept right on until it smacked the goblin in the chin, knocking the creature backward to land in a heap on the floor.

"Stick, return!" Peter commanded and his staff flew back to his outstretched hand. Peter hurried out of the room and into another tunnel. This one was much larger than the one he had followed from the sea and was thankfully illuminated by torchlight. He hurried along the tunnel quickly, but carefully, not wanting to run right into a trap. Peter heard the sounds of goblin feet pounding on the stone floor and moving toward him. He froze and glanced around, frantically searching for a place to hide until he remembered his cloak. He pulled the hood over his head and crouched beside the wall. The cloak blended in with the dark stone of the cavern and a squad of armed goblins hurried past without noticing him.

Peter watched the goblins disappear around a bend in the tunnel before straightening and hurrying away. The goblins had probably heard the screams of the guards Peter's staff had knocked unconscious and were investigating. When they found their comrades, they would come back searching for him.

Peter ran along the tunnel quickly, but still not as fast as his boots could carry him. He soon came to a large room with tunnels branching in many different directions. The middle one had stairs leading upward. Peter didn't know which way to go. He remembered that when Father Joe and Ms. Naomi couldn't decide what to do, they always "let the Holy Spirit guide them." Peter wasn't sure exactly what that meant, but he knew it involved trusting God, much like when he trusted Christ to reveal His light in the Shadow Wood.

CHAPTER TWENTY-TWO

Peter took a deep breath and tried to clear his thoughts. "Which way, Lord?" he asked silently. He surrendered his own thoughts and desires, giving in and allowing the Holy Spirit to guide him. He felt the Spirit leading him up the stairs, and Peter climbed and climbed. Peter eventually emerged from the tunnels to the surface of the goblin's world.

It was dark, but unlike in Evermore, Peter did see a moon shining in the sky illuminating the night. There were trees, but they reminded Peter of those in the Shadow Wood—black, gnarled and twisted. A small path wound through the trees, and Peter followed it. He soon came to a clearing and could see a dark castle atop a rocky hill in the distance. The top of the castle was made of black twisted spirals stabbing menacingly into the air.

"The amulet must be there," Peter said to himself and continued through the clearing toward the castle. He walked for a long time before he finally emerged from the trees into what appeared to be a small village of mud huts made of earth, sticks, and stones. There he saw lots of goblins. It was an entire town full of goblins. They all stared at him in horror as he passed through. He also noticed several fauns, small creatures with horns, tails, and two legs that looked like a goat, but with bodies and a head that looked human. He also saw centaurs, creatures with lower bodies like a horse, but with upper bodies like those of men.

The fauns and centaurs appeared to be slaves to the goblins who whipped them mercilessly. Peter's eyes met those of a faun, and the creature's brown eyes held complete sadness. Peter noticed a leash around the faun's neck and a goblin holding the other end.

The goblins stopped whatever they were doing to stare at Peter, but did not interfere with him until he reached the center of town. There two goblins armed with short swords stepped into his path.

"Halt, boy!" one sneered. "You're the one His Highness is looking for."

Peter stopped dead in his tracks and stared at the two goblins before him. "Am I?"

"Yes," the goblin said.

"And who is His Highness?" Peter asked.

"Igwurm, Prince of the goblins of course," the second goblin replied.

"Why would a prince be looking for me?" Peter asked. "I'm a nobody."

The two goblins glanced at one another and then back at Peter as their lips spread into large but wicked smiles. "Likely to eat you," one of them cackled.

Peter didn't like the sound of that at all. "Stick, attack the goblins!" he shouted, and his staff flew from his hand and smacked one of the goblins in the face and then the other one. The two goblin soldiers were taken care of quickly. "Stick, return!" Peter commanded and the staff flew back into his hand. He smiled proudly to himself, having defeated four goblins without any help at all. In fact, he became so proud of himself, that he did not notice the entire village had surrounded him and just as he was about to continue on his journey they pounced. Peter had no hope of escape as the goblins overwhelmed him, stripping him of his staff and binding him with rope.

"So the Prince wants him, does he?" one of the goblins snarled.

"Fetch us a proper reward," laughed another.

Then singing and laughing a dark song about stewing a little boy in a pot, a score of goblins carried Peter out of the village and up the hill to the castle. Peter cursed his own foolishness. He had become too confident in his own abilities, forgetting that it was not he who controlled the miraculous staff, but the Lord. Now he was once again in danger of being eaten.

The goblins carried Peter into the throne room of Prince Igwurm. The room was dark except for a few torches, but Peter could see the heads of bulls, bears, and lions adorning the walls as trophies. He assumed that Igwurm had killed them. Peter noticed the prince himself sitting on the throne. The prince was larger than the other goblins, with a round belly and a pointy nose at least a foot long. He wore a silver crown on his head and in his hand he held a scepter as long as a spear. All of the goblins with Peter quickly fell down on their faces before the prince.

Prince Igwurm stared at the mass of goblins bowing before him. He sneered, clearly unhappy to have been disturbed by such common filth as these. "Lower," he said in a hoarse voice, and Peter saw all of the goblins lie down on their bellies, groveling before the prince.

"That's better," Igwurm sneered. "And why have you disturbed my royal greatness?"

"W-we h-have the b-boy," stammered one of the goblins.

Igwurm quickly rose to his feet. They had his attention now. He spotted Peter and a wickedly gleeful grin spread across his face. "Oh yes, there he is," Igwurm cackled. "The little boy that King Apollyon is so afraid of."

Afraid? Peter couldn't understand why Apollyon would be afraid of him. Igwurm made his way down the steps from his throne to the cold stone floor below. He walked over to Peter, his metal scepter clanging against the stones with every other step. He reached Peter and stood over him, looking at the boy lying on the floor bound in ropes.

"What is your name boy?" the prince asked.

"Peter," he replied.

Igwurm threw back his head and laughed a terrifying laugh. "This is the boy!" He shook his head, but then turned back to Peter. "Why is Apollyon so afraid of you, boy?"

"I don't know," Peter said honestly.

"Are you really an angel in disguise?" the prince asked as he took a wary step backward.

"No, sir," Peter said. "I'm just an ordinary boy."

"Is that right?" Igwurm asked.

"Yes, sir," Peter said.

Igwurm turned to the goblins still lying on their bellies before him. "You have done well," he said.

"Do we get a reward?" one of the goblins asked.

"Yes, I think so," the prince smiled. "For doing such a good job, you may kiss my royal feet." Gleeful cheers rose from the prostrate goblins, and they all crawled toward him to press their lips against Igwurm's claw-like toes. "Am I not magnanimous?" Some even began to fight for their spot at the prince's feet.

"Enough!" Igwurm shouted, suddenly annoyed. "Get out!"

The goblins rose from their bellies and hurried out of the throne room. Igwurm turned away from Peter and began to ascend to his throne once again. When he reached the throne, he turned and plopped himself down. "Lift him up," the prince commanded and two guards rushed forward to lift Peter to his feet where he could see the prince.

"Tell me boy, why did you come to my realm?" he asked. "Did you travel all of the way here to kiss my royal feet?" At that, the prince pointed to the floor in front of him and the guards chuckled as they threw Peter to his belly before Igwurm. "Beg me, and I may let you."

"Actually no, I didn't," Peter said.

"Oh?" Igwurm said as if he were surprised. But then he reached behind him and pulled out a small metal box, the same box a goblin had taken to King Apollyon. "Did you come for this?"

"The Amulet of Eternity!" Peter exclaimed as he looked up from his belly.

"Yes," the goblin prince sneered. "It is mine. One of my most prized possessions."

"Please may I have it, Your Highness?" Peter asked.

Igwurm threw his head back and laughed. "No!" he shouted. "You will no doubt use it for some horrifying purpose!"

"I simply want to use it to save my mother," Peter said.

"EXACTLY!" Igwurm roared. "How terrible that would be if your mother were saved! How disgusting it is when little boys like you do a nice thing for others! How horrible it is for you to be filled with joy! If you saved your mother you would no doubt throw your arms around her and cry on her shoulder all happy to see her alive."

"Yes!" Peter exclaimed.

"Yuck!" the goblin said as he spat on the ground beside his throne. "It would be ever so much more splendid if she died. It would be so much more beautiful if you wept for years and years because you would never see your little mommy again!" the prince cackled. "I have half a mind to let you go, so that you can return home and watch her die. Oh how I would love nothing more than to see you weeping, knowing you had failed. Knowing how close you had come, before being defeated by Igwurm, prince of goblins."

THE REALM OF GOBLINS

Igwurm thought about that with a broad, but twisted smile on his rotten face. Then his smile turned into a frown. "Unfortunately, Apollyon would likely skin me alive if I let you go." He turned to stare at Peter. "So I'll just have to be satisfied with watching you die knowing you failed. That will be good enough." He turned to the guards "Take him..." he began, but was interrupted when a door leading to the throne room opened and two goblins strolled in arguing with one another.

"Ugh," the prince said. He looked down at Peter. "My own children," he informed Peter, as if hoping Peter would be sympathetic with the fact that he had two such miserable kids.

"Father!" shrieked one. "It's true, you've captured the boy."

"I knew you would, Father!" exclaimed the other. They circled Peter and motioned for the guards to lift him to his feet again. Peter was relieved to be off his belly.

One of the goblins leaned in close, his pointy nose almost touching Peter's. "You are hideous," it sneered. He then backed up. "I am Pusglob, the prince's only son!" he said as if Peter should be deeply honored to be in his presence.

The other goblin pushed Pusglob aside. "And I am Stankle, his royal daughter!"

Peter's eyes danced back and forth from Pusglob to Stankle, but could not tell that Stankle was female. "You're a girl?" Peter asked somewhat surprised.

"Of course," Stankle replied as she leaned in close to Peter while batting her eyelids. "Aren't I beautiful?"

Peter almost threw up from the smell of her breath, but was somehow able to keep it down. "You're gorgeous," he replied, coughing.

This pleased Stankle immensely. "You are so sweet!" She

turned to her father's throne. "Can I keep him?" she asked.

Pusglob pushed her out of the way. "No!" he shouted and then placed his nose near Peter and sniffed him. "He smells delicious. Let's eat him!"

"No!" cried Stankle as she punched her brother in the eye. "You can't! I want to keep him as a pet." She wrapped her arms around Peter and pulled him tight to her. Her body odor was even worse than her breath. "I'll love on him and play with him every day." Peter imagined it might be better to be eaten.

Pusglob stepped behind his sister and grabbed her by her long pointy ears. "We're going to eat him, maggot teeth!" he shouted as he pulled her away from Peter. Stankle reached up and poked a bony finger in her brother's eye causing Pusglob to cry out in pain. Stankle then spun around and leapt on her brother, knocking him to the ground. The two goblin siblings rolled around on the floor, punching and biting one another.

"Stop this!" Igwurm commanded, and the two stopped fighting immediately and stared up at their father. "I have a way to solve this. We will send him to the arena. If he lives, Stankle may keep him as a pet. But if he dies," the prince leaned forward staring at Peter as a wicked smile spread across his face, "we eat him."

CHAPTER TWENTY-THREE
THE ARENA

Peter stood in the center of the arena staring up at the thousands of goblins surrounding him, cheering wildly. As Peter scanned the crowd, he noticed Prince Igwurm and his two children sitting together. The prince held his long scepter in his hand, but beside him, leaning against his chair, was Peter's miraculous staff.

The prince rose from his seat and held his arms up high into the air, silencing the crowd of cheering goblins. "My fellow goblins," the prince shouted in a hideous voice. "In the arena today is a fierce human boy. A boy so terrifying that Apollyon himself trembles at his name." The crowd gasped in unison.

"The boy shall face off against our champion...Taurus!" The crowd went wild with excitement at the champion's name. There were hoots and hollers and shouts of praise for Taurus and cries cursing the boy challenger. The prince held his hands up once again, quieting the crowd. As the cheers and screaming ceased, the prince continued. "If the boy defeats the champion, he shall win the honor of serving as a pet to my beautiful daughter Stankle. If he should fall to Taurus, tonight we shall feast on his flesh!"

The arena again erupted into uproarious cheering. "Let the fight begin!" the prince shouted.

Peter was scared. He was no fighter. He was just a boy. He was not a "fierce boy" as Igwurm had described him. He was just a normal kid. However, even though Peter was not a fighter, he did have a fighter in his corner. One Who had come through for him time and again. As the arena shook with the cheers of the roaring crowd, Peter lowered himself to his knees, folded his hands together and prayed. "Lord Jesus, please help me. I know I got too proud and thought I was defeating the goblins by myself. It was You who was really doing it. I can't do anything without You. I need You for everything and I especially need You now!"

Peter's prayer was interrupted by the sounds of stone grinding against stone as a large granite door was raised. Peter opened his eyes and rose to his feet as he stared at the opening of the door. He heard a grunt and snort emanating from the darkness inside. Then he saw a figure striding through the door. It was an enormous creature with a head and legs like that of a bull, but the body and arms of a man. It was not a normal-sized man though, but a huge man, with rippling muscles. The beast carried a two-edged battle-axe in his giant hands. Peter's mouth fell open as he recognized the creature from a mythology book his teacher had read them. It was a minotaur—a real life minotaur!

The crowd chanted "Taurus! Taurus!" The beast released a blood-curdling sound as it charged toward Peter, lowering its head, its enormous horns set to impale the boy. Peter stood firm, not moving at all. He had faith that if his Lord wanted him spared, he would be spared. If the Lord was ready to take Peter to Heaven, the boy would die. The minotaur charged faster and faster toward Peter, thundering closer and closer. Fear suddenly washed over Peter, but he pushed it away and instead fell back down on his knees to pray the prayer Jesus had taught His disciples to pray.

"Our Father, who art in heaven," he prayed as the beast thundered.

"Hallowed be thy name." The minotaur charged closer.

"Thy kingdom come, thy will be done, on earth as it is in Heaven." The ground shook with the pounding of the beast's hooves.

"Give us this day our daily bread and forgive us our trespasses as we forgive those who trespass against us." The minotaur was almost upon him, but Peter did not flinch.

"And lead us not into temptation, but deliver us from evil." Peter trusted in God as he readied himself to be run through by the beast, but the minotaur did not ram Peter. Instead it darted right past him.

Peter turned his head to see the minotaur charging toward the wall. No, not the wall—the gate. The gate that had been closed behind Peter, after the goblins forced him into the arena. Peter's eyes went wide as the minotaur rammed into the gate. The iron bars could not stop the beast, and it busted through the gate, trampling the goblin guards on the other side. Only then did the minotaur stop. With a grunt, it turned its bull face toward Peter and waved its human looking hand as if to say "follow me!"

"Amen," Peter said finishing his prayer. He leapt to his feet and turned his gaze toward the goblin prince. Igwurm screamed for the guards to do something about the minotaur and the boy. Peter held out his hand. "Stick, return!" he shouted, and his staff leapt up from beside the prince and flew down into the arena and into Peter's waiting hand. Peter then darted off after the minotaur, his boots propelling him forward at an incredible speed.

The minotaur had already cleared a path of goblin soldiers and Peter simply had to follow their trampled bodies. Peter wanted to escape, to simply flee the castle and the Realm of the Goblins, but he knew he could not leave just yet—not without the Amulet of Eternity. Peter found the minotaur outside the castle, fighting half a dozen armed goblins.

"Stick, attack the goblins!" Peter shouted. The stick did just that. With the stick's assistance, the minotaur quickly defeated the goblins and then turned to Peter.

"We must hurry my small friend," the great bull-headed beast grunted. "I am tired of being a slave to goblins and fighting for their entertainment."

"I can't leave yet!" Peter exclaimed. "Not without the Amulet of Eternity."

The minotaur snorted. "Where is this amulet?"

"Prince Igwurm has it," Peter told him.

The minotaur nodded. "You hide here," he said. "I will lead the soldiers away. Once they are gone, you will have a better chance to get this amulet of yours."

"Thank you!" Peter exclaimed. "Why are you helping me?"

The minotaur grunted. "Because, I stepped into the arena to see a little boy on his knees praying to God. How evil must one be to put a small child into the arena? I decided I would no longer entertain these wicked creatures, even if it meant my death." He patted Peter on the head. "Hurry and hide!" he said and then with a snort, the minotaur disappeared, running down the hill.

THE ARENA

Peter pulled the hood of his cloak over his head and crouched down by the stone walls. He waited for the soldiers to pour out of the castle after the minotaur and then he slowly rose and crept back inside to find the Amulet of Eternity. Peter made his way through the castle, hiding behind his cloak whenever he heard the sounds of approaching goblins. He eventually arrived in the throne room where he found Prince Igwurm screaming furiously at two of his soldiers. His children—Pusglob and Stankle—stood behind him, chuckling at the soldier's faces.

Peter's eyes rose to the goblin prince's throne and noticed the silver box containing the Amulet of Eternity on the arm rest. The boy stood up and darted out of the shadows, past Igwurm, and up the steps to the throne as quickly as his miraculous boots would carry him. He scooped up the small box and turned to see the goblin prince and the others staring at him.

Igwurm was furious. "Seize him!" he shouted.

"Stick, attack the goblins!" Peter commanded, and the stick sprang from his hand, slamming into the guards charging up the steps toward him. While the guards were distracted, Peter dashed past them much too quickly for anyone to catch. He paused briefly at the door. "Stick, return!" he said with a smile and the stick flew back to his outstretched hand. He gave Princess Stankle a wink and then dashed off once again.

"Isn't he dreamy?" Stankle sighed like a love sick school girl. Her father ignored her.

"I want every goblin in the realm after that boy!" Igwurm screamed. "If he escapes, I will have everyone's head!"

Peter's miraculous boots carried him through the castle

gates and down the hill much faster than even the fastest goblin could run. He navigated the terrain by moonlight until he came to the small goblin village at the foot of the hill where he had been captured. The entire village was in an uproar and when he arrived he realized why.

The minotaur stood in the center of the village swinging his mighty battle axe at a troop of goblins bearing spears, swords, and other weapons. But it wasn't just the goblin soldiers that the minotaur had to worry about. It was also the villagers. The village goblins had surrounded the minotaur and a group came at him from behind slinging a noose around his neck and dragging him down to the ground. Then the rest of the village piled on. As strong as the minotaur was, he was not strong enough to defeat the entire goblin village.

Peter whisked into the village at an incredible speed. He zipped past the goblins holding down the minotaur and as he did so, struck one of the goblins with his staff. He then turned and zipped past again, striking another. He did this again and again until enough of the goblins had been knocked off of the minotaur that the mighty beast was able to force himself back to his feet. Then Peter slid to a stop beside his new friend. The two surveyed the mass of goblins ready to attack and kill them.

Taurus the minotaur snorted. "They may kill me, but I'll take a lot of them with me!"

Just as the goblins were about to attack something wonderful happened. The goblins' slaves—fauns, centaurs, and the like—suddenly attacked their masters. The goblins closing in on Peter and Taurus were beset on all sides. Taurus took that opportunity to lower his head and charge the goblins, trampling many beneath his giant hooves. Peter smiled, relieved that the slaves were rebelling against the goblins, and quickly joined the fray. He zipped back and forth, too quickly for the goblins to catch, while smacking the wicked creatures with his staff as he passed.

A group of goblins attempted to spring a net on Peter, trapping him so that they might kill him. But Peter turned and ran straight up the side of a tree, performed a back flip off the trunk, and landed on the ground before dashing away in the opposite direction. He continued to fight the goblins alongside his new allies, and soon had them fleeing into the forest. A cheer went up from Peter's new friends, and more than one patted him on the back.

"Thank you for helping us," Taurus said. "We have been slaves of the goblins for too long."

"It was my pleasure," Peter replied. "And thank you for not running me through in the arena." He then looked at the crowd of fauns, centaurs, and others pressing in on him. "But I am afraid I need to go. If I do not get back to my mother with the Amulet of Eternity, she will die."

Peter's words were interrupted by a great thunder shaking the ground and he turned to see an army of goblins charging down the mountain astride terrifying beasts. He'd call them wolves, except they were three times the size and had horns sticking out of their heads.

"Go!" Taurus said to Peter. "Save your mother. We shall hold the goblins off for as long as we can." Peter glanced around to see the others nodding in agreement.

"Thank you," Peter said. He swallowed hard as he watched the goblins descending the hill. "I will never forget you."

Taurus smiled. "The Lord be with you," he said softly.

"And with your spirit," Peter replied before dashing away from the village through the dark forest until he found the entrance to the tunnels once again. Peter hurried down the steps and made his way through the tunnel as quickly as he dared. Fortunately, no goblins were inside, at least not yet. He knew that a horde of them were coming. He grabbed a torch from the wall, found the small hole through which he had entered the tunnel, got down on his hands and knees and crawled through it. Inside, he held the torch up, illuminating the path through the tunnel.

Peter hurried through the tunnel until he emerged inside the cave with the pool. He expected to find the mermaid Amatheia waiting for him as she had promised, but she was not there. "Amatheia!" he cried out. He feared that he could not make it back to the surface alone. "Amatheia!" he cried again. Where could she be? He began to worry, and his worry soon gave way to panic as he heard the sounds of goblins in the tunnels behind him. They had fought their way through Taurus and the others in the village and would find him soon.

Peter glanced behind him at the tunnel, expecting the wicked creatures to appear any second. Suddenly, he heard a splash in the water and turned back around to see Amatheia. Peter breathed a sigh of relief. "Where have you been?" he asked.

"Watching for the Leviathan," she told him. "We cannot go now, the beast is too near."

Peter turned around as the sounds of the goblins grew closer and closer. "We have no choice," he said. "If we don't go now, the goblins will kill us both."

Amatheia gasped at the predicament they were in. "All right," she relented. "Come into the water. We will try our luck with the Leviathan." Peter nodded, tossed the torch aside, took a deep breath and jumped into the water with a splash. "May the Lord protect us," Amatheia said softly before diving after the boy.

THE ARENA

Amatheia swam down to catch hold of Peter's hand. She swished her tail and pulled him from the cave and into the open ocean. She stopped and waited. "We must be careful," she told him with her mind. She then turned to him and pressed her lips to his, once again filling his lungs with air. Peter smiled. The mermaid's kiss had quickly become his favorite part of the entire quest.

Amatheia glanced about, and believing the coast to be clear, quickly emerged from the mouth of the cave, pulling Peter into the open ocean. She swam as fast as she could, but it was hard with the boy weighing her down. Peter held onto the mermaid's hand, and as he did so, he scanned the dark water, fearful that the Leviathan would appear.

"We're almost there," came Amatheia's voice in Peter's head. He smiled. It looked as though they were going to make it. Thanks be to God! Then suddenly, Peter saw something moving in the distance. It was like a giant black shadow. His heart began to pound in his chest. The shadow appeared to be moving toward them. As it grew closer, Peter noticed glowing yellow eyes and the giant head of a sea serpent.

"The Leviathan!" Peter thought. "It's right behind us."

Hearing Peter's thoughts, Amatheia turned her head to see the creature in the distance. Fear shot through her as she swished her tail faster trying to reach the surface before the Leviathan caught them. Peter kept his eyes on the massive beast as it moved quickly toward them.

"It's almost on us!" Peter told Amatheia. The great sea serpent opened its mighty jaws as it swam. Peter could see rows of enormous teeth and down its long throat. Peter screamed in terror causing bubbles to escape his mouth. Just as the mighty jaws were about to chomp down on Peter, the boy shoved his staff into the monster's mouth. The

CHAPTER TWENTY-THREE

Leviathan's jaws got stuck on the staff and it stopped chasing them. The monster began to wiggle its massive head back and forth trying to dislodge the staff from its mouth. Finally, the Leviathan crushed the staff in its mouth, breaking it in two with its mighty jaws.

Amatheia pulled Peter close to her, smiled sweetly at him, and then pressed her lips to his one last time. She filled his mouth and lungs with oxygen and then shoved him toward the surface. "Swim, Peter!" he heard her voice in his head. He obeyed, swimming as quickly as he could to the surface.

Peter glanced back below him to see Amatheia swimming away, toward the Leviathan. She swam straight at the creature's face, but just as the monster was about to chomp her, she darted away. The Leviathan turned and chased the mermaid, forgetting about Peter. Peter finally broke through the surface gasping for air, but soon began to sink again, weighed down by his clothes and boots. He struggled to keep his head above the water and realized that the shore was too far—he'd never make it. He had survived demons and goblins and a sea serpent but was going to die drowning. Suddenly, Peter felt an arm slip around him from behind.

"I've got ya!" came a voice, and Peter turned his head to see the old homeless veteran. "Just stay calm," the man said. Peter obeyed and allowed the old man to pull him to the shore. Once they were in shallow enough water, the veteran stood, scooped Peter up into his arms and carried him onto the beach. He laid Peter down in the soft white sand and knelt beside him. "Are you all right, Peter?" the man asked.

Peter coughed up some water. He then looked the man in the eyes and nodded. The man smiled. "Good."

Suddenly, there was a giant splash and Peter sat up to see Amatheia leaping from the water. She was not alone. The

THE ARENA

Leviathan was behind her, and as its giant head burst forth, it thrust Amatheia forward. The mermaid flew through the air high above Peter's head, to land on the beach behind him.

"Amatheia!" Peter shouted and scrambled to his feet. He ran to the mermaid's side and fell to his knees in the sand beside her. "Amatheia," he said again as he shook her, but she did not move.

The Leviathan released a terrifying roar as its long serpent-like body rose from the water staring at Peter, Amatheia, and the old man. Peter watched as the homeless veteran stood up and returned the monster's glare. "You are not allowed here!" the old man shouted defiantly. "Return to your depths!" The monster roared again and looked as though it was about to strike the old man, when the man suddenly rose into the air. He was illuminated by blinding light, and when Peter could see again he did not see the old veteran, but instead saw a dazzling angel dressed in white with golden armor. The angel flew toward the Leviathan, striking the beast on its snout with his shining sword and the Leviathan pulled away.

"I am Michael, Archangel to Almighty God and General of Heaven's Armies!" the angel cried in a large booming voice. "Leave here now, or I shall strike you down!"

The Leviathan shrieked at Michael, but then dove back into the water with a massive splash. Michael turned to see Peter and Amatheia. He flew down to them, his enormous white wings beating the air. Michael landed on the sand and knelt down beside Peter.

"I think she's dead," Peter sniffed as tears welled in his eyes.

Michael reached forward and touched her.

"Can you save her?" Peter asked.

Michael turned to Peter. "Salvation comes through God

alone." He then looked at the box-shaped bulge in Peter's pants pocket. "But He has given you the power to save in that little box."

Peter's eyes lit up! "The Amulet of Eternity!" he shouted. "Would that save her?" he asked.

"As I said, only God can save," Michael repeated himself. "But would you be willing to trade that amulet for Amatheia's life? If you opened the box and used the amulet on Amatheia, you could not use it on your mother."

"But then how could I save my mother?" Peter asked.

Michael placed a hand on Peter's shoulder. "You can't save your mother either way, Peter."

Peter understood. It was not him or the amulet that would save his mother. Only God could do that. Would God still save his mother even if he didn't have the amulet? Peter started to cry. He didn't want Amatheia to die, but he didn't want his mother to die either. Then he reasoned that if God wanted his mother alive He would save her, whether or not Peter had the amulet.

Peter picked up the box and held it out for Michael. "Save her please," he said.

"But what about your mother?" Michael asked.

"God will save my mother," Peter said. "Or he won't. Either way, I cannot hold the power to save Amatheia in my hand and selfishly let her die."

"Well done, Peter," Michael said warmly. "You have passed your final test. You have shown not only selflessness, but most important of all, you have trusted God and His will for your life and your mother's life." He then turned to Amatheia. "But do not worry. Your friend is not dead. She is only asleep."

Michael took Amatheia by the hand and lifted her up.

THE ARENA

"Time to wake up, Amatheia," he said gently and Peter saw the mermaid blink her eyes open. When she saw Michael, she smiled brightly.

"Am I in Heaven?" she asked.

"Not yet," Michael said.

Peter threw his arms around her neck. "Amatheia, you're all right!" he cried.

Amatheia looked at him. "Barely!" she said. "The Leviathan almost had me for breakfast."

"Breakfast!" Peter said. "Is it almost morning?"

Michael nodded. "On the East coast it *is* morning," he said letting Peter know that Father Joe and Ms. Naomi would be up soon.

"Oh no, I've got to hurry!" Peter exclaimed. "Thank you again," he said to Amatheia. He then turned to Michael. "I cannot believe I met *the* Michael."

"If God wills it, I'm sure we will see each other again, my young friend. But for now you must go!"

Peter nodded and stood up. With the small box in his hand, Peter sprinted from the beach and back toward the small church as quickly as he could. When he reached the church's parking lot, he saw Ariel standing in front of the large windows, smiling at him. He rushed to her and threw his arms around her in a tight embrace.

"I have the amulet," he said.

"Then we must hurry and get you home to your mother before it's too late."

"Back through Evermore?" Peter asked.

"No," the angel replied. "The Lord has graciously healed my wing, so I thought we'd go back a quicker way."

"You mean we're going to fly?" Peter asked.

"Yes," she smiled. "Besides, you're soaking wet, and the

wind will dry you off."

Peter laughed. "Good," he said.

"Now hold on tight," Ariel cautioned. "We're going to move faster than any jet ever could."

She wrapped her arms around him as he wrapped his around her. Her wings spread out wide, and when she flapped them, she launched into the air like a rocket, disappearing into the dark sky.

CHAPTER TWENTY-FOUR
GOING HOME

The sun was already rising on the East Coast when Ariel flapped her wings to slow herself down as she neared the home where Peter and his mother lived with Father Joe and Ms. Naomi. Peter gripped Ariel so tightly he wasn't sure if he'd be able to pry his arms off her. When she had told him they would fly faster than the fastest jet, she had not exaggerated. She had flown the entire length of the country in a matter of minutes.

Ariel landed in the back yard and set Peter on the ground. His legs were wobbly, and when he finally released her, he toppled over onto his behind. "Are you all right?" Ariel asked, trying to hide her amusement.

Peter nodded. "I think so," he said through dry lips. He looked up at her, but she was no longer the tall, beautiful, shining angel she had been. Ariel had transformed back into a little girl, in a flowered dress and oversized glasses.

"Let me help you up," she smiled and extended a small

hand. Peter accepted it, and Ariel yanked him to his feet. Her form may have changed, but her angelic strength remained. "The Parsons should be up."

Peter nodded. "Yeah," he agreed. He then noticed the nurse's car parked in the driveway. "The nurse is here early," he frowned.

"Are you ready?" Ariel asked.

"Yes," Peter said as he flashed a huge grin. How could he not be ready to save his mother?

Ariel stepped close to him and placed a hand on each shoulder. "I'm here with you," she said. "Don't forget that."

"I won't," he replied.

"And no matter what happens, remember to trust in the Lord."

Peter chuckled. "Of course," he said. After all he'd been through and survived, he didn't see how he could ever not trust in God ever again. "C'mon," he said and took hold of Ariel's hand, pulling her toward the house. They climbed the steps to the kitchen entrance and opened the door stepping inside. The kitchen was empty and Peter took off his cloak and hung it over the back of one of the chairs set around the breakfast table.

Holding the box containing the amulet in one hand and gripping Ariel's hand in the other, Peter hurried from the kitchen, through the living room and into his mother's room. There he found Father Joe, Ms. Naomi, and the nurse standing around his mother's bed. Ms. Naomi was sobbing into a tissue as she stared at Peter's mother.

Suddenly, Father Joe noticed Peter and Ariel. "Peter!" he exclaimed. "I thought you were still in bed." He looked the boy up and down. "You're filthy. Where have you been?"

Before Peter could answer another voice stopped him.

GOING HOME

"Peter," his mother said weakly.

"She's talking," Ms. Naomi smiled. She then turned to Peter. "Go see your mother, sweetheart—she doesn't have long."

Peter approached the bed and saw his mother turn her head toward him. "Peter," she said again, her voice very weak.

"I'm here, Momma," he replied as he stepped close to her and lifted the little silver box up and placed it on the bedside.

"What's this?" his mother asked.

"It's an amulet, Momma," Peter said with tears in his eyes. "It's gonna save you."

Tears welled up in Peter's mother's eyes as well. "Oh, baby, that's sweet, but it's too late for me."

"No, Momma, God promised me," he said and then turned to point at Ariel. "Ariel is an angel—a real angel, and we went on an amazing quest through the land of Evermore and the Realm of the Goblins. I met dwarfs and giants, a small elvish knight, and a dancing gopher that could talk. He could really talk Momma! And we were chased by demons and goblins and all kinds of scary things. But I got it, Momma. I got the Amulet of Eternity, and it will save you. Well, the Holy Spirit will save you, but He's going to use the amulet."

Peter's mother placed a cold hand against his cheek. "What a wonderful imagination you have," she smiled.

"But it's real, Momma," he said. He then flipped the small latch on the little silver box, opened it, and reached inside. Peter could feel the cool metal of the amulet in the palm of his hand. He raised his hand close to his mother's face and then opened his fingers. She looked down at his open hand and her eyes grew wide.

"Where did you get this?" she asked.

"From the Realm of Goblins," Peter said. "I had to jump

off of the pier in California where you and Daddy used to take me when I was a kid," he said as if he were all grown up now.

Peter's mother started to cry as she reached down and lifted the small necklace from her son's hand.

"What is it, Joanna?" Ms. Naomi asked Peter's mother.

Peter's mother held it up so that everyone could see it. The amulet was not really an amulet at all, but a small silver locket that appeared to be two angel's wings formed together in the shape of a heart. "This belonged to my grandmother," Joanna explained. "My grandfather gave it to me after she died, and it's what brought me to God." She flipped the tiny clasp and opened the locket up. A small folded piece of paper fell out onto the bed.

"I don't believe it," she said as her voice cracked. She lifted the tiny piece of paper with trembling fingers and handed it to Peter. "Read it," she said softly as tears streamed down her cheeks.

Peter gently unfolded the small piece of paper and read the faded words written there. "I believe in the sun, even when it is not shining," he read, struggling to make out the words. "I believe in love even when I don't feel it. I believe in God, even when he is silent."

Peter's mother burst into tears. "How can this be?" she asked. "I threw that locket off the pier in California after David died," she said referring to Peter's father. "I didn't want to believe in a God that would let my husband be killed like so many others in endless war." She looked at her son. "How did you get this?"

"I told you, Momma," Peter whispered. "I jumped off the end of the pier in California and swam to the Realm of Goblins."

Joanna rolled onto her back as she wept. She squeezed her

eyes closed tightly and placed a bony hand over her face. Peter saw her lips move but could not make out what she was saying. Eventually her eyes opened, and she looked at Father Joe.

"Will He forgive me?" she asked. "Even after I cursed Him for letting David die?"

The priest nodded. "He already has Joanna," Father Joe assured her. "And I promise you, there will be more joy in Heaven because you've returned to God than over ninety-nine others who never left."

Joanna wiped tears away from her eyes and turned to look at her son. "I love you so much," she said. "I'm going to miss you when I'm gone."

"You're not going, Momma," Peter smiled. "God promised the amulet will save you, Momma."

Joanna nodded. "I know He did, and He was right baby," she replied. "It has saved me."

Peter smiled. "You feel better?" he asked excitedly.

"No, Peter," his mother said. "Your Momma's about to die." She then looked past Peter at Ariel, but instead of seeing the little girl that stood in the room, she saw the angel, tall and brilliant. "I am going home, aren't I?" she asked.

Ariel smiled. "Yes, Joanna," she assured her. "You are going home."

Peter's mother inclined her head toward Peter. "Thank you, my darling boy," she said as the breath was leaving her. "I love you so much. I will miss you." Peter watched his mother as the life faded from her eyes. Suddenly, Peter saw his father standing beside his mother's bed dressed in his blue uniform.

"Daddy," Peter said as he started to cry. His father was younger looking than he remembered. He didn't say a word, but turned toward Peter and gave him a little wink. His father then reached his hand out to Peter's mother. Peter saw his mother take his father's hand and stand up, but it wasn't her body. His mother's body lay still in the bed, eyes wide staring at him. The person who stood up looked young and healthy, like Peter remembered his mother looking in her wedding pictures. Peter's father led her past Peter and Ariel toward the living room.

"Momma!" Peter shouted and saw his mother turn. She blew him a kiss and then a bright light appeared in the center of the living room, as if a door had opened. Peter's dad gave his son one last wave before leading his wife into the light and disappearing. "No!" Peter shouted and then turned to see Ariel—the little girl with the oversized glasses—standing in the doorway. "You lied to me!" he screamed angrily.

"Peter," Ariel began, but Peter wasn't listening. He took off at a sprint through the living room and into the kitchen. As he pulled the kitchen door open he heard Father Joe call his name, but he ignored him. Peter rushed down the steps outside and sprinted across the yard to the little church. He flung the doors to the church open and stepped inside.

Peter stared at the sculpture of Jesus on the crucifix. He stomped down the aisle between the pews, toward the altar. He was angry—furiously angry! He wanted to smash the crucifix to tiny bits, but instead he collapsed in a heap on the floor of the church and wept.

"Peter," he heard Ariel's voice say and turned to see the full grown angel standing behind him. She slowly knelt down beside him on the wooden floor.

"God lied!" Peter spat. "And you lied to me. You told me the amulet would save my mother!"

Ariel frowned and placed a comforting hand on his shoulder. "God never lies," she said. "And neither do I."

"The amulet didn't save her!" Peter shouted.

GOING HOME

"Oh, yes it did, Peter," Ariel replied softly. "After your father's death, your mother turned away from God. She wanted nothing to do with Him. She cursed His name. She hated Him, blaming Him for her husband's death. The amulet reminded her that God's plans are not always our plans, but He loves us and works all things for good. Even death." Ariel wiped a tear from Peter's eye. "Your mother put her trust in God again because she saw that locket and the poem inside. Her soul was saved, and she went to live with God and your father in Heaven."

"But I wanted her body to be saved!" Peter cried. "Not her soul!"

"Really?" Ariel asked. "You would rather spend a few more years on earth with your mother than an eternity with her in Heaven?" Peter sniffed. "The human body is temporary, Peter. Your mother's, your father's, yours, they all die. What really matters is not whether your body dies, for it certainly will. What really matters is what happens to your soul. Bringing your mother that amulet saved her soul, Peter. That is the most important and wonderful thing you could ever do for anyone."

"Will I ever get to see her again?" he asked.

"Of course," Ariel smiled. "And your father. All three of you will get to spend eternity together and never die. And the best part, you'll get to live in the presence of God."

Peter leaned over and hugged Ariel tight, burying his face in her bosom. "But I miss her so much," he sobbed.

"I know you do, Peter," Ariel said. "And that's all right. It's all right to cry, but be comforted by the fact that her soul lives on and as long as you continue to trust in Jesus, so will yours. And one day, when Jesus returns, he will raise the bodies of all of God's children from the grave."

"Really?" Peter asked as he wiped his nose with his sleeve.

"Yes, Peter. God will bring Heaven down to Earth, and all who were faithful and loved Him will live with Him forever."

Peter looked up at her and she wiped his tears away. "I've got to be going, too, Peter," she said softly.

"What?" Peter said. "You can't leave me now! I'll be all alone."

"You're not alone, Peter," Ariel said. "I will always be watching you. And so will your parents. And so will Jesus. Remember that Jesus is always with you."

"But I don't have anyone to take care of me!" he cried, in a cracking voice.

"Yes, you do," Ariel whispered, and then she was gone. Disappeared. Peter looked around the church but didn't see her anywhere. He laid his face in his hands and wept. Then he heard something.

"Peter!" a voice said softly. He looked up and saw Father Joe and Ms. Naomi walking into the church. "Peter are you all right?" Ms. Naomi asked. Peter pushed himself to his feet and rushed over to her as she knelt down with arms wide. He threw his arms around her and sobbed onto her shoulder as she petted his hair. "It is all right, darling," Ms. Naomi said in her sweet English accent. "I know you miss her."

"Am I…" Peter said between sobs "gonna have to…go live…in an orphanage?"

Father Joe knelt down beside Peter and his wife. "Actually, Ms. Naomi and I were rather hoping you'd want to live here with us."

"Really?" Peter asked as he lifted his head to see Ms. Naomi nodding with tears in her eyes.

"Yes, Peter, we really want you to stay here with us," Ms. Naomi said. "Would you like that?"

GOING HOME

Peter nodded his head up and down. "Yes," he said and then wrapped his arms back around Ms. Naomi. Father Joe wrapped his arms around both of them, and all three sat in the church for a long time, crying.

A couple of months later, Peter knelt beside Ms. Naomi inside the little church as they prayed the closing prayer for their Christmas Eve service celebrating Jesus' birthday. Jesus had been born to poor parents in a stable where animals slept, and laid in a feeding trough for horses and donkeys because they had no crib. Born that day was the King of Kings, the Prince of the Universe, the Son of God, who would one day bring salvation to the entire planet. But on that night over two thousand years ago, few humans cared. Only a handful of shepherds came to pay him homage. However, the angels in Heaven sang praises to Jesus, and Peter couldn't help but wonder if Ariel had been among those singing.

"Amen," the congregation said as the prayer ended. Then the organist began to play and everyone stood and sang.

Hark the Herald Angels Sing

Glory to the newborn King.

Peace on Earth and mercy mild,

God and sinners reconciled.

As Father Joe processed up the center aisle, he bade Peter to join him, and the boy happily did, wrapping an arm around the priest. Ms. Naomi gave her husband a wink as he and Peter walked to the front of the church where they greeted the congregants as they left.

"Merry Christmas," Father Joe would say as he shook hands and hugged necks. Then a woman Peter had never seen before stepped up and extended her hand.

"Hello, Father, I'm Sarah Walker," she smiled, and Peter noticed two children about his age standing with her.

"Nice to meet you," Father Joe smiled warmly as he shook her hand.

"I'm going to be the new principal at the elementary school down the street," she said.

"Oh, excellent!" Father Joe smiled. "Let me introduce you to Peter Puckett. He's one of your pupils."

Ms. Walker smiled at Peter. "It's very nice to meet you, Peter," she said. "What grade are you in?"

"Fourth," he said.

Ms. Walker turned to her children. "Well, you will have to show my kids around. They are in fourth grade, too," she said as she coaxed her children—a boy and a girl out to meet Peter.

"Are you twins?" Peter asked.

"Yep," the girl smiled. "But I'm the oldest."

"Only by two minutes," her brother reminded her.

"I'm Lizzie," the girl smiled. "And that's James."

"I'm Peter," he said. "It sure will be nice to have new friends at school."

"We don't live far from here. Maybe you could come over tomorrow and see what we get for Christmas!" James said excitedly.

"That would be fun," Peter smiled.

"And we'd better hurry if we don't want Santa Claus to pass us by," Ms. Walker reminded them.

James leaned over to Peter. "I don't really believe in Santa Claus anymore," he whispered.

"You should," Peter smiled, "because I promise you he is real."

Ms. Walker led her children to the car, and they drove out of the parking lot. Peter stood on the front steps of the church waving to them as they left. He was about to turn away when his eyes saw a little girl with oversized glasses and golden hair smiling at him from across the lawn.

"Ariel!" Peter shouted excitedly as he leapt off the church steps and rushed to his friend, throwing his arms around her neck.

"Merry Christmas, Peter," she said, but did not return his hug, instead keeping her arms behind her back.

"I've missed you so much!" Peter exclaimed. "Can you spend the night?"

Ariel shook her head. "Actually, I cannot stay," she said disappointing Peter. "But I've brought you a Christmas present."

Peter's eyes lit up. "What is it?" he asked excitedly.

Ariel brought her hands from behind her back, and Peter shouted with excitement when he noticed she held a small gopher.

"Euripides!" he shouted gleefully.

The gopher did not say a word but leapt from Ariel's hands and landed in Peter's. He crawled all over Peter like a crazy squirrel.

"What is going on?" he asked the gopher. "How are Strom and Sir Palamedes?" But Euripides did not answer.

"I'm afraid the Holy Spirit has not given you the gift of tongues in this world, Peter," Ariel said. "You will not be able to talk to Euripides."

Peter frowned, but then his frown turned into a smile. "That's okay, we can still have lots of fun."

Euripides jumped up and down excitedly on Peter's shoulder.

"Peter," came a voice, and Peter turned to see Ms. Naomi walking up behind him. She looked past him to Ariel. "Merry

Christmas, Ariel," she smiled. "It's good to see you."

"You, too, Ms. Naomi," Ariel replied.

Ms. Naomi's eyes then fell on Euripides perched on Peter's shoulder. "And what's this?" she asked hesitantly. "Some kind of chipmunk?"

Peter laughed. "This is Euripides," he said. "He's a gopher."

"Oh, lovely," Ms. Naomi replied in a voice that said she didn't really believe it was lovely at all.

"Can I keep him?" Peter asked.

"Peter, I..." Ms. Naomi began, but before she could finish, Euripides leapt from Peter's shoulder to land on Ms. Naomi's. He planted a big kiss on her cheek, causing her to laugh out loud. "Well, I guess so."

"Yay!" Peter exclaimed. "Don't worry, he's a really good gopher and wait until you see him dance."

"I can't wait," Ms. Naomi sighed as she pulled the gopher from her shoulder and handed him back to Peter. She then turned to Ariel. "Would you like to come inside for some hot chocolate?"

Ariel shook her head. "Thank you, but I should be getting home now."

"Already?" Peter whined.

"Yes, Peter," Ariel said. She leaned over and gave the boy a hug and kiss on the cheek.

"Will I ever see you again?" he whispered into her ear.

"I sure hope so," she whispered back. "But you aren't the only one who needs me."

"I know," Peter said.

Ariel pulled away and then leaned over and kissed Euripides on the cheek. "Merry Christmas, Euripides," she said as the gopher blushed.

GOING HOME

"Let me drive you home, Ariel. It's getting late," Ms. Naomi said.

"Thank you, but I'm all right," she said.

"No, I insist," Ms. Naomi said and then turned back toward the church. "Joseph!" she called to Father Joe. "I'm going to take Ariel home." She turned back, but the girl was gone. Ms. Naomi turned to Peter. "Where did she go?"

Peter shrugged. "Probably back to Heaven," he said and then turned and jogged to the rectory, holding Euripides in his hands.

Ms. Naomi looked around but could not find Ariel anywhere. She gave up—assuming the girl had gone home—and returned to the rectory to put Peter to bed while Father Joe locked up the church. She frowned when she saw the gopher curled up on the pillow beside Peter.

"Don't we have a cage or something for that thing?" she asked.

"He'll be fine," Peter promised. "We've done this before."

Ms. Naomi relented and sat down on the side of his bed and tucked the blankets under Peter's chin. "Did you say your prayers?" she asked.

"Yes, ma'am," he smiled.

She stared at him for a moment and tears began to well up in her eyes.

"What's wrong?" Peter asked.

"Nothing," she said and bent down and kissed him on the forehead. "I love you, Peter."

"I love you, too."

Ms. Naomi stood and crossed to his door, flipped off the light, and pulled the door closed behind her. Peter was in complete darkness, but he wasn't scared. He had Euripides, and he knew that his parents were watching. He knew he had a guardian angel. And he knew that Jesus was always with him.

The next morning, Peter rose early, excited to see what he got for Christmas. He rushed down the stairs with Euripides at his heels, to the living room and there under the tree were several packages beautifully wrapped in various colors. Peter smiled as he hurried to the tree. He spun around as he heard footsteps behind him and saw Ms. Naomi and Father Joe coming down the stairs wiping sleep from their eyes. They were tired, but truth be told, they were just as excited as Peter. This was their first Christmas as a family, and Ms. Naomi couldn't wait to see Peter open his presents.

He did so, ripping the paper, and tossing it on the floor. He got some video games, a toy robot that transformed into a car, and a bicycle helmet. "But I don't have a bike," Peter frowned.

"Uh-oh!" Father Joe said. "We must have messed up." He then rose from the couch and walked around the corner and rolled a green and red bike into the living room. Peter leapt to his feet with excitement and rushed over to it. "Now you can ride your bike to school," Father Joe said.

"Thank you," Peter smiled and gave the priest a big hug. He then rushed over to Ms. Naomi and gave her a hug as well. He sat down on the couch by Ms. Naomi. "I forgot to get you anything," he said.

Ms. Naomi laughed. "That's okay, Peter," she smiled as she placed an arm around his shoulder. "You are the best present I could hope for anyway." She squeezed him tight and pressed her lips to his head.

"Hey, what's that?" Father Joe asked, pointing to the back of the tree.

GOING HOME

"What?" Peter asked as he stood from the couch and walked over to the tree.

"Behind the tree," Father Joe said.

Peter ducked down to look behind the branches, and when he saw what it was, his mouth fell open. There behind the tree was a shining silver shield with a ruby red cross on the front. "The Shield of Faith!" Peter exclaimed, hoping he could lift it this time. He quickly reached behind the tree, grabbed hold of the shield, and pulled it out. It was much lighter than the last time he'd tried to lift it.

Attached to the shield was a little card that read:

To Peter,

You've earned this.

Merry Christmas,

Nicholas

"Well, who is that from?" Father Joe asked, a bit perplexed.

Peter smiled. "Santa Claus brought it to me," he said. "But it's really a gift from the Holy Spirit!"

Peter heard Euripides squeak with delight and he turned to smile at the small gopher. Both of them realized what this meant—they were not yet done with their adventures in Evermore. Peter couldn't wait to see what God had in store next!

THE ADVENTURE CONTINUES IN

Peter Puckett & The Enchanted Chalice

AVAILABLE NOW!

THE WORLD OF PETER PUCKETT

I am so honored that you took the time to read *Peter Puckett and the Amulet of Eternity*! Peter and his world were born from an idea to write a wholesome, Christian story that my children could enjoy and which could further form them as disciples of Christ. To accomplish that somewhat lofty goal, I prayed over many months for the Holy Spirit to inspire a story that God would be pleased with—a story that would bring glory to His holy name, demonstrate the beauty and joy of Jesus Christ, and help bring people to salvation through Jesus Christ. I continued to pray for those things every time I sat down to write this book and I believe the Holy Spirit delivered.

Writing *Peter Puckett* was the most amazing writing experience of my life. I easily wrote 5,000-6,000 words a day when I normally only averaged 2,000-3,000. Beyond that, *Peter Puckett & The Amulet of Eternity* is without question the best story I have ever written and I must give all credit for that to the Holy Spirit.

I do not believe the Lord is done with the World of Peter Puckett just yet. because I've already begun writing more! If you would like to see more of Peter Puckett and all of the fantastic creatures of Evermore, I'm going to ask you to help me out by doing four simple things.

First, **write a review on Amazon.com**, Goodreads.com, and anywhere else you think would be appropriate. Good Amazon reviews help more than you can imagine, so please do not neglect this. Second, **tell your church, family, and friends (including those on social media) about this book** and encourage them to buy it. Word of mouth will be very important to the success of Peter Puckett. Third, **visit my website at www.RCVANLANDINGHAM.com and sign up for my email list**. You will get early news on all the happenings of Peter Puckett, special offers, and even FREE stories!

Finally—and most importantly—**please pray that this book bears much good fruit.** Ask the Holy Spirit to use the story of Peter Puckett for the glory of God's holy name, to show the world the beauty and joy of Jesus Christ, and to bring people to salvation through Jesus Christ. Please do not underestimate the power of prayer. If this book is a success, it will be a credit to the Holy Spirit!

Thank you so much! I appreciate all of you more than you realize. Together, and with God's guidance, we can turn Peter Puckett into a fruitful ministry, spreading the love of Jesus to those who currently live in darkness.

Yours in Christ,
R.C. VanLandingham

ABOUT THE AUTHOR

R.C. VanLandingham lives in Florida with his beautiful wife Elena and three boys—Dixon, Stafford, and Maxwell.

Visit him **ONLINE** at
www.**RCVANLANDINGHAM**.com.

Made in the USA
Columbia, SC
19 November 2020

24933706R00183